THE
FUGITIVE BLACKSMITH

In the Sand-house

THE
FUGITIVE BLACKSMITH

BY

CHARLES D. STEWART

NEW YORK
THE CENTURY CO.
1905

THE DEVINNE PRESS

THE
FUGITIVE BLACKSMITH

THE
FUGITIVE BLACKSMITH

CHAPTER I

T HE Finerty household, like all Gaul, was divided into three parts: the kitchen, the "middle room," and the parlor.

As Mrs. Finerty used to say, "We have two rooms to live in, an' wan for Michael. 'T is a pity that MAN"—and she would say it as if she were emphasizing the whole human race—"w'u'd not lave things th' way God thried to have thim, an' not be invintin' locomotives to be kapin' all kinds av hours. We 're atin' an' shlapin' from hand to mouth; an' 't is little I hear av Michael's voice but whin he shnores. But sometimes I shtop in me worruk an' think how thankful I ought to be to hear *that;* for wid him always laid out in th' dark parlor, 't is th' only thing that kapes him from bein' dead to his family intirely."

The sacred parlor seldom had its green

blinds raised, for it was here that Michael re-
posed in daytime darkness. Had it not thus
been used, the parlor, it is safe to say, would
never have been invaded except on rare company occasions. So Michael was laid by in it
as an entirely "out-of-the-way" place. It was
chilly and still, as befitted its household alti-
tude; and, principal among its grandeurs, there
looked down from the wall over Michael's bed
a framed relic of preserved flowers, and a cher-
ished coffin-plate in a sort of show-case picture-
frame. And the coffin-plate, as if in continual
reference to the sleeping Michael, hung over
him with the one word "Rest."

Finerty, as night keeper of the sand-house
and coal-chutes in the Memphis "yards," was
called foreman, although, as he explained, "I
do all th' worruk mesilf." But there had to
be some title for a man who put his official
signature in lead-pencil on the tickets that
showed how much coal and sand each engineer had taken. This clerical phase of his
labors with the shovel was what made him a
"raysponsible man," and as strict and vigi-
lant an official as could be wished for.

As Finerty used to explain whenever a visitor was shown inside the sand-house, "'T is
f'r th' hoomps on th' backs av locomotives.

Ye see,'' he would continue, demonstrating the matter on two fingers, "there are two hoomps on th' back av a locomotive. Th' wan is for dry shteam an' th' other is for dry sand. An' if ye don't belave it about th' dry shteam ye can ask Halloran, that has run on th' division for twinty year, an' he 'll tell ye 't is thrue. But there 's no wan iver saw *ginooine* shteam; f'r whin ye can see it 't is not shteam, an' 't is no good. An' so they have th' hoomp on top av th' biler where th' gassy shteam will rise intil. An' th' pipe gets it there, shkimmin' th' cream off th' top like. An' th' other hoomp is where th' pipe gets th' sand that it shpills down on th' rails on a shlippery day. 'T is that way a locomotive *goes*.''

And frequently he would add, pointing himself out with the demonstrative finger, "An' 't is me that pits th' sand into thim.''

One spring day Mrs. Finerty applied her ear frequently to the keyhole, and each time announced to Agnes, "Yer father is shnorin'. I do hope,'' she said, "that *yer fa-a-ather* will wake up airly enough to tell me th' news—if ther' be's anny.''

That was Mrs. Finerty's day for the weekly baking; and early in the afternoon, when she had her bread and biscuit to the right point of lightness, she again began her struggle with the fire, which persisted in burning only at one end.

While she was so employed, Michael awoke and came out into the kitchen, his suspenders draping his trousers and the sleeves of his red undershirt rolled up to his elbows. Having looked sleepily at the clock, he sat down on the step that descended from the middle room to the kitchen, with his elbows on his knees, blinking at the daylight and waiting for his senses to gather themselves together.

When Mrs. Finerty had patted a potato pancake into shape, and given the stove an admonitory punching with the poker, she turned her attention to her spouse.

"Why don't ye shpeak? Why don't ye be tellin' me what ye were doin' yestherday afthernoon?"

He had risen early the day before to go across the Mississippi and see Mary Ann and her cousin on the "widdy's farm," for Mary had a letter from "acrost th' wather."

"Did ye see Mary Ann?" Mrs. Finerty insisted.

"I did not. She was away. But I saw her cousin, an' I saw no wan but him, an' I wint nowhere."

"An' what were ye doin'?"

"I was mindin' th' farm. An' I w'u'd want to be no farmer. 'T is too dangerous. I nearly had a wreck."

"A *wreck!*" she exclaimed. "How w'u'd ye have a wreck on a farm?"

"'T is not annything ye w'u'd undhershtand."

"I w'u'd be listenin' to it, annyway."

"Well, befure Jawn wint away, he shtarted to explain about th' throttle av th' plow. 'Ye don't need to be delayin' yersilf showin' me annything about that,' says I; 'for 't is little I don't know about a throttle, an' me worrukin' twinty year on th' railroad. I know that all; an' whin ye throw it till th' last notch here, 't is turned off; an' whin ye throw it till th' last notch there, 't is turned on. But ye might be inthrojoocin' me to th' four cows,' says I; 'for, seein' there is no lines nor bridle nor annything, I 'd want to be knowin' their names so that they 'll be mindin' what I tell them to do.'

"'I will,' says he; 'an' I don't doubt but, from what ye know, ye 'll be gettin' along all right. I am only goin' acrost th' river to get some seed.'

"'Ye need n't be apologizin' at all,' says I,

'an' ye th' cousin av Mary Ann McBride. For it 's little I w'u'd n't be doin' for Mary Ann's cousin,' says I.

" 'Well,' says he, 'th' near leader is called Coaly.'

" 'D' ye mane th' black runt av a wan to th' lift side in front, wid only th' shtoomp av a tail?' says I.

" 'Yis,' says he; 'I got him off a load from Texas. An' that was all th' coyotes left av his tail. An' ye 'll soon see that he leans sideways on th' yoke to be pullin' away from worruk all th' time he is doin' it; an' that makes it twice as hard for him, so that he gets blowed. If ye notice him shwellin' up in th' shtummick, 't is a sign he is gettin' blowed. An' ye 'll be givin' him a rest till it goes down a little,' says he.

" 'I can raymimber that,' says I.

" 'An' th' off leader is named Shpot,' says he.

" 'Is it th' tall rid-and-white wan that is parthner av th' little black runt?' says I.

" 'Ye 're right,' says he.

"An' he p'inted him out to me wid th' ind av a shtick. He was a bony old woman av a baste, all marked over in rid like th' map av a sthrange counthry, wid gulfs an' bays in white. Th' lift side av his face was rid, like ye 'd think he had nosed himsilf befure th' map was dry, an' he got half av Florida on his face. An' th' rump av him propped his hide out like th' centher-pole av a tent, he was that thin.

" 'D' ye iver let him shtand out in th' rain?' says I.

" 'Why wor ye askin'?' says he.

" 'I 'm thinkin' it w'u'd not do; for th' basins in th' flanks av him w'u'd be fillin' wid rain-wather, an' 't w'u'd be bad f'r his rheumatism,' says I.

" 'I have n't noticed that it dooes,' says he; 'although ye might think so. Th' shtiff walk is only his natheral way, from bein' tall an' thin.'

" 'I can raymimber he is Shpot, aisy enough,' says I.

" 'An' th' off wheeler is named Nig,' says he.

" " 'T is th' big black wan to th' right behind that ye mane,' says I. 'Nig will be th' wan wid th' right side av his face bigger nor th' other,' says I. For ye 'd think some wan had shlapped him wid th' thrunk av a three till he was Roman-nosed on wan side wid th' shwellin' av it.

" " 'T is only what 's called a warble,' says he, 'an' 't is no hurt to him at all. An',' says he, 'th' other is th' near wheeler, that ye 'll be handlin' thim all wid, an' his name is Shquat. Ye see there is nothin' th' matter wid him.'

" 'He is th' fine, able-bodied wan; an' 't is a pity ye did n't have thim all like that, so that they w'u'd match,' says I.

" 'They are matched perfect,' says he. 'In th' first place,' says he, puttin' his finger into th' palm av his hand, ''t is only because they are shtandin' on th' level ground; an' they 're a plow-team,' says he. With that he geed thim all over till th' right-hand wans were shtandin' down in th' furrow.

" 'I see,' says I. 'They are all out av joint on th' smooth land, like a fish out av wather. An' now, wan is no higher than his parthner, although he is taller. But ye 'd hardly call thim matched at that; for they 're av all shapes an' hefts an' thinnesses—not shpakin' av color. An' th' wan to th' right behind is not only taller, but is sthronger-lookin' acrost th' back nor his parthner.'

" 'Ye see,' says he, shtartin' to rattle away, like th' catechism av th' locomotive, 'how they were matched for size an' sthren'th, foorward and back, an' right an' lift, th' way ye 'd have to take th' side av a shlate to be figurin' it out.'

" 'Do I have to know much av that?' says I, lookin' at him wid his fingers matched together like th' rails av a log fince to be showin' how mixed up an' perfect it all was.

" 'Ye have only to drive thim an' tind to th' throttle,' says he.

" 'Ivery man to his thrade,' says I; 'for I can tind th' throttle. An' it 'll be gee an' haw for a signal at th' curves, an' they can tind to th' rist.'

" 'Ye need not say, "Gee!" an' "Haw!" at all,' says he; 'for th' leaders have been out to grass an' are too ignorant to know it. Ye have only to say "wo" at th' ind av th' furrow, an' th' wheeler will sit down an' hould thim all back. An' whin he brings thim to a shtop, ye whip th' leaders round where ye want thim, for they 're intilligint enough to know that.'

" ' 'T is Shquat holds thim back,' says I.

" 'Yis,' says he; ' 't is for that rayson th' sthrong an' intilligint wan is put behind on the land side o' th' furrow. 'T is so that whin he "wo's," th' front wans will have to. An' they can't be runnin' away, because an ox can hould back as much as half a dozen can pull.'

" ' 'T w'u'd be no use for th' front wans to "wo," wid th' hind wans havin' horns to push thim wid,' says I.

" ' 'T is that exactly; ye 'll have no throuble at all,' says he.

" 'I 'm thinkin' th' wheeler behind is a good wan at quittin' worruk, an' is always willin' to do it,' says I.

" 'Ye have th' saycrit av th' thrade,' says he. 'He 'd break his neck to shtop thim.'

" 'He is th' foreman av th' gang,' says I.

" 'Now ye have it,' says he.

"Wid that, he wint away an' lift me. An' sorra th' day he did.

"I shtarted thim up, an' they all folleyed down th' furrow as sthraight an' aisy as if 't was th' way home from worruk. At th' ind I did what he tould me, an' we crossed over an' got into th' thrack av th' down furrow back again. 'T was an aisy thrade to l'arn. An' 't was a long field wid a five-minute thrip acrost it, an' nothin' to do but sit on th' iron sate, wid yer hands to yersilf, an' look at th' scenery. So I lit me pipe an' sat, wid me hands on me knees, shmellin' th' fine air and thinkin' what was in me mind.

"Back an' foorward we wint, wid no throuble at all, but to raymind the big wan whin we come to th' fince, an' thin show thim all th' lift hand wid th' whip. The medlarks was all folleyin' behind in a sthring, takin' th' worms from th' sod, like pancakes that I 'd be turnin' over for their breakfast. An' they

kept that close 't w'u'd surprise ye, to be gettin' th' worms befure they c'u'd shrink up
short into their holes again. All av us med a
procission half a block long, an' 't was no more
worruk than St. Pathrick's day whin ye 're on
th' committee an' ridin' on a float.

" 'Had I knowed about farmin',' says I to
mesilf, 'I w'u'd niver have l'arned to shovel
sand an' coal at the chutes—an' I 'd niver be
an ingineer that has to look ahead all th' time,
an' bother about shtayin' on th' thrack. For
cows,' thinks I, 'are more intilligint nor a horse
or a locomotive.'

"They w'u'd go through th' black land as
aisy as makin' a mark in ashes. An' whin ye
come to a tough place, wid th' plow a-crunchin'
through th' woven grass, an' th' chain shtiff
as a crowbar, ye w'u'd not know 't was anny
worruk at all, from lookin' at thim. For they
w'u'd nayther lean nor pull, but w'u'd ramble
along like an ould woman out for her health
—an' th' plow comin' afther thim. 'T is that
sthrong they are.

"An' at th' ind av ivery furrow th' wan
called Shquat w'u'd hear me, an' he w'u'd sit
back an' hould thim like a bulldog that w'u'd
not lave go if ye pulled his head off. I 'm
thinkin' that befure they 'd 'a' dragged him

he 'd 'a' plowed a furrow wid each av his hoofs, an' thin he 'd not give in. For they 're shtill sthronger that way. An' he was like th' felly said.

''Whin it was they shtarted to run away wid me I dunno. For they did n't run at all, but just wint on wid th' same furrow acrost th' counthry to th' southwest a mile or so, an' thin east again to th' place they all had in mind to be spindin' th' afthernoon. I did n't get what ye might call mad till they had gone a quarther av a mile or so—an' thim not pretindin' they noticed me, wid all I c'u'd say or do, but only lavin' me to me own foolishness. 'T was thin I lifted th' plow out av th' ground, to see thim go fasther. An' they did not. An' 't was thin I was what ye w'u'd call mad. For they 're not like horses that has to run away in a hurry for fear some wan might ask thim to shtop. 'T is a case av 'We know our own minds; an' what are ye goin' to do about it?' 'T is that makes ye mad. An' they give ye plenty av time to show what ye 're good for. An' ye 're good for nothin'.

''But 't was all like this it kem about. Whilst I was puttin' a furrow acrost th' field, th' sthrong wan dropped down on his belly, wid his legs folded, an' he throws a swally up his neck to his mouth, an' shtarts his jaw to worrukin', like takin' a chew. I let thim rest a while, for th' leader was gettin' blowed up in th' shtummick, an' I thought I w'u'd not be intherferin' for a while. But whin th' time was up, I gave th' sthrong wan a dig in th' ribs, an' says, 'Get up. We will now be goin' along.'

"He took another swally from th' inside av him an' shtarted in to be chewin' that up. I gave him another dig, an' a rap wid th' butt av th' whip; an' whin I saw that did n't shcare him at all I laid it on till him harder. He swallied down his cud again, whin he had it to suit him, and thin I saw another come up his throat; an' he shtarted up his jaw as cool as ye plase. He was kapin' on wid his own worruk.

"'Git up, now,' says I. 'Ye can be chewin' yer breakfast to-night. I worruk nights mesilf, an' ye are no betther nor I am,' says I. 'We will now be doin' th' plowin'.'

"'T was thin I shtarted at him wid th' heel av me boot. But whilst I w'u'd be kickin' him at wan ind, he w'u'd kape on chewin' gum, like me daughther Agnes, an' lookin' about as if 't was fine weather he thought we were havin' th' day.

"An' whilst I was shtandin' off, thinkin'

how I c'u'd hurt him widout killin' him, his hind legs shtands up whilst th' front wans was shtill layin' down wid him chewin'; an' thin he rises up at th' front ind an' shtands there, like 't was now time for me to tind to me business again—an' him havin' th' say. So I got on me sate again an' we shtarted off plowin'.

"Or mabby 't was thin they were shtarted to where they were goin' to spind th' day—for I thought 't was plowin' till we got out av th' field. Annyway, I gave him a rap wid th' butt-ind av th' whip an' a taste av th' cracker.

" " 'T is always th' way,' says I, 'that an aisy boss will be imposed upon. An' 't is that I get for me good-natured way.' So whin we were gettin' to th' ind av th' furrow I hammered him again be way av lettin' him know I had a mind av me own, an' so that he w'u'd tind to his houldin' back whin I 'd say, 'Wo!'

"An' that time he did n't do it at all. Th' leaders wint on till they run into th' fince; an' him pullin' an' helpin' along. Whin they turned they brought th' plow so close they broke off a fince-post; an' they kept goin' along th' fince, wid th' iron axle av th' plow shnappin' off wan post an' thin another. An' on account av th' barb-wire I c'u'd not get to th' right side av thim to be shooin' thim back from it. So I shtood up on th' sate an' jumped over th' fince, an' I whipped thim away from there. 'Wo, to th' lift!' says I. 'Turn to th' lift! D' ye think 't is a-reapin' fince-posts I want ye for?' Wid that they med a circle back, and thin kem out av th' hole they had med in th' fince. An' away they plowed acrost th' land that was no farm at all.

"'T was thin I saw that th' barb-wire was caught in th' axle by the wheel an' was ravelin' off th' posts as they wint along. An' I wint along, hollerin' 'Wo!' into th' sthrong wan's ear. But he kept on plowin' away to where he was goin'. Wid that an idee kem to me at wanst. I w'u'd sink th' plow so deep 't w'u'd anchor thim to th' earth. So I jumped up on th' sate an' put on th' emergency brake, throwin' th' throttle over till th' last notch. An' thin th' plow threw a furrow that ye c'u'd 'a' berrid a man in; but divil a bit did they know it was tied to thim at all. Th' yoke wint a bit deeper into their bull necks, an' that was all. An' they kept pokin' on, nayther fasther nor shlower.

"Whin I looked back a quarther av a mile, I c'u'd see th' other ind av th' wire shnappin' off from post to post an' lettin' us out like th' sthring av a kite. 'This won't do at all. We 'll

2

be unwindin' th' whole farm,' says I. 'An'
I 'll have to be shtoppin' thim.' Wid that I
ran ahead an' shtood wavin' me arms an'
threatenin' thim back. But they kem sthraight
on, waggin' their horns befure thim; an' I had
to get out av th' way to kape from bein' kilt
an' berrid at wan operation.

"I 'll not be tellin' ye th' whole av it; for
't is n't a thing ye can tell about to some wan
ilse. Whin a horse does it, 't is somethin' to
shpake av; but what is it whin ye 're dragged
off by a parcel av cows? 'T is only a walk-out,
an' not a word av where ye 're goin' to.

"Whin I had been mad two or three times I
sat down on me sate; an' there were the medlarks hoppin' along behind an' chirpin' like
ye 'd think I was doin' it all for thim. 'Git
back, ye dom birds; d' ye want to be insultin'
me too?' says I. 'Git back to your field an'
mind yer business.' An' I cut out at thim wid
th' whip. An' there was th' wire as far back
as ye c'u'd see; an' it thrailin' in th' furrow
like ye 'd think I was layin' a cable.

"'T was an open, level counthry for a while,
wid here an' there a shtump or a hummock, an'
no sound but th' tinkle av a cow-bell in th' distance an' th' sound av th' grasshopper callin'
to his mate. Whin we were out av sight av

our own land, th' counthry sloped more till th' east, wid here an' there a bush or a young three that w'u'd bind befure th' axle an' thin shnap up sthraight again. There was an oak-three ahead, an' I was hopin' we 'd run sthraddle av that; but we changed our coorse befure that an' wint sthraight east.

"Th' cows were now settled down, tendin' sthrictly to th' business av walkin' away wid me; an' I thinks to mesilf, ' 'T is now mabby th' heavy-set cow will be listenin' to rayson.' So I got down an' wint alongside an' pounded him on th' nose, tellin' him to shtop.

" 'Wo! ye ould shtir-pot av a trouble-maker,' says I. 'Woe to ye, if ye don't wo!' says I.

"But he only nodded his head up an' down, as if he undhershtood what I was sayin' but did n't think much av me advice. An' nixt we crossed a counthry road. An' we put a thank-ye-ma'am acrost it that 'll be joltin' th' farmers for years to come.

"Whin I saw th' railroad ahead, I climbed up on me sate to be mindin' th' throttle; for I did n't want to be pullin' up th' thracks an' makin' that kind av throuble. So I put it foorward wid all me sthren'th to the last notch, an' threw her wide open wid th' plow 'way off th' ground intirely. An' we wint over th' rail-road widout doin' anny damage at all; th' iron wheels only bumpin' over th' rails.

"On th' other side av th' thracks we came to a sthrip av woods; an' we wint into thim, wid here an' there a thin pig lookin' at us in alarrm an' runnin' away like a deer. An' be-fure long we were headed for a naygur cabin that was shtandin' up high on props, like four legs, to be kapin' it out av th' shpring rises. Whin we were nearly to it I shtood up, an' got ready to jump; for I c'u'd see that th' iron axle w'u'd be catchin' wan av th' tall posts, an' I 'd be havin' the house down on top av me. We only shkinned it wid th' hub—but 't was a close escape, I 'm thinkin'.

"'T was thin I saw th' sight that brought th' satisfaction back to me again, an' med me feel like a man wanst more. For there was th' wather av th' river that I c'u'd see shpark-lin' bechune th' leaves av th' threes sthraight ahead an' shinin' in th' sun. 'T was th' Mis-sissippi; an' now we 'd be seein' was I th' boss or not.

"'I 'm thinkin' ye 'll be shtoppin' a while now,' says I. An' I got ready to be sayin', 'Wo!' whin they 'd have to be shtoppin'—just for th' satisfaction av it. An' whin we got to th' edge av it I shtood up an' said, 'Wo, now!'

"They kept sthraight on. They wint in it fasther than iver; an' befure I c'u'd get me mind we was plowin' into th' river, wid me holdin' me feet up out av th' wather an' thinkin' I w'u'd dive back to shore whin th' wather w'u'd be comin' up to me neck. An' they wint on till th' wather was half-way up their bellies, where they c'u'd take a dhrink widout th' throuble av shtoopin' their heads. An' whin I thought they were through dhrinkin' they w'u'd nayther go foorward nor back, but shtood there, mindin' th' scenery, wid th' river coolin' their legs, an' thim daddlin' their noses in th' wather. Whither th' little wan was shtandin' or floatin', I dunno; but I 'm thinkin' 't was a good thing he was blowed up like a bladder, he had to go in so deep to suit th' tall wan.

"An' there they shtood, peaceful-like; an' I c'u'd now see 't was this they had in mind to be doin' all th' time. An' I sat wid me legs up on th' sate, wonderin' if I w'u'd shwim off or wait till they 'd be goin' to grass an' take me along.

"Th' river was lappin' against th' throttle an' gushin' in the chain; an' I sat wid th' whip

in me hand in a way that I w'u'd only need a
hook on it to be catchin' catfish. An' behind
me was the fince-wire ladin' out av th' wather
like a throllin'-line. Had th' barbs on it wint
into a few av th' worms I had been turnin'
up, 't w'u'd be all ready to catch a sthring av
thim. An' thin I 'd 'a' been fishin'. An' th'
medlarks were cleanin' up th' last av their
meal.

"Afther a while (for I had now plenty av
time to mesilf) th' *Creole Belle* kem down th'
river an' called out wid th' base whistle av
her. An' th' tall wan looked out acrost th'
wather an' answered, 'Moo!' like givin' a signal for th' pilot to be passin' us on th' lift.

"I 'll not be tellin' ye all I thought, for I
can't; but th' ind av it was that I saw a man
comin' acrost in a shkiff, wid his back to us.
'T was th' cousin av Mary Ann bringin' back
the seed; an' I waited till he 'd be arrivin'.

" 'Halloo!' says I, shtandin' up in th' sate
on th' wather; 'we thought we 'd all be comin'
down to meet ye,' says I. 'Had ye been a little later, we 'd 'a' passed ye in th' middle.'

"He rowed around th' cows in th' boat, lookin' to see was iverything right.

" ' 'T is all right,' says I, 'for I have been
tindin' th' throttle; an' 't is now turned off.

If 't wa'n't for that we 'd be anchored to the bottom, I 'm thinkin'. An' I handled it bist av all on th' railroad.'

" 'How did ye get here?' says he.

" 'Th' same way that ye 'll be goin' back,' says I. 'An' ye 'll have no throuble at all figurin' it out, for a blind man c'u'd find th' way we kem.'

" 'Throw me th' whip,' says he.

" Whin he had it he rowed off a piece till he was in firin' range, an' thin he worked it at thim, wid explosions av hair flyin' off their backs—rid hair off wan av thim and black off another.

" 'Huddah, ye shtub-tailed Coaly! Huddah, ye Shpot! Get out av there, ye ramblin' carcass!' says he. An' th' dust av th' cracker wint off like fireworks befure their eyes, an' him sayin' their fav'rit' shwear-words till ye 'd think 't w'u'd sink th' boat. Wid that they med up their minds to be hurryin' out. An' they turned so short they upset th' plow an' sint me to th' bottom. Whin I kem up I took a few sthrokes down-sthream to be gettin' rid av their company; an' thin I turned to land.

"Whin he had thim shtarted back I got into th' boat an' headed for Tinnissee an' th' sandhouse—for 't was time for me to go.

"That was all that happened till me at farm-in'. But there 's manny kinds av throttles, an' it much depinds on what kind av power ye are turnin' on. I don't care to be tearin' up th' earth like that again; but, annyway, what-iver I do, it can't be said that I have n't med me mark in th' worruld."

CHAPTER II

HEN Michael had finished this explanation of why he had not seen Mary Ann, to which Mrs. Finerty listened with a rapt seriousness that sometimes arose to horror, he opened the door of the wall-clock and fumbled about inside until he found the stump of a lead-pencil, stopping the pendulum in his search. Then he started the pendulum again, dampened the point of the pencil on his tongue, and sat down on the step. While he was engaged with the pencil and a piece of paper that he had torn from a bag of sugar, Mrs. Finerty turned her attention to the stubborn stove, and deciding that it needed coaxing along, she went out into the yard to split kindling-wood. Presently she came in to procure a case-knife and a flat-iron, with which to get through a knot.

"What is it ye are figurin' on, Michael?"

"How much have ye now put away, Marg'ret?"

"Elivin dollars an' forty cints," she replied.

"Twinty dooes n't go intil that manny times. D' ye know, had I th' money, what I w'u'd do? I w'u'd sind Agnes away to college."

"College!" exclaimed Mrs. Finerty.

"Yis; to be a stinnygrafter. I hear ye can go intil it for twinty dollars to shtart. An' mabby they 'd be comin' down till tin."

"She w'u'd be wearin' silks an' satins," mused Mrs. Finerty. And, having contemplated the problem with her finger at the corner of her mouth, she continued: "But 't w'u'd n't be safe, Michael, to be takin' all th' money at wanst. Ye can't tell."

"No," remarked Michael; "I was only jist figurin' on it. 'T w'u'd not do, for ye can't tell whin th' hard times might be comin' on. I 'm hopin'—and fearin'—that th' Dimmycrats will get in again. An' ye can't tell what another administhration might be doin'."

"'T is uncertain," she replied.

"But 't is th' fine worruk, an' had I th' money 't is that I w'u'd do."

He put the pencil back in the clock, again interfering with the pendulum and starting it up again. And then he shut the door on the pencil and resumed his seat on the step.

IN one corner of Mrs. Finerty's kitchen was the flour-barrel on a three-legged stool that had each of its feet in a cup of water to keep the ants away—or, rather, there were but two cups; for the third leg, that was out of the way in the corner, stood in a broken yellow bowl. Against another wall was the wash-bench before a small mirror; and the wash-basin was set down in the center of Mrs. Finerty's largest tub, an arrangement calculated to save her immaculate household from the splashing that Michael indulged in when he came home early in the morning and got the coal-dust off him, washing always "down to the belt." In its proper place under the bench was half a cocoanut-shell nailed to a block of wood, from which bowl the cat had learned to take her occasional sup of milk in a cleanly manner. Before the cook-stove was a round "twist" mat; and where its circumvolutions of twisted and sewed rags came to a vortex in the middle, the cat was always attracted; and there she would "cuddle," as if by a law of nature, and purr in unison with the tea-kettle. Besides the drop-leaf table and the cupboard, whose tin front had ornamental holes in it and was called a "safe," there was little else for her to scrub and scour, which caused her to go over them the more often with added particularity. And in the bottom compartment of the "safe" was a sort of yellow earthenware caster intended to hold medicines, as if its manufacturer had designed it, not only to keep company with the food, but also to follow it to the table. In it was the "black oil" that cured all superficial disasters, either bruise or cut; and there was the ipecac, the most sovereign remedy for almost anything else that a Finerty could be afflicted with. And whether Mrs. Finerty always diagnosed right or not, the ipecac was at least sufficient to make Michael forget any other ailment after she made him take it.

The floor of the kitchen was lower than the general level of the house, so that she went into the middle room by taking a step up; and the sense of the kitchen's comfortable abasement from the higher plane of the carpeted portion made Mrs. Finerty often declare that it was "cozy-like and aisy."

In the middle room was the high chest of drawers supporting an ancient brass candlestick and a pair of snuffers; and balancing it off on the opposite side of the room was the

American invasion of a "what-not," whose shelves bore a mock orange, a piece of glass in a curious chunk from a glass-house, and other inutiles, which kept their place merely because long occupancy had given them a˙ permanent right of existence, even though they had behind them the history of ten thousand dustings. Here, also, was the high-posted bed in which Mrs. Finerty and Agnes slept while Michael was working; and under it was the hatchet which had given them the confidence to sleep unprotected for many years. It had certainly been there every night as long as Agnes could remember; and she, with a lifelong confidence in her mother's prowess, dropped early to rest, in the assurance that when the long-delayed tramp or burglar got round to his job of robbing them he would come to grief at the hands of her mother.

Going out again to take a look at the elbow of stovepipe that topped the low brick chimney,—an experiment of Michael's at fixing her troubles,—Mrs. Finerty made puzzled observation of the direction of the wind; and then she came in and took the hatchet out from under the bed, resolved to conquer the stove. She fell to splitting, or, rather, hammering, wood on the cinder-path, occasionally shying away the goat that persisted in investigating her doings.

Failing in her efforts with the hatchet, she recollected the use of the case-knife; and now, by dint of it and the flat-iron, she resolved to finish splitting the wood. Michael came out, and stood for a while watching her operations.

"Lave go an' let me do it fur ye wid th' hatchet. 'T is no way to be goin' at it."

He took up the hatchet and battered away without accomplishing more than smooth welts on the side of the stick. Then he paused and examined the dull, rounded edge of the hatchet.

"'T is time 't was fixed," he remarked. "'T was time tin years ago. I think I will sind a thramp up an' lave him rub it an hour or two on th' brick to put an edge on it."

"A *thramp!*" exclaimed Mrs. Finerty. "An' to be sharpenin' th' *hatchet!* Ye 'll not be doin' that. 'T is well ye know, Michael," —and she said it in a tone of injury and admonishment,—"that th' hatchet is not only for choppin' th' kindlin'-wood. 'T is th' only protiction I have; an' I will have no edge on it for th' burglars. I w'u'd be wantin' to shtun thim aisy. If 't was th' kind that w'u'd draw th' blood, I w'u'd *not* have th' *heart* to do it."

To this Michael was unable to reply. Giving

the implement another critical examination, he continued to hack at the wood with breaking blows. When he came in with the splintered reward of his labor he saw that she had put the "skittle" on the hot end of the stove, and he disappeared into the other part of the house while she made further preparation for his "afther-dinner breakfast."

As Mrs. Finerty busied herself she heard a sound as of stamping and stumbling; and as it kept up with a sort of regularity she abandoned her cooking to look through the door of the middle room. Michael was standing in the center of the room, making experimental tappings and stampings with his feet, stopping and starting over again repeatedly, and maintaining an upright clog-step posture with his head well up, but his eyes bent down, as if, to use her expression, "he did not want his fate to notice that he was lookin' at thim."

"What are ye up to, Michael?"

"I 'm thryin' this," he replied, executing a cross-step. "'T is th' fine shtep, c'u'd I get it. I think I now have it." And to exhibit it to her he attacked the movement in such style that he set the house rattling. As the flimsy floor began to quake, Mrs. Finerty made a sudden dash across the room.

"Th' china *duck!*" she exclaimed in alarm. "Th' DUCK! Shtop it quick!" And by the time Michael had seized the situation and checked himself, she grabbed it from the edge of the shelf and had it safely in her hand.

"'T will be broke yet wid th' foolishness. Th' other night, whin ye had young Barney over here doin' his jiggin' for th' company, I looked up jist in time, for there was th' duck shwimmin' off th' what-not. 'T is th' second time I have saved it," she commented, as she set it where it could swim safely in the middle of the flowered bed. "We 'll be losin' it yet," she continued. "An' Agnes says 't is th' finest piece av brick-a-bat we have."

Before Michael could make any extenuating remarks on his "foolishness," Mrs. Finerty's experienced nose sensed something wrong in the kitchen, and she hastened to the rescue. Michael sat down on the edge of his wife's bed, with his back to the duck, and looked about in a bereft and unresolved state of mentality.

"Come on out now," said Mrs. Finerty, looking in through the door. "Come and ate what is lift av th' mate. Ye have made me burn it. An' it has gone up half a cint—which is good-by to th' other half a cint."

Michael placed his erring feet under the

table, and began the solemn ceremonial of eating the singed meat, the while Mrs. Finerty sat down opposite to have her daily look at him.

"What is it that has put th' jiggin' into yer fate, Michael,—an' that befure ye 've had bite or sup?"

" 'T is a sand-jig that wan av th' byes was showin' me."

"Faith, 't is little ye don't know about sand, Michael."

"Had n't I ought to?" he replied; "an' me bein' guardeen av sand now for sixteen year. An' befure I sint for ye was n't I tindin' it on th' Santy Fay, where 't was nothin' but sand —an' th' desert med av it. 'T was often I felt foolish settin' there wid me little houseful— an' no wan but mesilf in sight as far as I c'u'd see. 'T was a lucky day whin I quit th' job, for I c'u'd niver be gettin' away from me business. Was Agnes a bye, I 'm thinkin' I 'd call her Sandy. What shtory is she radin' now?"

"Th' wan of thim is about 'Lola, th' Belle av th' Bindery.' An' jukes an' countesses. I have read a few worruds out av it, and she must shtop that wan. F'r there is a countess in it that can be doin' nothin' but she must switch her shkirt an' be off till th' grand saloon. 'T is

3

bad enough for ye min to be goin' to Rafferty's, without weemen comin' till it.''

Having thus been led into a subject up to his chin, Michael had to close his mouth and be silent. When the clock struck four he looked at his watch to see what time it was; then he donned his corduroy coat and limp hat and departed to get his jury money from the city, and, if he had time, to see Dennis, the plain-clothesman at the police station, who was brother-in-law to Michael's cousin.

Mrs. Finerty followed him to the gate, calling after him: ''Michael dear! Be careful, an' don't be run over be th' pony-injine.''

By half-past seven o'clock, Finerty was back at the yards, and making his way along the tracks. He stopped where a rail was beginning to feather at the end and a tie had grown uneasy in its bed. ''There 's *another* thing has got to be fixed,'' he soliloquized, inspecting it critically with his foot. He contemplated it a while and then proceeded on his way, as if the management of a railroad were a perplexing burden to carry through the world. Arriving at the sand-house, he unlocked it and left the hasp hanging; and while he worked around the chutes he looked up occasionally with the interest of a man who has set a trap.

"Oh, Halloran," said Finerty to the engineer of Number Twenty, as he threw on the last scoopful of coal that the tender would hold, "d' ye know that me daughther Agnes is a great wan at th' bukes?"

"So?" remarked Halloran, contriving to delay himself with unnecessary work around the side-rods.

"Yis. An' whin 't is n't bukes 't is th' continual-shtory papers—but there 's manny big worruds in thim. How she raymimbers thim all I dunno, for th' way they are printed she won't be finished wid wan till she 'll be shtartin' another wan an' her different ways through all th' rist av thim. I 'm thinkin' she has more brains nor th' thrain-despatcher to be kapin' thrack av thim—for they 're runnin' all on each other's time."

As Halloran climbed up into the cab Finerty followed and stayed on the engine while she ran up the track to "hook on," himself taking a hand at the bell while the fireman threw in some of the newly acquired coal.

"Oh, Halloran!" he shouted, as the engine rumbled along and swerved onto the main track.

"Yes, Mike."

"D' ye know what I 'm goin' to make av

her?''—yelling it loud enough to overcome the tread of the wheels and the din of the bell.

''What?''

''A *stinnygrafter*,'' he answered, checking the bell to give the word a chance. ''An' there 'll be th' way av gettin' her a job in th' *coort*.''

He attended to his ringing for some time, leaning out and watching the track ahead. Then he suddenly drew in his head and added: '' 'T is her w'u'd have th' *intilligince*. She 's th' bist in school in *algeberry*.'' At this he gave the bell a jerk that turned it a complete somersault and caused it to lose tongue as he said the word. And then he was silent until Number Twenty had coupled up to the train.

''Yis, Halloran,'' he continued, as the engineer got down with the oiler and made final inspection for the run, '' 't is her w'u'd have th' intilligince. An' she can write compositions about annything. Th' wan av thim is called, '' 'T is a Good Wind that Blows Nobody Ill.' An', be th' same token, I 'm thinkin' 't was a good wan that put me intil th' jury business. 'T was there I saw th' stinnygraftin'. There was a fine bit av a girl that c'u'd take th' worruds right out av yer mouth—an' I was talkin' till her. So I asked her to put down wan worrud while I c'u'd see her do it. 'Will ye jist write down *me?*' says I. An' d' ye know, Halloran, she made a dot wid an eyebrow on it, an' there 't was lookin' right at ye. 'T was quick as a wink.''

"I think there 's a hobo in the sand-house, Mike," said Halloran. "You 'd better look in when you go back.''

"'T is me that knows it," said Michael. "'T is wan I 'll have divertin' me th' night.''

CHAPTER III

HAT evening, Mrs. Michael Finerty came down the tracks of the Memphis "yards," bearing on her arm Michael's big bright dinner-pail, which winked familiarly at the switch-lights as it passed. As regularly as the sun went down, Michael's pail, being destined to shine at night, took on a brilliance of its own from the rubbing of brick-dust which she gave it before it received those two large nameless meals which Michael consumed between nightfall and morning. She was bound for the little sand-house.

The sand-house and the coal-chutes, stilted and somber, were situated on the Memphis levee where the tracks run parallel with the river. The house itself was about fifteen feet square. The bank of drying sand occupied about half this area, being held back at its base by a board; and in the middle of the other half was the stove. The coal-box and the bucket occupied the two remaining corners. It being necessary for the sand to flow freely through the pipe whenever the engineer opens the valve, it is kept so dry that a handful will escape through the fingers as steadily as the flow of an hour-glass. And many a tramp, having knowledge of the prosperous railway stove that dwelt therein, would approach Finerty during the cold spells that occasionally invade even the balmy clime of Tennessee; knowing which, Mrs. Finerty had worried until the idea of tramps had become the bane of her life. When she woke up in her bed at night it would be to worry about Michael braving death between tramps and locomotives.

But Finerty, not being alive to danger, would parley with them if it suited his fancy; and sometimes he would inspect the horny palm that was usually extended in proof that the applicant was in the habit of working. Thus he had truly predicted so many a man's fate that he prided himself on being quite a "hand-rader." It was Halloran who used to tell tales of Finerty's feats in prescience. "Ye are a man av an aisy-goin' disposition, an' nothin' is like to worry ye much till ye feel it. Ye have come from a distance, an' ye are goin' on a journey. An' if ye don't shtart soon ye 'll be recayvin' a prisint from a man about my size."

When Mrs. Finerty had arrived at the sand-house, which goal she had kept steadily in eye, she set the bucket on the bench outside and began to touch up her person primly. Having assured herself, by stroking her palms on her head, that no hairs had strayed from their slick arrangement, accurately parted, she folded her arms and composed herself in the knowledge that she would be presentable to any of the yard-hands that might chance to pass.

"Yis," she replied to a switchman who greeted her, "I have brought it mesilf th' night. Michael was goin' up t' th' station t' see Dinnis, th' plain-clothesman,—he that is brother-in-law t' Michael's cousin,—an' thin he was goin' t' thry t' get his jury money from th' city, which has now been owin' him four months. He has served for thim five times a'ready; an' if they don't be payin' up I 'll have him shtop worrukin' at it."

Noticing that the door of the sand-house was unlocked, she pulled it open by the hasp and went in and set the bucket by the warm stove. What was her amazement, when she looked about in the faint light of the glowing stove, to see the figure of a man reclining half-way up the side of the steep sand-pile! He was lying full length on his back, with his hands clasped behind his head; and he was looking down on things below in evident content of his superior advantages. When Mrs. Finerty looked him over curiously, trying to see how he rested with such easy security on such an impossible place, she observed that one leg was driven to the knee in the sand, anchoring him, as it were, to the unstable declivity. But where he got the power to drive it in like that was a more striking mystery. The man ventured an uncertain smile. Mrs. Finerty immediately took up her bucket and gave him another moment of very foreign contemplation. And when the two had made a mutual exchange of silence, she marched out of the door again, closed it behind her, and stood waiting in the chill air.

Having waited what seemed a long time to her, she went over to the chutes to look about, thinking that perchance her husband had gone there directly on his return. But he had not appeared; and already she noticed among the day men premonitions of the moment for quitting work. After a few minutes she began to be visibly perturbed. She walked a short distance down the tracks, looking before her as if she expected to find traces of Michael on every tie, and looking back apprehensively now and then to assure herself that she was not in the road of the switch-engine. "The pony-injine," she often declared, "is too soft-futted to be allowed in a yard where th' childer do be playin'." When she got back to the chutes after her aimless walk, eight o'clock was ominously near, and still Michael had not come. She hurried across the tracks to the sand-house again, making inquiries of every "hand" she met. Here she took her final stand beside the shining pail, looking solemnly at the tracks, with her needle-marked finger pressed to the corner of her mouth, and expressing her fears to the switchman and several of the "day min."

"I have th' feelin' that somethin' has happened him. What is kapin' him from worruk is nothin' nathral. He has n't been late for six year come th' sivinteenth av nixt Mar-r-r-ch. I was thinkin' he 'd be back in time to have a cup av tay to nourish him. 'T w'u'd give him sthren'th to coal up Number Twinty-wan."

At that instant the "soft-futted" pony-engine added itself to her audience, and Finerty stepped off the foot-board with a package in his hand. Giving his wife a quick glance, he slapped the package down on the bench; and while he gave the pony-engine a "go-ahead" signal with one hand, the other reached out and grabbed the shovel at exactly eight o'clock. And he was away with the tool of his trade on his shoulder.

"Michael," she called after him, "what was ailin' ye?"

"Don't be hinderin' me," he called back, with a wave of his hand; "I have me worruk to do."

And indeed he had; for the engineer of Number Twenty-one had just brought her to a well-calculated stop at the chutes, and the air was in a tremor for a block around as her vibrant boilers trembled like a racer before the start. Mrs. Finerty sat down in company of the tin bucket, to which she knew he must inevitably return. When Number Twenty-one had been coaled up and seen off, he came ambling leisurely across the tracks; and, having arrived at the bench, he seated himself on the other side of the tin pail. Mrs. Finerty held her peace for a while, taking in shrewdly that some of the men who were loitering about seemed to have a curiosity as to her family affairs. But seeing that they did not depart, she began:

"What has happened till ye, Michael?"

"*What* has happened?" he replied equivocally, having also an eye to the audience, whom he would in nowise have think that he was a henpecked man.

"That ye were nearly late, Michael."

"*Nearly* late! 'T is that th' superintindent w'u'd promote ye for. He w'u'd call it roonin' on time."

Michael very deliberately produced an abbreviated pipe from an inside pocket, and, having filled it, he packed it methodically with the head of a nail that he picked out of the cinders before the door. Mrs. Finerty, seeing how the land lay, now turned her attention to inspecting the package; and she brought to light three slices of bread and a link of smoked sausage. This disclosure forced him immediately out of his equivocation.

"Well, I will tell ye," he said. "I had th' pony run me down opposite Rafferty's place whilst I w'u'd be goin' in an' takin' some av his free lunch f'r th' thramp."

"A *thramp!*" exclaimed Mrs. Finerty, bridling up and looking fixedly. "Is he *that?* What has come over ye, Michael?"

"*What* has come over me?" he replied, assuming his mood again.

"That *ye* sh'u'd be kapin' a thramp! Afther ye promisin' me ye w'u'd niver take in a single *wan* av thim."

"Right ye are!" said Michael, striking a match, as if by way of emphasis. "An' so I will not. He is only three quarthers av a wan."

He took a philosophic puff or two, as if this settled the case beyond rebuttal. "Come on, now, and have yer say about it," he said, leading the way into the sand-house and shutting the door by way of privacy. He threw open the doors of the stove for illumination, and the two stood looking at the elevated stranger as if he were a picture hung up for their critical inspection.

"Tell us, now, did ye iver do anny worruk?" said Finerty.

"Why, yes; I was tellin' you I—" began the wanderer, extending down the calloused hand that he thought was expected of him.

"Ye nade not be showin' us that at all," said Mrs. Finerty, giving her head a perverse turn. "Manny av yees get that from hangin' on th' rods."

"*Hand* us yer leg," said Finerty, peremptorily.

The vagrant put his hands to his knee and pulled out that part of himself that had been serving as a post in the sand-pile; and, deftly undoing a buckle or two, he handed down the wooden member.

"Now d'ye see, Marg'ret?" said Finerty, taking it in his hand and putting his forefinger on a part of the peg-leg. "D'ye see th' saw-marks on it—like on th' sthraddle-beam av a sawbuck? 'T is this leg he holds th' shticks wid, an' 't is from th' saw slippin' sudden-like. 'T is for *that* I have let him in." Then, after a pause and a look of seriousness that was only a smile in disguise, he added: "An' if he was n't th' bright boy he might 'a' sawed aff his leg."

But this was entirely lost on Mrs. Finerty, who was absorbed in considering the man himself, the other half of his leg being of more import to her than the one that Finerty held. The tramp now had both hands dug into the sand to keep himself from sliding down to their feet, and he returned her gaze with a humorous expression of doubt and appreciation. And there was that in his blue eyes—which Mrs. Finerty regarded especially—which showed that he was rather disposed to side with the world in any jovial view it might take of his misfortune.

"I 'll not be sayin' annything at all, Michael," she finally concluded. "'T is ye that runs th' sand-house." And when they had gone out she added, as she took her leave, "He has n't a bad eye in his head. Annyway, I 'll not have it on *me* to be puttin' a wan-legged 'bye out in th' cold.''

When Finerty had given sand and coal to Number Twenty-two, he returned to the warm sand-house to avail himself of an ''aisy spell.'' Having hung his lantern in the corner, he turned the bucket upside down and seated himself on it. Then he brought forth the short-stemmed clay pipe and filled it with scrapings from various pockets. As he threw his head back to avoid the flames of the sulphur match so close to his face, he regarded his lone guest, and stopped puffing long enough to remark: '' 'T is th' handy leg ye have, th' way ye are usin' it.''

''Yes, it is. And it ought to be a famous leg, too, considering how much it got into the newspapers a few years back. There was one paper that had it, 'Human Brute Holds Up Four Citizens with a Club.' And the carriage-shop being broken into that night made it all the worse. Another paper said it was a 'Carnival of Crime.' But Bill was n't doing things polite just then. He was about disgusted with having to dodge around the country ready to fight the police all the time. This leg was the spoke of a barouche. It was polished till you could see your nose in it, with a green stripe down the side. It was a Sunday-go-to-meetin' leg about eight years ago. But it is about worn out, and I wish I knew where Bill is now. I think that if he made me another it would n't be such a long story."

"Is ther' a shtory to it?" said Finerty, taking out his Brobdingnagian watch and staring into the face of it, to calculate how much time he had to spare. Settling himself with his elbows on his knees, he looked up and simply remarked, "We will be havin' th' shtory."

CHAPTER IV

ND "Stumpy," knowing what was required of him in return for the lodging, began:

"Bill was a partner of mine. At the time I met him they wanted him in New Orleans for a murder—which he did n't do. Bill was a natural mechanic and an all-round workman. When he got into trouble he was doing some blacksmith work on the brig *Lion,* a Liverpool vessel that had come within an inch of being lost rounding the Horn. Lying next to the *Lion* was the bark *Betsy* of Boston. Bill became friends with the bo's'n of the *Betsy,* and they used to go out evenings together. The bo's'n was a bad-tempered one when things did n't go right; but mostly he was a good fellow, except when he had too much whisky aboard. One day he was in a bad state of mind for a good many reasons, and he was mad at the captain. And then the weather went against him. When he was painting some canvas on top of the galley it began to rain. That did n't suit him at all and he got madder and madder. He would stop painting and shake his brush at the sky like he was trying to pick a quarrel with it, yelling, 'Rain, damn ye; rain! That 's it; rain!' Then he would take a drink and cuss more. But he would n't stop painting. He 'd rassle the rolling raindrops around on the greasy paint and dab it all in and cuss.''

''Ye w'u'd n't be gettin' th' best av that felly if he had a *fair show,*'' remarked Finerty.

''This fellow,'' continued Stumpy, ''was named Tiffin; and he used to drink his water out of a 'monkey'—a sort of stoneware tea-kettle with a cork atop of it instead of a lid, such as they use for sailors to drink out of at sea. For a sailor can't very well drink out of a bucket with a tin cup when she 's rolling hard and pitching—fresh water being too valuable to be spilled around. And Tiffin was so used to it that he could hold the monkey about six inches above his face, and pour a stream straight down into his stomach without spilling a drop or stopping to swallow. He liked his whisky straight out of the bottle, and would drink it in the same way. On this day he had whisky mixed with the water.''

''Th' wather was more vallyble at that,'' remarked Finerty.

''When it stopped raining he stopped working. Then he came over to the *Betsy's* wharf to tell his troubles to Bill, carrying the whisky and water under his arm. Because Bill would n't take a drink with him he hauled off and hit Bill a welt in the forehead with the monkey. But it struck on the cork, driving it in without doing Bill much damage. Bill was n't the kind that liked fighting just for the sake of it; but when he was caught suddenly there was a good deal of the devil in him, and if he got started on any kind of a job he would be bound to see it through. He hit the bo's'n a welt in the nose, and then took after him with a cotton-hook, never saying a word—but looking it. Just as he put the cotton-hook through the bo's'n's coat-tail, Tiffin tore away and dodged into the galley, where he shut himself in. Bill pounded the door of the galley with his fist and tried to break it open, until the crew came to the rescue. As they dragged him off the ship Bill kept shaking his fist at the galley and telling what he would do to the bo's'n.

''This Tiffin used to roll aboard late at night

and sleep in the galley whenever the cook had a night off. The cook's bunk was a sort of shelf fastened to the wall with hinges, and it was a cool place for the mate to sleep with the doors open. On the morning after the fight the bo's'n was gone. One of his old shirts, all torn and bloody, showed that he had slept in the galley. And there were spots of blood that led out of the door and over the side of the ship—the offshore side. It didn't take them long to calculate that Tiffin's body was on its way to the Gulf of Mexico. And when three policemen got the best of Bill and took him up to the jail and searched him, they didn't have to think long before they made up their minds who had done it.

"Tiffin had a brass-handled knife and a coin that was a pocket-piece. The coin had three legs on it running like a wheel. He got it in the Isle of Man. He had carried it for years, and he showed it whenever he got to talking about his voyages. They found the knife and the coin in Bill's pocket. When they asked him about the knife he told them he had borrowed it from Tiffin; but when they brought out the coin Bill hadn't a word to say. All he could say was that he didn't know how it could have got into his pocket; it was a mystery to him."

"They'd be thinkin' 't was runnin' in on its three legs—for to help the knife whittle a shtick," said Finerty, significantly. "'T is that th' police have a way av thinkin'."

"The long and short of it was," continued Stumpy, "that he was held over to the grand jury."

"And are yez thryin' to tell me this felly didn't kill th' bo's'n av th' ship? 'T is that ye were sayin' when ye shtarted," said Finerty, shrewdly.

"That's what I did say."

"An' 't was him that was tellin' ye."

"Whether it was him that was telling me or not, that's how it was. He took up with me for a partner, and I knew he didn't kill him because he *told* me so. It was a puzzle to him. But what I started to tell is how he got me this leg."

"Verra well. Don't let me be hindtherin' ye."

"As I was saying, Bill was put in jail and held over to the grand jury. He sat in jail and contented himself a couple of weeks, hoping that some day they would find who killed Tiffin and let him out. But nothing turned up; and he began to see that it was not likely that they would do much to help him, because they had

their minds made up that they had caught the
murderer. And Bill, when he studied it over
and thought what he would say to the jury,
made up his mind that if he was on the jury
himself in the same kind of a case, he would
say, Guilty. Every way he looked at it he
could n't see anything but a sure case. And
every day he saw he was getting to be more of
a criminal to the rest of them just by sitting
in the cage holding his hands together. And
sitting idle like that came hard on him, anyway,
because he was always used to being at work
on some kind of a hard job. Bill could always
hold a job in almost any kind of a shop, and
nothing pleased him better than to be put at
something that had puzzled the rest of them.
Then he would show them some trick that they
had n't heard of. As Bill used to say, 'It 's
the little things that count.' And he had got to
be a whole cyclopedia of wrinkles from what
he had thought out himself and what he had
learned from traveling around. And what he
had n't seen he 'd think of. And if it was a
risky thing to be done Bill would sail in, for he
was n't afraid of anything as long as it was a
job of work.''

"Some av thim is mighty scared av that,"
remarked Finerty, significantly.

"I remember one time he got a job fixing a broken shaft on a stern-wheeler. One of the helpers dropped the monkey-wrench into the river about twenty feet from shore—a big wrench two feet long. Bill threw off his shoes and dived in after it while the rest were trying to tell him he might be drifted under the boat. While they were standing ready to give him a hand if he came up, and thinking what a fool he was to go after a chunk of iron he could n't rise with, Bill called to them from the shore with the wrench across his shoulder. He had walked ashore on bottom with it, not having to crawl more than eight or ten feet before he could stand up with his head out. Then he went to work as if he did such things every day.

"But, as I was about to say, when he had thought over the trial until he saw plainly that there was no way out of it but being hung, according to law, he made up his mind he might as well die by shooting as by hanging. Anyway, he had loafed as long as he could stand it. His mind had been working on the cell at times when he was n't particularly intending to get out, for his brains had to be always working on a job. And now that it was a case of live or die, he set about it. First he got the steel springs out of the soles of his shoes. Then he went to work at his heel-plates. Bill used to run his shoes over at the heel, and he did n't like the soft iron plates sold in the stores, because they wore out on stone as quick as lea-ther. So he made himself a pair out of a file which he had softened up so that he could shape and bore it, and then tempered again, glass-hard. That was how he had the face of a good file on the inner side of his heel-plates. With the steel springs he unscrewed them and turned them over and screwed them on his shoes again, so that he had two files with good solid handles. Then he went to work with the two files, and the knife and the saw he had made from the springs. Bill used to say that the rest of the job of breaking out of jail was n't half as hard as breaking into the in-soles of his shoes with a piece of steak-bone to get something to start with.''

''I have *seen* shteak,'' remarked Finerty, ''that w'u'd be as ha-ard to break into befure he did *that*.''

''One night,'' continued Stumpy, ''when everything was right, he got out of the cell and ran to a side passage where there was a door that opened into a blind hallway. The door was locked. He cut around the edge of the panel where it was thinnest, making a V-shaped slit, the way a Norwegian wood-carver does. It was a soft panel, and in about two times round he had it out and laid it on the floor as soft as serving a pancake for breakfast. At the end of the hall he found there was a window. It was swelled and jammed so tight he could n't raise it. On the floor was an old awning and a bucket of asphaltum that the painters had been using. He cut a piece out of the canvas and gave it a coat of the sticky asphaltum. Then he pasted it up like wall-paper against the glass, leaving a tuck in the middle of the canvas. By the time he had untied an iron pulley from the awning the asphaltum was set. He tapped the glass once with the sharp edge of the pulley, starting it to crack. Then he took hold of the tuck in the middle of the canvas and pulled out the pane, breaking it to bits, without dropping a piece or making any noise. He rolled up the window-pane and threw it down a narrow place between two walls; for just then the dev-ilment came over him to have the police wondering how a window could be broken out without a noise and no glass around. He dropped to the roof of another building, slid down the legs of a cistern to the alley, and started north."

"Is this shtory supposed to be thrue?" queried Finerty.

"Of course. I'm just telling you what he did, so that you will understand the rest."

"Th' legs av a *wha-a-at?*" said Finerty, withdrawing his pipe for the nonce.

"Of a cistern. You see, in New Orleans the cisterns are all up on props in the air because they can't dig in the ground. It is below the level of the river."

"Go on wid yer shtory," said Finerty.

CHAPTER V

"A that time I had a job watching a coal-barge that the *Vineland* had dropped ashore about fifteen miles below Memphis in the Arkansaw woods. In those days I used to be always looking out for a job of work, thinking I would strike something steady. I had n't found out that there was n't any use in me trying to get ahead. I had got on the *Vineland* at St. Louis to work around the cabin and peel potatoes, without any pay except my keep and the ride to New Orleans. The *Vineland* was one of the big boats that push the wheat-barges down the Mississippi—those big barges that look like Noah's Arks, lashed together by twos in a train with the power-boat pushing them from behind with her flat nose."

"'T is like railroadin' on the river," said Finerty.

"The *Vineland* was loaded down to the waterline with the weight of her own machinery, and the coal-barges were lashed along her sides, as she made the twelve-hundred-mile trip. One day when she dropped an empty, the captain told me that watching a barge would be a good job for a one-legged fellow, and he would give me a chance to make a couple of dollars. And that was how I came to be lying there with plenty of provisions in the Arkansaw woods, about fifteen miles from anywheres.

"One evening, when I was sitting on the barge feeling lonesome and looking ahead on two more weeks of the same kind of life, there came a fellow out of the woods who looked tired and hungry.

" 'Good evening, captain,' said he.

" 'Evening,' said I.

" 'How 's navigation?' said he.

" 'Rather slow,' said I. 'Do you live around these parts—or are you hunting?'

" 'Well, you might say I 'm hunting,' said he. 'You don't happen to know where I could find a piece of bread and butter,—in change for a good pipe of tobacco, do you?'

" 'Sure thing,' said I. 'But where are you from and where are you going?'

" 'Well, I 'll tell you, partner,' said he. 'I 've just escaped from behind the bars. They caught me riding on the cow-catcher back here in the woods a few miles, and they put me out while they were side-tracked for a passenger to pass. It was the first time I was ever invited from behind the bars in my life. And just at the present time I am lost. I don't suppose you ever traveled that way, did you?'

" 'Once or twice,' said I.

" 'Well, I ain't making any apologies,' said he; 'but this was my first time. And if you 've got the bread and butter to spare I would really appreciate it.' So I gave him the bread and butter.

"And that was how I met Bill.

"The first thing that made me warm up to him was his sitting up nights to keep the gnats off me. It was after the spring rise, and the woods were full of them, so I had n't had a good night's rest since I could remember. 'I 'll give you first sleep,' says he. He took a box of sulphur matches out of his pocket—the kind that make you turn your head till they stop burning blue and yellow. I was a little slow about going to sleep. Every once in a while I would wake up out of a doze and open one eye.. And there would be Bill keeping the gnats off me. I lay there a long time with one eye part open when he thought I was sleeping, and every time he lit a match I would take a good look at him. And the more I looked at him the better I liked him.

"In the morning when I woke up and looked around I thought he was gone. But pretty soon he came out of the dark hole from where he had been sleeping inside the hold of the scow on a board that he had fixed up to keep him off the bilge-water. He stayed that day and then another, keeping me company. And the upshot of it was that we got to feeling like shipmates.

"One day—I 'll never forget it—he sat quiet a long time, sizing me up with a peculiar look in his eyes. Then he said, very slow and deliberate, 'Well, partner, I see you 're the kind I can be honest with.' And he told me fair and square what had happened to him. 'Now, honest,' says he, 'can you believe it 's true when I say I did n't kill Tiffin—or can't you?'

" 'I know you did n't,' says I. 'I can see you 're on the square.' And I 'll never forget, if I live to be a thousand years old, the look in his eye when he said, in a sort of quiet way, 'Well, I 've got somebody that believes me.'

"We sat and smoked a while. Then he said: 'I guess I 've boarded off you about long enough. It 's about time for me to be moving

on to the back country. You see how it is, partner—it 's a case of dead or alive; and with me
it 's going to be dead.' "

"He w'u'd be good for th' reward, all th'
same," remarked Finerty; "but they 're not
like to bring so much whin they 're dead."

" 'But,' he says to me, 'I 'm glad I know
you. And it 's hoping that I 'll get the best of
them and some day come across you again.'
With that he put his hand behind his back
under his coat-tails, and pulled his belt around.
He had a holster with a revolver in it, and a
pocket made of the top of a boot-leg filled with
cartridges. He took out the revolver and
cleaned it up, examining its action, and putting
it in shape in a way that showed he knew all
about its workings.

" 'Better stay on a couple of days, anyhow,'
said I.

" 'Think so?' said he, looking up from his
work.

" 'I ain't supposed to know anything about
you,' said I. 'And if anybody comes along
you can lay low in the dark hole.'

" 'Well, I ought to be getting farther away;
but if you look at it that way I guess I *will* stay
a while. I ain't very anxious to be saying
good-by myself.'

"So he stayed on and we spent the time together, he telling me more about the hard jobs he 'd done, and me letting him know some of the hard times I 'd seen. About a week after that the *Vineland* showed up down-river. He jumped up and got ready to leave. Then he turned to me and, looking me in the eye, he said: 'Maybe you 'd better change your mind and go on with the boat instead of coming with me. I 'm bad company.'

" 'I 'll go along,' said I.

" ' Anyway, I 'll say good-by,' said he. 'I 'll go back in the woods and wait a while. But of course,' says he, as if he was afraid I might change my mind when the boat came, 'if I got into trouble it would n't be any trouble of yours. And you could go on your way at any time.'

"And I could see that it was harder for him to give me up than he was saying.

" 'You ain't as bad company as I am,' said I, kicking up my bad leg.

" 'Then it 's a go,' said he, brightening up. 'I 'll take care of you, and don't you forget it. Maybe I will have a chance to show you a trade that will put you on the way of being something. I don't like to be saying good-by, and maybe we won't have to at all. Anyway,

I can make a good umbrella-and-boiler man out of you before my time comes.'

"When I had drawn my two dollars from the boat and seen the scow away, I met him back in the woods. We caught a freight across the river, and were switched off about three miles below Memphis. As we intended to buy some things that Bill needed before we crossed the river again and took the train for the Southwest, we had to walk to town. It was a hard walk for me, because my shoe was giving out and my old leg needed fixing—being splintered at the end and a little short and beginning to split. As we walked along, the sole of my shoe got looser, and every time I stepped it would yawn open and hang down."

"Like th' mouth av an alligathor," interpolated Finerty. "Kape on wid yer shtory an' don't let me be intherruptin' ye."

"As I was saying, I would have to lift my foot high and kick it forward and slap it down every time I took a step. Bill tied it up with a piece of string, but as we got near the levee I stubbed my toe and the sole hung almost straight down. Then it took so long between steps that if I had n't been pretty good at balancing on the peg I could n't have walked at all."

"Thin ye could n't shtand a while on wan leg at all if 't was only a wooden wan, I 'm thinkin'. 'T is only good for bechune times av th' other wan, is it?" queried Finerty.

"Of course; and it was too long between times. But we were almost to a wharf-boat, where Bill would have a chance to get some more string and fix it up right. So I managed to get along with him helping me. But as we turned into the levee, where the walking was rough, I stumbled and fell, and the peg-leg, being caught between two cobblestones, broke off in the middle. There I sat on the levee without a leg to walk on.

"I never had anything come over me and take the heart out of me just the way that did. I guess that if I had n't knocked around considerable I would have cried about it—and I ain't saying that I did n't feel like it then. It was n't that I was tired and hungry, and it was n't that I was broke down—although it always went against me to be brought to crawling. It was something else about it all that got the best of me. I wiped off my eyes with my coat-sleeve and sat looking up at Bill.

" 'Well, I guess it 's all off between us, Bill,' says I.

" 'I won't leave a partner crawling,' said he.

He caught me under the arms and threw me on his back and took me farther down the levee. He set me up against a pile of freight. 'You sit there till I come back,' he said. 'I 'll get something for you to walk on.' He gave me a piece of torn newspaper to read, and then hurried away up town.

"I sat and waited for over two hours. It grew dark, and still Bill did not come back. Then it clouded up and began to rain with a chilly mist that set me to shivering. I buttoned my coat up and got around on the lee side of the freight. When I had stood the wet and cold a long time I made up my mind that something had happened to Bill, and that there wasn't any use in my waiting any longer. I took off my shoe, intending to hop away; for, as I was saying, it always made the bottom drop out of my feelings to be brought down to crawling. But I found I couldn't hop on the big cobblestones. So I went on all fours till I came to the smooth street. Then I hopped across the street to a long row of commission-houses, carrying the shoe in my hand—thinking I could get it fixed up some way—and wearing what was left of my leg.

"There was a wooden awning stretching away for a block over the brick sidewalk in front of the wholesale houses. It was a dark, deserted, tunnel-like sort of place—which I was glad of, being fixed the way I was. I kept on, although I could hardly see where I was going, thinking I would find a good place to lie down. At the other end of it I came to five or six others standing in out of the wet, and passing round a bottle with five cents' worth of alcohol in the bottom of it. I took up with them for company, and stretched myself out on the tongue of a new wagon which was standing under the awning, hoping to get shivered up warm again and wondering what had happened to Bill.''

"'T was th' polis was shtoppin' him, I 'm thinkin','' commented Finerty.

CHAPTER VI

"NO; it was two women and a little girl," replied Stumpy. "I 'll tell you what happened to him. I know the story so well that I can say it by heart. After he left me he went up into the residence part of town, thinking he would do some work for somebody who would give him a good right shoe. Then he would cast about and find a good piece of timber to make me a new leg. When he was walking past a brick house with rose-bushes and a magnolia-tree in the front yard, who does he see but Mrs. Thorne, waving her hand and calling, delighted to see him. You see, Bill had worked in this town for a machine-shop that kept him around the levee a good deal, fixing things on boats. And there he got acquainted with some well-to-do church ladies who were interested in a sort of mission where Bill dropped in one day to listen to the singing—for he was a great hand to listen to good singing. When they came around in the meeting to talk to him and ask him if he wanted to be a Christian, Bill sort of took them on a different tack; for he did n't count himself in on the kind that was getting converted, but just a visitor. And he got them interested in telling him how the place was run. He took a liking to them, and offered to put in a broken window that he noticed was out. He came round after the meeting was over and did it, and after that he used to drop in once in a while and the ladies would always have something that needed to be fixed. He got to be a sort of a partner in the place, and he would take his pay out by sitting down at the back whenever he felt like it of evenings and listening to the singing, saying, 'How do?' to the ladies and getting to be good friends, so that they did n't bother him about being a Christian. And the ladies used to leave all their trouble to William. Finally, when they saw how much he knew about fixing things, they got to asking his advice about things that were going wrong at their homes. And some afternoon he would take a walk out to the house and look it over. Then he would stay and fix whatever it was, for Bill was the kind that could n't stand it to see anything working wrong.

"As I was saying, Mrs. Thorne waved her hand and called, 'William, William!' She was delighted to see him again. And after they had talked things over she happened to remember that the bath-room faucet was out of order. And could he explain why it was, and how it could be that when you turned off a faucet it would n't stop running?

" 'That 's easy enough fixed,' said Bill.

"He went into the bath-room to explain what was the matter. Then he shut off the water and unscrewed the top of the faucet to show her. He packed it with candle-wicking and put the valve in order with a new rubber. And then it did n't leak a drop. 'That 's what was the matter with it,' said Bill; for he was better on doing a thing than explaining it. Then, while he was taking leave and pretending he would drop in and see the mission again, she happened to think of the music-box that had n't played for months.

" 'I don't suppose anybody can fix that,' she said. 'They told me I would have to send it to Chicago, where there is a man from Switzerland.'

"Bill stopped to take a look at it with the reading-glass, poking around in the works with a toothpick. 'There is n't anything broken about it,' he said. 'And I don't see any lost motion that ought to hurt any. If you give me the bicycle-pump and some gasolene, maybe I can fix it.' He unscrewed it out of the box and took it out into the summer kitchen, where he squirted gasolene through the works. Suddenly it started to play a tune that she said was 'Home Again.' He fanned it till it was dry, oiled it up with the end of the toothpick, and screwed it back into the rosewood case again.

" 'That 's what was the matter with it,' said Bill. 'It was gummed in the fan-pivot and had dirt in the cage-wheel. After this, only use a low-proof oil on it.' Then he said good-by, with her standing on the porch telling him how kind it was of him, and the music-box playing the 'Blue Danube' in the parlor. And all she could do was to invite him back again; for when she used to know him he made too much money to be paid like a tinker for doing a favor. And all *he* could do was to promise to come again, and then go away to find a stranger that would give him a right-footed shoe.

" And walking up the next street, who did he run across but the Widow Brown, sitting out in front of her candy-store. She no more than set eyes on him than she jumped up and made him come in, asking him where he had been and how he was getting along, and telling him about the mission, and stopping to catch her breath so that she could go on and tell him how all the ladies had missed him and how glad she was to see him. When Bill was looking for a chance to move on without being impolite—for he wanted to find the timber for the leg before it got dark—the widow jumped up from her chair and asked him if he would mind tending the store a little while. 'I have been wanting to get away a few minutes all day. I have to run down and telephone for some of the new jaw-breaker candies that the children have been inquiring for.' She put on her shawl and bonnet, and before Bill could think up a way to say no she had pointed out that everything in the store had the price marked on it, and was away down the street.

"Bill sat down behind the counter. A policeman went past. He was one that used to have a beat on the levee, so Bill moved his chair down where he would be behind a taller show-case. Pretty soon he saw that the policeman passed regularly, walking up and down his beat, striking his club on the sidewalk and enjoying the afternoon sun. Bill sat with his head down behind the show-case, thinking of his revolver and wondering whether the officer might know he was wanted. And he hoped no customers would come in.

"Before long a little girl stopped and looked into the show-window. She held a cent against the glass, and moved it about as if she used it to mark her place as she looked over the different kinds of candy. Then she stood and pressed her nose against the window, so that her face, as Bill sat watching her, was a flat white spot surrounded by red cheeks and golden hair. After a while she decided to come in; and Bill had to stand up behind the counter, keeping his eye out for the policeman.

" 'What do you want, little girl?' said Bill.

" 'How many of them do you give for a cent?'

" 'Three for a cent,' answered Bill, looking at the ticket.

" 'How much is them candy marbles?'

" 'Candy marbles, two for a cent,' said Bill.

" 'How much is them lozingers?'

" 'Six for a cent.'

" 'Ain't you got any eight for a cent?' asked the little girl.

"Bill looked all over the show-case, but did n't find any at that price.

" 'Guess not, little girl. We 're all out of lozingers eight for a cent.'

"Just then Bill saw the policeman coming, and he bent down behind the show-case until he had passed. When he stood up the little girl was standing with her nose pressed flat against the show-case, and holding her cent against the glass with one finger. Then she looked up at the shelves.

" 'What kind of candy is them in that jar?' she asked.

" 'Them 's just sticks of candy, little girl.'

" 'Is they lemon or hoarhound?'

" 'Don't know,' said Bill, looking the jar over to find a label.

" 'Why don't you taste them? That 's how you can find out,' said the little girl.

" Bill handed her a stick and said: 'I guess you had better taste it yourself.'

" 'Them 's hoarhound. Ain't you got any lemon?' she said, chewing the bite she had taken.

" 'Guess not. Guess we 're all out of lemon,' said Bill, putting the jar back and keeping his eye out of the front window.

" 'What 's inside them marbles, two for a cent?'

" 'Which? Them red ones?'

" 'No; them white ones.'

" 'Don't know; I never ate any,' said Bill.

" 'Wisht I knew if they was nuts in them,' she said, pressing her nose against the glass again.

" 'Well, I guess the only way to find out is to try one,' said Bill.

"He stood and waited until she got through eating it, keeping his eye out for the policeman and hoping he would n't take a notion to come in.

" 'Them ain't got any nuts inside. I likes them with nuts inside. What 's in them red ones?'

" 'Don't know,' said Bill.

" 'Let me see one of them,' she said.

"Bill handed it out, hoping she would find something to suit her and go home.

" 'Them red ones has nuts in. Ain't you got any white ones with nuts in?' she said, as she swallowed the red one.

" 'Look here, little girl,' said Bill, 'you 'd better make up your mind what you want.'

" 'Well, then, I 'll take some red ones with nuts in.'

"Bill counted the red ones out into a bag. But before she gave him the cent she showed him the inside of the bag and said: 'I only got four.'

" 'Yes, of course you got four. Don't you know you ate two?' said Bill. 'And two from six leaves four.'

" 'No, they don't,' she said. 'They leaves five; 'cause one was a white one, and them red ones is six for a cent.'

" 'Well,' said Bill, 'you 've got me beat. Here 's the other one. Now trot along with you, because I 've got something to 'tend to.'

"When the widow came back Bill got away in a hurry. By that time it was raining and drizzling. As he walked down a dark street thinking things over—of me sitting all this time in the wet waiting for him, and of his hurry to get away, and of me not having any leg to walk on, and then of how he had been wasting his time—he began to get mad, blaming himself and everybody else. He went into a saloon and drank a big glass of whisky, and came out swearing that the leg and shoe would have to come soon. As he was passing a carriage-maker's shop that was locked for the night, he suddenly came to a stop, and it flashed across his mind that he would get a good hickory leg in there and tools to work with. And that was where he got it.

"Then, as he was coming down the street, with the whisky and his troubles working inside of him, he met two citizens who were walking abreast and taking up the whole sidewalk, leaving him the gutter. The bull-headed idea came over him that here was where he would get the shoe. He was looking for trouble, anyway. He whirled the spoke around his head and backed them into a corner. I guess they must have been able to see that he meant what he said to them; for, when he told them to pass over their right shoes, they did it. That was how he got the one that suited him.''

''Then ye was n't th' only wan that had to do some hoppin','' commented Finerty, manifesting a more lively interest in the tale.

''While this was going on,'' continued Stumpy, ''I was lying on the wagon-tongue in front of the commission-houses. The others stood in a dark doorway, waiting for some one to come along and give them another nickel to get alcohol with. They found it was a good place; for, although few passed that way, the ones who did pass were prompt about giving something to charity. Seeing this, one of them would suddenly step forth and ask for the nickel in a way that you could see that he expected to get it—and so he would.

''Presently I heard some one coming in the distance. His footsteps echoed in the big, quiet building and under the long tunnel of awning.

I could hear them whispering among themselves—deciding who should stop him. And when he was opposite the wagon one of them stepped out in front of him. I heard him say, 'We are needing a little money, stranger.'

" '*We* do, do we?' He roared it like a bull. He gave the fellow a push that sent him about ten feet away. Then he cast about for the others, and went at them with the spoke of the barouche; and he sent them flying up the street. Then he stood flourishing the hickory and saying to himself, '*We* need the money. *We* do.'

" 'Bill,' said I, rolling off the wagon-tongue on to my right leg.

" 'Lord, boy! is it you?' he exclaimed. 'I was beginning to feel bad; I thought I had lost you.' He dropped his club to his side and stood thinking. Then he said: 'Well, partner, we have no time to lose now; we must hunt a hole.'

"He threw me across his back and started away, holding my leg in his hammer arm.

"We followed the edge of the levee, where we would n't be likely to meet any one; and we kept going till we came to an old wharf-boat about half a mile south. Here we found a hole and got below decks.

"Bill lit a lantern that he found, and laid down the spoke, some extract of beef, and six Scandinavian crackers about a foot in diameter. He unloaded his pockets of a kit of tools, with nails and screws and brass-headed tacks, and started to work.

" 'A part of your old leg will do,' he said, 'with a little fixing. But I am going to put a wider strap on this one,' said he, putting a string along my leg and marking off the measure. 'And I'll make the leg about a quarter of an inch too long. Then, after you have it on, I'll keep skiving it off till it feels right before I put the ferrule on. Then it will be sure to fit.'

"He set to work with hammer and awl and jack-knife; and pretty soon he was as happy as a shoemaker, talking away about what had happened to him. And whenever he told about the time with the little girl he would smile to himself and peg away faster, whistling under his breath. 'We'll make a good job of this to-night,' said he; 'and in the morning we will do a little thinking and make ourselves scarce. They'll be looking for me.'

"Before morning came it was all done, and I was standing again in a good grain-leather shoe and on a leg that fit me as if it grew there.

And it had a good ferrule at the bottom—an iron band that was made for the end of a breast-yoke.

"It suited Bill every way but one. 'I 'm sorry,' said he, when he saw me standing on it and walking around in the hold of the boat to try it—'I 'm sorry that I had to drive the ferrule on. It ought to be heated and shrunk.'"

"D'ye know," said Finerty, withdrawing his pipe and straightening up, "ye could n't be makin' me belave 't is thrue if 't was n't that I see it is. An' did th' polis get th' felly?"

"Well," continued Stumpy, "the next morning, when we came out of the wharf-boat—"

"*Shtop!* 't is shtartin'-time f'r Twinty-three. Ye can tell me th' rist again," exclaimed Finerty, jumping up with the big silverine watch in his hand. There came a murmuring of the rails before the door. He grabbed his lantern and bolted out, slamming the door behind him.

Stumpy made himself easy on the sand, and went to sleep for the night.

CHAPTER VII

HEN Michael appeared at the breakfast-table on the following afternoon, Mrs. Finerty seated herself opposite to "have a look at him." She made many inconsequential inquiries in hope of finding a subject for conversation. This reminded Finerty of the tramp's tale, and he repeated it all to her, setting forth the facts in his own way.

"An' *ye* a-sittin' an' talkin' to Shtoompy! An' why was he goin' wid a murd'rer an' not tellin' th' polis?"

"He is th' innocint wan for ye. Ye can see he is good at th' bukes, but he 'll not be goin' far in this worruld. He says he knew th' blackshmith did n't do it. An' he knows it th' way 't w'u'd be no use denyin' him, because th' blackshmith tould him so."

"Sometimes ye *can* tell a thing just by knowin' it," commented Mrs. Finerty. And after a moment's thought she continued: "'T was good av him to do that for th' poor wan-legged bye. If 't was n't that he was a murd'rer, I 'd be thinkin' he was kind-hear-r-rted," she said. "An' why w'u'd a murd'rer do it, d' ye think?"

"'T was because th' wan-legged bye w'u'd belave what he tould him. 'T is a quare worruld."

"I see," mused Mrs. Finerty. "People must be havin' those that belave in thim; 't is that weemen are for—an' worrukin'. If 't was n't for me belavin' in ye, ye 'd niver be what ye are at th' chutes, Michael."

Whenever his wife's conversation took this turn, Finerty made excuse to end it. Looking at the clock, which was always kept ahead of time and then interpreted by his watch, he seized his hat and bucket and started for work. Mrs. Finerty hailed him from the gate, as usual, and reminded him to "be careful." "And," she added, "find out about th' indin' of th' blackshmith."

That evening was chilly, and Stumpy came promptly to the sand-house, where Finerty was awaiting him.

Stumpy settled himself in the accommodating sand, with his arms behind his head; and looking down on his auditor, he resumed the tale.

"As I was saying, when we crawled out of the hold of the wharf-boat early in the morning, Bill said to me, 'We 've got to get across this river right now!' He had been happy-go-lucky all night while he was tinkering on my leg, but now I could see the business look come back into his eye again. Bill was one of the kind that did n't bother much about trouble till the time came; then he would take hold of it like a job of work when the whistle blows. There was five hundred dollars reward offered on the bills that were pasted up in the police stations; and Bill said to me, 'I 'm good for just so much money, ready to be cashed in New Orleans. On account of what I did last night in this town they will be hauling in the likes of us on suspicion. And it won't do for me to be taken up for this, because then they would find that I 'm both men that 's wanted.'

"We walked down the levee and found a skiff. It was chained and locked to a post, and there were no oars. Bill opened the lock with two big rocks for hammer and anvil, cracking it like a nut. We headed for Arkansaw with a fence-rail, Bill shoving her along strong, canoe fashion, and letting the board trail after each stroke to keep her course right. He did n't know how to run a canoe with one oar when he started, but after a few strokes he said he saw how it was. Out in the middle the spring flood was running like a mill-race, but we got over without drifting down more than a quarter of a mile. When we landed Bill shoved her out again, hoping she would ground on shore somewhere below and put them on the wrong trail.

"The river was going down after the worst of the flood, and the mud on the trees showed that the eastern part of Arkansaw had been about five feet under water. The woods were damp, and the air was alive with gnats. Bill took the fence-rail along on his shoulder, saying we would need the dry end of it to cook breakfast with. They were just beginning to repair the washouts on the railroad, banking it up with bags of dirt. We skirted around a wrecking crew and struck the railroad again, following a spur that led to the Iron Mountain, where we would strike the main line to the Southwest. We walked the tracks through the muddy woods all morning; a cloud of gnats going along with us.

" 'These gnats seem to know the way,' said Bill, pointing to the ones that kept ahead. So

I could see that he was beginning to feel like himself again.

"The tracks gradually sloped away from the river, so that, as we got deeper into the State, the road-bed was in better condition. But there was a washout here and there, and trains were not running because connection had not been made at the Memphis end. Toward noon we came to a string of wrecked freight-cars that had gone off the raised track and rolled over in the woods. Here we took a rest and had dinner, making soup with the beef extract in a peach-can full of water. We threw damp leaves on the coals till we had a smudge fire, and then we sat down in the smoke to eat dinner, dipping the Scandinavian cracker in the soup, and getting a rest from the gnats.

"Toward sundown, when I was about tired out, we came to a hand-car.

" 'I wish it was the kind we could pump. My arms are not so tired as this leg is,' said I.

" 'If that 's the case, it 's luck as it is,' said Bill. 'I 'll keep it a-going while you rest. Give me a hand to put it on the rails. You can ride and I 'll push.'

"He kept it going at a brisk walk; sometimes running till it had a good start and then jumping aboard to catch a ride himself. But before dark he steadied down to a regular walk. After a while I got to thinking things over, lying on my back rolling along and looking up at the stars. And I did n't like the idea.

" 'Say, Bill,' said I, sitting up of a sudden, but not seeing him very plainly because the woods were so dark; 'set it off the track. I can sleep on it, and you can keep on. If it was me that was running away it would be different, and this would be all right.'

"He did n't answer right away. The car gradually slowed down, and finally it came to a dead stop. Then I heard him say, 'You know I did n't kill Tiffin, don't you?'

" 'Sure I do,' said I.

" 'And you 're a partner of mine, ain't you?'

" 'Of course,' said I. 'If I was n't I would have gone on the boat.'

" 'And if you was n't you would n't 'a' met me behind the tree—seeing you did n't have to,' said he.

" 'I should say not,' said I.

" 'Well, then, roll over and go to sleep.'

"With that he started the car up again and got it rattling along; and it made so much noise we could n't talk. But after a little while, when I had rolled over to rest, the car slowed down and stopped again.

" 'I wish it *was* you that was running away. Then maybe we 'd get along together.' And he started it up again, pushing hard.

"I laid on my back looking up at the stars and thinking it over till I saw how he felt about it, and I felt kind of cheap for not wanting him to push me. And finally I rolled over and went to sleep.

"When I woke it was beginning to grow light. I was still rolling along. I sat up and rubbed my eyes till I got myself awake. I found he had been pushing me steady all night. He had struck a washout and carried me across it, laying me easy on the ground till he got the car over. And I was so dead tired that I never woke up.

" 'Well, partner, how are you feeling?' said he.

" 'Pretty fair,' said I.

" 'That 's good. Here 's where we stop fifteen minutes for refreshments.' "

"He must have been th' sthrong, healt'y bye to be kapin' it up like that," remarked Finerty.

"Yes," replied Stumpy. "But I could see he was pretty near worn out. He had lots of grit. When we had eaten the cracker and beef juice he was about ready to shut his eyes and roll over for want of sleep. So I says, 'Get on the car, Bill. I 'll push it along while you get some sleep.'

"He looked me over a while, as if he was studying something out. Then he said, 'You 've got the power, but you ain't got the gearin'.' He went off into the woods and came back whittling a long pole. 'You 'll get along better working it like a flatboat,' he said. 'You have the back and arms for it; and that 'll save your legs till you need them.' And pretty soon I had her going at a fair clip, shoving her along with the pole, and dragging it between strokes, with Bill laying on the car watching me.

" 'Well, I guess you could n't go that fast on a stiff leg, stooping over,' said he, looking up at me, with his arms behind his head.

" 'I could n't keep up to it,' said I.

" 'Now you 've got the power *with* the gearin'; and you 're getting to be a perfessor,' said Bill. Then he laid down flat, putting his coat over his head, and went to sleep.

"I rolled along pretty well all morning, changing arms and getting rested one side and then the other. The gnats—and whether they were the same ones kept me guessing—followed us still. At noon Bill woke and sat up, frowning as he looked at the sun, and smiling when he looked at me. He pushed me along again for a couple of hours to even things up between us. Then we dumped the car off the tracks; for Bill said that as we were both in shape again, and as we would get to Hoxie before my leg gave out, the car would be a dead weight now, seeing that we would n't need it again. Toward night we struck the Iron Mountain road at a little station where there were some country stores and a depot platform sitting in the middle of a big circle of thick woods. And just as we reached the main line a freight-train showed up in the distance. It was going the right direction for us,—toward Texas,—and we stood near the platform waiting for a chance to get on when she came to a stop. But the train, instead of stopping, put on more speed and went past, with the engineer and fireman leaning out and watching both sides of the train, and the crew keeping a lookout along the length of it. There were fifteen or twenty tramps lying around on the grass back of the platform. They paid no attention to the train—no more than if they had never had any idea of traveling.

" 'What does this mean?' said Bill to an old fellow who was lying on the grass, with a rusty coffee-pot under his arm.

" 'It 's the strike,' he answered.

" 'Ain't there any of you that can flip a train going at that speed?' asked Bill.

" 'There 's some. But they don't want to. Down at Little Rock the soldiers are holding the yards like a fort and searching the cars—and they are the regulars. So we don't want to take the chances. Besides that, the crew keeps close watch for fear strikers will get on and do them up when they get out in the country. We 're all afraid of each other—us and them.' The old fellow shifted his coffee-pot under the other arm and went on: 'We 're blocked front and back, and it 's too far to walk anywhere. There ain't enough grub around these parts to feed the chickens. I have a pocketful of coffee, and I have to sleep with this coffee-pot and hug it all night to be sure that I 'll have it in the morning. That 's how it is.'

"Bill walked up and down the tracks and looked around at the circle of woods like an animal in a cage. If the army had figured on getting Bill into a pocket where the police could catch him, it could n't have been done better than in the strike of '86. I could see the devil come back into him again. When Bill was himself and talking friendly there would

be little wrinkles at the corners of his eyes that
made you think he was smiling. And when he
was working on a job he looked at it the same
way, except that he closed his eyes a little more,
as if he was looking deep into crooked places,
and building things in his mind. I used to
think Bill could look into a keyhole and tell
what kind of a key would fit the works. But
when he was on the war-path his eyes would
open up and set like a steel trap ready to go off.
This day I guess he would have looked a fine
hole through a Texas ranger. It would have
been a hard job to pull a gun on him.

"I sat down on the edge of the platform
while he paced up and down the tracks. Finally he went so far that I lost sight of him.
In about an hour he came back and motioned
me to follow.

" 'They slow up about a mile above here and
come almost to a stop. There 's a bad track,'
he said.

"We went up to the place, and sat under a
culvert and waited. Before long a train slowed
down and came almost to a stop over our heads.
Bill took off his hat and peeped out of the culvert along the tracks. The crew were leaning
out along the top of the train. But as she
started up again they stopped watching, think-

ing there was no one in sight. Bill hurried me up the bank and gave me a lift to a cattle-car, running along and almost carrying me till I got my fingers in the slats. He swung up and helped me to the bumpers between the cattle-car and the box-car ahead, and then up through the end window of the cattle-car. The car carried a few barrels of kerosene and some boxes of soap, for there had been such a blockade on account of the strike and the floods that they were sending the return cattle-cars back to Texas with freight. We shifted the load around till we had a clear space surrounded by barrels. But as we sat down in it Bill saw that when the brakeman walked along on top he could see down through the end window into our place. He piled some soap-boxes up in a careless way, to shut off the view.

" 'Now we have a fort of our own,' said Bill.

"As we rolled through the little town we looked out between the barrels and through the slats and saw the others lying about the platform. The old fellow was sitting with the coffee-pot under his arm.

" 'This was the only opening on the train, and we struck it,' said Bill.

" 'But how about Little Rock?' I asked.

" 'We 'll take our chances,' said Bill.

"It was growing dusk. We rolled along, talking about the chances and the luck we had been having, good and bad. After a while Bill sat quiet for a spell, not giving me more than an answer when I spoke to him. I saw he was studying something out.

" 'What are you thinking so hard about, Bill?' I asked.

" 'I 've been thinking that Little Rock is the end of this division, and Texarkana is the next. We 've only got that one division after this—if we don't have trouble with them soldiers; and when we get down there in God's country we 'll stop running. When you get to Texas there ain't nowhere else to run to that 's worth while. I want to get to work again. So when we get down there we 'll settle down somewhere, and then we 'll mix up with folks instead of running away from them. I will have to take another name. I 've been trying to think up a name. But I 'll be hanged if I can think of one that sounds right.'

" 'How would John do?' said I.

" 'It 's too much like Bill. It 's what anybody would think of.'

" 'You want one that sounds as if you did n't pick it out yourself.'

" 'That 's it,' said he. 'I can't come across

one that don't seem suspicious. None of 'em sound right to me.'

" 'Charlie would n't fit you right, would it?' said I.

" 'No; that don't suit me at all. It don't seem to be on the square.'

" 'Or Aleck or Henry or Jim?'

" 'No; I 've thought of them. I don't like them.'

"I thought of twenty or thirty more, but he would n't have them.

" 'I know a name—Cecil,' said I. 'That 's different from the others.'

" 'Yes; it 's good enough some ways; but it ain't a name my mother would 'a' called me. And me a blacksmith. I 've got to pick out a name that I 'll have to keep; that 's why I am so particular.'

" 'How about your second name?' said I.

" 'I 've made it Dalton. That was easy enough. It 's only the first I can't decide on.'

"I thought a long time, and at last I struck it.

" 'How would Alonzo do?' said I. 'Your mother *might* have called you that. And you can make it Lon for short.' I saw that that struck him.

" 'That is n't a bad one,' said he. 'It ain't a clerk's sort of name. I guess I could answer to Lon all right. I 've noticed you 're mighty handy with words, perfessor.'

" 'Then,' said I, 'when we get to water—and I 'm mighty thirsty now—I 'll sprinkle a few drops on your head, and we 'll make it Alonzo.'

" 'And if they find us when they search the cars,' said he, 'you 'd better make it Alonzo right away without the water. And you are supposed to have met me at Hoxie. And you don't know anything about me except that my name is Lon. That 'll keep us from getting our lies mixed.'

"We sat talking and watching the lights of farm-houses and stations through the chinks between the barrels. And late at night I fell asleep.

"In the morning, when I woke, the car was standing dead still; and Bill was gone. I was afraid for a while to get out and take my chances. But as I could not stay there until the strike was over, I decided to pile out the end window and trust to luck, thinking the army would be easy on a man with a wooden leg. When I had climbed out I saw Bill sitting on the edge of a grassy bank along the track, looking down at a negro mammy washing clothes beside a spring. And from the way he smiled when he said, 'Good morning,' I saw that this trouble was over.

" 'Where are the soldiers?' I asked.

" 'Back in Little Rock, I suppose; I only saw one of them. He held up his lantern and showed me his face when he looked through the slats. But I guess he did n't recognize us through the barrels. This is Texarkana. I 've been taking a walk in Texas; I just got back to Arkansaw.'

"He brought me a drink of the spring water in a gourd dipper, and then we went up town. I was hungry, and I knew Bill was; but neither of us said anything about it, for we had spent our last forty cents in Hoxie.

"The principal thing I remember about Texarkana was a shanty restaurant called 'John's Place.' John had some pork-chops showing off in his window. Bill and I both stopped and looked in at them."

"Was Bill afther holdin' up that place?" inquired Finerty.

CHAPTER VIII

"**N**O," replied Stumpy, paying little attention to the interruption. "Bill and I both stopped and stood looking in at them. John came from the kitchen, walking lame, with a plate of ham and eggs that he set down before a fellow in a blue flannel shirt. John had on a bed-tick apron, and you could see that he had cooked for a cattle outfit till he got rheumatism, or a bullet, and started in business for himself. The door was open, and we could smell the ham and eggs.

"Bill and I watched the fellow start to eat them. Then we took another look at the pork-chops and walked away, saying nothing.

"As we went up town Bill kept looking around, this way and that, as if he expected to get breakfast out of the air. And that was about what he did.

"At a street corner we came across a crowd

of people around a tall flag-pole. The flag was about three quarters of the way up, probably seventy-five feet from the ground. The ropes were caught and tangled in the splicing of the pole near the top, so that they could n't get the flag down. They had given up trying to climb, and now they stood about, looking up at it. Bill went away in a hurry, telling me to wait. Pretty soon he came back with two short pieces of telegraph wire. He elbowed his way into the crowd, saying, 'Where 's the boss?' They pointed out a man who was commissioner of something, and Bill asked him for the job.

" 'Have you got a pair of climbers?' said he, looking Bill over.

" 'No,' said Bill.

" 'Then how would you hang on to do the work, if you *did* get up there?'

" 'It 's the knowing how that I am supposed to be paid for, ain't it?' said Bill.

" 'Go ahead; let 's see you try. I 'll put a dollar on the flag when you come down.'

"Bill looked around in the street and found a cobblestone. He bent one piece of wire round the pole and fastened the ends together, making a ring around the pole just loose enough to slide up and down. When the ring was held level it would slide, but when it was pulled up or down on only one side it would bind and stick. Then he cut the other piece of wire in two by hammering it on the edge of the curbing with the cobblestone. And he used the pieces to put two smaller rings on the one around the pole, like links of a chain, one on each side. Then he took his coat off; and the way Bill walked up that pole was a wonder. He put one foot in each of the little links, like stirrups, and threw his arms around the pole, hugging it while he drew his knees up under his armpits. And he went up like a monkey on a stick, drawing both legs up together and then standing on one foot; and when he straightened out he would go up three feet at a time. When he was at the top he leaned out and waved his hat with one hand to show the commissioner how he could stand on the side of a smooth pole. He did the job in about half a minute. Then he put his arms around the pole, letting his legs hang down straight, with the ring level, and slid down in a jiffy, with the flag coming after him, and waving, and the crowd a-cheering. By the time he had got his feet out of the tight rings the dollar was on the flag. Some man in the crowd threw in a quarter. Bill picked up his wages, leaving the quarter lay, and pushed his way out of the crowd.

"When we were a distance away from them we looked back. One of the men had his feet in the loops and was trying to climb. But each time he lifted his legs and stretched them out the ring would only slide up and down the pole without lifting him from where he was.

" 'I 'll bet that fellow could n't get the flag down if it was up there now,' said Bill. 'There 's tricks in all trades; and that one is to lift one foot a little just as you are stepping on the other. That 's what makes the ring bind.'

" 'Did n't it feel funny to hang out up there with one arm?' said I.

" 'Sort of,' said Bill. 'They were all looking up, with their mouths open, like a flock of chickens drinking water. It was kind of funny.'

"We went back to 'John's Place' and ate the chops. And when we got through with the bill of fare the dollar was nearly gone. We went down to the railroad tracks again, and sat down on the grassy bank, and watched the negro mammy finishing her washing. After a while Bill left me to go up to the roundhouse and look on the call-board to see when the next freight pulled out. I did not see him again for almost an hour. Then he came running back.

" 'Hurry up,' he said, 'and get down to that string of cars; they pull out in about twenty minutes. I 'm going to get provisions.' He hurried away, taking just enough time to open his hand and show me another dollar that he had got.

" 'Don't make it extract of beef,' I called out after him.

" 'Pork-chops,' he called back, 'and pie.'

"We went away in a box-car half filled with lumber, and were put off by the crew in the middle of the afternoon—for the strikes made it bad. After that luck seemed to go against us in every way. It took us five days to make the next three hundred miles. Once we were put off at a country road where there was nothing but a saloon and an alkali well. The water we could n't drink; and in the saloon there seemed to be nothing but an ivory-handled revolver behind the bar. When the bartender got back he was surprised to see us. He made us some lemonade to show us that the lemon took the soapy taste out of the alkali water. Before long we were thirsty again, and had to buy more. After that we sat behind the saloon, waiting for a train to come along and take us away; and the bartender sat inside, waiting for us to get thirsty again and come in. By the time we got away from there we had spent our dollar for lemonade and had n't a cent left.

"Next we were put off at a watering-tank on a prairie, where there was nothing to be seen but the sun going down. We had no provisions left, and the only way we could get a drink was by holding our mouths open and catching the water that dripped down from a leaky place in the tank. We lay down on one of the foundation timbers, intending to sleep there. But a little after sundown a snake came and coiled on the timber opposite us. Bill killed the snake with a rock, and we lay down again. But we found we could n't sleep; we would think of snakes. As the snakes seemed to like the damp place under the tank, we went and stood up on the prairie. While we were standing out in the night, listening to the coyotes bark, I said, 'Bill, I 've been thinking it over.'

" 'Thinking which over?' said he.

" 'About you dragging me along. Why don't you travel passenger?'

" 'With you? You can't get off and on the blind baggage at stations—you 'd get left.'

" 'That 's it,' I said. 'Now, Bill, you came to Arkansaw in a cow-catcher yourself. You could have been across the continent by this time, doing it your own way.'

" 'I guess I could,' said he.

" 'Well, it ain't fair,' says I. 'You 'd better travel your own way and watch out for yourself.'

" 'And what would *you* do?'

" 'Do the same as always—the best I could.'

" 'And what would *I* do? Do you suppose any one would know I did n't kill Tiffin—seein' how it happened—if he was n't a partner of mine, like you?'

" 'I guess not. It looks like you did, and they 'd think you was lyin' about it,' said I.

" 'And I should leave a partner of mine bumming round the country when I can teach him a trade. That would be sense, would n't it? But if you want to make a try of it, we will get out of here on the Cannon Ball express.'

" 'And if I can't pile aboard at any station, and get left, you 'd better be going on, Bill, and not be staying back for me.'

" 'Aw, shut up!' he said.

"I did n't say anything for a while, but stood with my hands in my pockets, looking up at the stars. The more I looked the more it seemed I could see—some of them so deep in the sky that my eye would have to go out after them, finding more and more—like as if I was getting used to looking down a well.

" 'Bill,' said I, 'did you ever notice that there are so many stars as there are?'

" 'There 's plenty more where them come from,' he said.

"We did n't say anything for about a half an hour after that. And then Bill found his tongue again.

" 'Yes,' he said. 'We 'll strike a likely sort of place somewhere and make harbor; and we 'll settle down and do any kind of a job they can bring in at the door. Then I 'll have to throw my old name on the scrap-pile and break in a new one. What name was that, perfessor? I 've been trying to see if I could think of it for an hour.'

"It had gone clean out of my head, and I could n't think of it again.

" 'Well, anyway,' said he, 'Bill will have to throw up his job and give it to what 's-his-name. We 'll have to think of that name. I 'll want to put it on before long.'

"I stood out most of the night, looking up at the stars, trying to think of Bill's name. And once in a while I would hear him saying names over, as if he was calling the roll of himself.

"It was long after midnight when the Cannon Ball express came to the tank, and we got on the front end of the baggage-car. When the sparks began raining back on us, we sat low and braced our feet, holding our coats before us and stooping down behind them to keep the fire out of our faces and the wrinkles of our clothes. Bill made me take his coat because it was wool and would n't burn. Once he got afire with my thin cotton one, and the wind was pushing us so hard he could n't slap it out. So he rolled it up in a ball and put it out that way. Every time the engine blew at the crossings—and the roads sailed by so fast that she was shrieking in our ears half the time—it did me good to think how we were leaving that water-tank behind.

"Whenever we made a station Bill and I would get off and hide in the shadow of the truck, stooping down on the side away from the platform until the conductor had swung up his lantern on the blind baggage and seen that it was empty. That night the conductor seemed to be very particular. After he had given the engineer the signal he would stand on the blind baggage until she was in motion, to make sure. That made it hard for me—running along and half hanging to the handle. But always, as the conductor got off, Bill would give me a boost that would put me aboard again. We made six stations that way, until finally we came to a place called Upton.

"There the conductor stayed on longer than usual after she started. And just as she was getting too swift for me to hang on, he swung off on our side. Bill was running low beside the truck and behind me. He swung aboard almost under the conductor's arm, intending to give me a quick hand and bring me up after him. But I had to let go, and the conductor ran against me about the middle of the car, knocking me down, and stopping himself so that he had to do quick work to catch the platform of the next car himself. As I got up the train was past me and well under way. I saw Bill jump. He fell, rolled over on the ground, and I ran toward him. But before I got to him he was up; and seeing me coming, he stood and waited.

" 'Are you hurt, Bill?' said I.

" 'Not much. I struck the edge of this hole. It looks as if it was filled with long grass a-purpose to catch me.'

" 'That 's a buffalo wallow,' said I.

" 'Well, I 'm glad it was n't me that made the hole. From what I 've laid down in it, it seems to be a pretty good bed. Seein' the buffaloes ain't usin' it, we 'll roll in. When we wake up we 'll see where we are.'

"We woke up in Upton. Upton consisted of one street—a dirt road—with the railroad running along one side of it and a row of stores along the other. It was a country of rolling, low hills, with pines standing scattered on the high places, and small scrub-oak gathered together in the hollows. A dusty road crossed the street at one end of town and led off into the country across a patch of prairie. We heard an anvil. Bill perked up as if it was a breakfast-bell and went off to investigate.

" 'It 's not for me,' he said when he came back. 'It 's a little shoeing-shop that belongs to an old negro. He 's calking a mule.'

"We followed the dusty cross-road away from the tracks. Just back of town, and at one end of it, we came to a bigger blacksmith-shop that was locked with a padlock. Some rusty tires and an old wagon-wheel were leaned up near the door. We put our eyes to a crack, and we could see the inside plain by the light that leaked in between the boarding.

"Everything—anvils, sledges, mandrels, and tongs, and the shoes that hung like rows of fringe, brown and red, on the rafters—was rusty. Two letters of a branding-iron—an A on the anvil and an O in the jaws of the tongs on the forge—were lying just as some one had left them when he quit work. The leather apron was lying on the floor beside the shoeing-kit.

Bill went around all four sides, putting his eye to cracks and finding more and more tools inside, and talking about two mandrels that seemed to strike him most—a big and a little one. It was a two-forge general-repair shop filled with tools and material. It gave me a lonesome feeling to look into the dark place and see all the tools, made for so many kinds of noisy work, lying quiet and rusty. It was what you might call a dead blacksmith-shop.

"'What's the matter with it—did n't it pay?' I asked Bill.

"'It must have been paying when he quit, seeing he knocked off in the middle of a job,' said Bill. 'And, judging from the outfit, he must have had a good trade.'

"'Then why is it sitting idle so long?'

"'It may not be very long. That's surface rust. Something has happened. We'll have to find out about this.'"

"''T is a long shtory av th' throubles ye had befure ye come till what happened," remarked Finerty. "I'm thinkin'—" He glanced at his big watch, slammed it shut, gave his pipe a sudden slap in his palm, and jumped to his feet. "Me time has come—I must be tindin' to Number Twinty-two. Mind ye, don't forget the place." And he hurried away to the chutes.

CHAPTER IX

EVERAL times that night Finerty went into the sand-house for an "aisy shpell," and finding his guest sleeping soundly, he did not disturb him for more of the story.

Toward morning, when the night was growing gray, thirteen tramps arrived in the yards under peculiar circumstances. A box-car laden to within a few inches of its roof with cottonseed was switched off on the levee. In the layer of darkness on top of the yielding freight the vagrants had stowed themselves away at New Orleans, crowded up against the roof, which lay upon them as a wooden covering of their common bed. The tramps, having got the door slightly ajar, had managed to squeeze themselves one by one through a small unboarded space at the top, those who entered first burrowing back to remote corners in order to make room for those who followed; and thus the lit-

tle hole, with its light and fresh air and con-
sciousness of liberty, became the sole property
of a venerable reprobate who had the foresight
to enter last. Thus they had bowled along in
mere bestial comfort and with little knowledge
of night or day, except what they learned from
the old fellow at the mouth of their burrow.
This one lay whiffing the brisk air of an unsea-
sonable cold spell with a grateful sense of the
contrast between the weather without and the
comfort within; for though it should have been
spring according to theories of the calendar,—
which the vagrants had too trustingly believed
in timing their pilgrimage north,—there was
little evidence of spring outside of the almanac.

Thus it was that, as Finerty was passing the
car at early morning, his attention was attracted by a puff of white breath coming forth
on the cold air like the exhaust of an engine;
and, looking up, he discovered a smooth, bald
head and a face with puffy features and patri-
archal amber-white whiskers, occupying the
dark port-hole under the eaves of the car.

"Did ye go in f'r th' winter?" said Finerty,
stopping and looking up.

"Good morning," said the other, blandly,
putting a good face on the matter. "What town
is this?".

"This is Mimphis, Tinnissee, United Shtates av Amerriky," replied Finerty, with a look that was intended to be ominously solemn.

"Memphis!" shouted the old man, drawing his head in.

At this there was a clamoring under the roof. The vagrants, having put themselves in an imprisonment to which one was the key, demanded that he should get out. He hesitated and looked down on Finerty till there came a more peremptory order: "Pile out, Pap Smith; Rochester Red says so." When Pap Smith had let himself carefully down, he began to parley about the weather to Finerty, with an air that was all quiet unconcern. The democratic Irishman, being taken in for the moment by Pap's art, replied in kind—and lost his chance to exercise his authority. As they came forth—ten, eleven, twelve of them—Finerty stood looking them over.

"Is there jist a dozen av yez?" he inquired.

This estimate was immediately proved wrong by the appearance of a freckled hand, and then the one called Rochester came forth head first and swung nimbly to the ground.

The full company now stood taking in the conditions to which the dark had delivered them. They were covered from head to foot

with cotton lint. And, what was more impor-
tant to them, their breath was white upon the
air.

"Yez look," remarked Finerty, "like yez
had been washed whiter—yis, whiter than
shnow."

Without paying any attention to his remarks, they fell to work to rid themselves of
the lint, some rubbing with soft felt hats, and
others, whose head-gear was less versatile, cur-
rying themselves with their coat-sleeves. But
cotton lint is not to be removed in this way—
as they finally observed. Much work made it
evident that the fine, short nap of the cottonseed was fastened deeper by rubbing; it had
the weaving nature; it had become part and
parcel of their clothes.

"This won't do," declared Rochester. "If
we all go up town like this, the police will have
us spotted."

"Well, if yez don't make out," said Finerty,
"come down till the chutes, an' I 'll give yez
lave to coal up a few ingines. That 'll change
yer color for ye." And seeing that his offer
was not likely to be taken, the foreman of the
coal-chutes walked away with a Milesian grin.

As Finerty worked around the chutes he
looked up the levee, now and then, keeping

8

track of the new arrivals. About an hour afterward he saw them sitting in a row by the river. The thirteen men were licking their palms and stroking themselves busily, having discovered that the telltale lint could be removed only by this slow process of rolling it into damp balls and picking it off. Finerty took the first opportunity to go back and entertain himself at their expense.

"Well, how are yees pussy-cats makin' out?" he asked, confronting the row. They made no rejoinder to his banter, but kept on with the irksome task, licking their palms and stroking themselves.

"It 's wor-r-rkin' ye are, ain't it?" said Finerty. He smiled broadly as this view-point of the situation grew upon him.

"Yez had bether thry the way I was tellin' yez about." Still no acceptance. And when Finerty had sufficiently "had his fling" at them, he went away again with a twinkle in his eye.

The tramps, having worked until they were cold and impatient, gave over the task to the spare moments of other days, and started up town, dispersing widely and understanding— without having to mention it—that they were to meet one another, and all other tramps, that night at the "White Elephant."

Finerty, having satisfied himself that they had all departed from his domain, unlocked the sand-house and roused his imprisoned guest. "We will now be lettin' out," he said. He secured the hasp again, and departed to take his daily sleep.

CHAPTER X

NORTHERN blizzard had come down upon the South, as if winter had rallied for a last charge; and Finerty betook himself, at the first opportunity, to the shelter of the sand-house. Having greeted Stumpy and seated himself inadvertently before a crack in the boards, he shifted over to get rid of the cold streak that was playing on his back, and went at the subject of the blacksmith immediately.

"Ye wor sayin' that ye an' th' felly Bill looked through th' cracks an' saw th' rusty blackshmith-shop. An' ye said ye must find out how 't was."

"Yes," replied Stumpy; "we could see that some one had quit work in the middle of a job. And Bill said: 'Something has happened; we will have to find out about this.' A half-used wagon-trail led from the main road past the shop and across a rolling stretch of green to-

116

ward a clump of oak at the foot of a steep little hill. The oak-trees were at the left of
the road, and at the edge of them was an old
frame-house of about the same color as the
bark of the trees. There was a little orchard,
and there was no fence around the orchard
or the house. Some of the apple-trees were
standing almost under the oaks, as if the big
trees were protecting them, and the house had
a hallway that ran clear through it. It looked
like two little houses set under one roof.

"Off to the other side of the road, quite a
distance back on the open, was another house—
a black-looking old cottage—with a garden
fence around it. We went up the wagon-trail
and struck off to the right toward the older
cottage. Inside the fence was a garden with
flowers and vines and rows of vegetables. Most
of the windows of the cottage were broken, and
we could see that it was empty. We lifted back
the little picket-gate, which had a broken hinge,
and went up the grassy path. The door was
partly open. Bill gave it a push with his finger, and it swung back, creaking. The front
room smelled musty and mushroomy, like all
old empty houses. There was a blackboard set
up in the corner, and on it there was marked
in chalk, 'H. W. Longfellow—The Skeleton in

Armor.' There were a dozen or so of chairs
set along the wall; and a long plank on two
soap-boxes made a bench along another wall.
There was a small hole broken in the old roof,
that the blue sky showed through. The
kitchen was in good condition, and had nothing
in it but an old cow-horn.

"When we had looked things over we came
out into the garden again. There were potatoes and tomatoes and peas and cabbage, all
hilled up and weeded out neat and clean.
There were flowers and vines that I did n't
know the name of, and there were morning-
glories climbing up the sides of the house,
showing off pretty blue and pink against the
black boards.

" 'This is queer doings,' said Bill. 'A blacksmith-shop where nobody works, and a kitchen-
garden where nobody lives.'

" 'It looks like they thought the place was
ha'nted,' says I.

" 'Well, if it is,' said Bill, 'the ghost seems
to be a better gardener than he is a blacksmith.
Maybe it belongs to that Henry What 's-his-
name. We 'll inquire.'

"I dug the end of my leg into a hill and
out rolled a potato. I put a few in my pocket,
thinking we would build a fire somewhere and
roast them, for we were both hungry.

''Going out of the gate, Bill picked up a piece of paper and read: 'Program—Afro-American C. L. S. C.' As he was figuring it out, and trying to think what the letters meant, I saw a young woman come out of the house by the little orchard. She came toward us, swinging a pink sunbonnet by the strings. She did not seem to notice us until she crossed the wagon-trail. She stopped a moment, and then she came on and stood about twenty feet away from us.

" 'Good morning,' said Bill, taking off his hat and dropping the piece of paper to the ground.

" 'Good morning. Were you looking for somebody?'

" 'Not anybody in particular,' answered Bill. 'We want to find out about the black-smith-shop.'

" 'If it 's shoeing you want done, you will have to go down to Ephraim—the old colored man. Our shop is closed.'

" 'Well,' said Bill, 'I happened to look in through a crack, and I saw the mandrels and other tools, and I thought it was a pretty good lay-out to be standing idle.'

" 'Yes, it is. But I don't know as we care to sell. My sister and I have thought it over, in case any one should make us an offer; but we can't make up our minds to part with it. If you want to buy the mandrels, I shall have to see her about it.'

" 'I was n't exactly thinking of buying,' answered Bill. 'I thought it might belong to some one who was looking for a blacksmith. I 'm from up North—looking round. Fact is, I have cast about for an opening till I 'm a little short of money; so I could hardly buy it.'

" 'A *blacksmith*—from up North!' she exclaimed.

"She had been swinging her sunbonnet round till the string was all wrapped tight around her finger. She dropped her arm, and stood looking at Bill, the sunbonnet unwinding and going down like a spider that seen a fly.

" 'Father was from up North. He used to be a machine blacksmith,' she said.

" 'Well, I 'm sort of that kind, too,' said Bill.

"She gathered up the bonnet-strings, and put the sunbonnet on her head. It had a ruffled top fastened on with a row of pearl buttons round the edge. As Bill said, she looked like her name ought to be Miss Hollyhock. And the way the sun shone on her face through the pink sunbonnet, and the way the dimples came into her cheeks when she put on the bonnet and smiled, she looked like she had just sprung into bloom. She stood looking at Bill, as if a machine blacksmith was good for the eyesight. She had been keeping her distance, but now she came closer and became sociable.

" 'We 're hardly situated to hire a smith and run the place again. Won't you come over to the house? I don't remember much about the North, but sister does. But I must get some vegetables for dinner.'

"She pulled up some radishes, and chopped off a head of cabbage with the blade of a hoe that had no handle.

" 'I broke my hoe-handle off short yesterday,' she said. 'I hit it on the top of the fence to get it clean. Sister Eva says I 'm too strong to be a farmer. She says I ought to be a blacksmith. But there are some weeds starting in the corner over there that I will have to clean out when I get the handle on again.'

"She looked up at us as she shook the dirt off some onions, and Bill smiled. She came out of the gate with the cabbage and radishes and onions, and said, 'Come along,' throwing the hoe-blade down beside its handle at the gate and going on ahead of us. Bill picked

them up and followed, carrying the blade in
one hand and the handle in the other. As we
crossed the road she ran ahead faster, so that
by the time we reached the house she was standing with her sister before the steps.

"The sister was six or seven years the oldest.
She was more trim and slender, with black hair
and large eyes that were deep and dark. As
Bill used to say, 'If they had growed on trees,
Nellie would be a peach and Eva an olive.' As
we stopped and stood before them Bill lifted
his hat, and I did the same as Bill.

" 'He 's a blacksmith,' said the younger one,
pointing to Bill. 'And he 's been looking all
over for work.'

"Bill seemed to lose his wits; and I could sort
of see why he was taken off his feet, knowing
him. Knowing Bill and how he felt about being good at his trade, I could see how he felt
about being introduced like that and standing like that before those girls—although I
could n't exactly say it in words. And whenever I thought he was getting his wits back
again, he would look up into the dark one's
eyes and lose them again. He looked down and
began to turn the hoe-blade over in his hands,
as if he was figuring on fixing it.

" 'He 's from up North,' said Nellie.

"Bill looked up at the dark-eyed one again, as if he intended to say something. Then he began to fit the handle onto the end of the hoe, pushing the splinters together.

" 'Did you try to get work down at Wilton?' said the older one in a kind voice.

" 'Wilton? Where is that?' asked Bill.

" 'It 's about twelve miles below—the next station. Since father died, most of the repair work he did has gone down there.'

" 'Did it?' said Bill, looking up suddenly.

" 'All but some of the shoeing. Of course we had to close the place. And I suppose we shall *have* to sell, if we get a good offer.'

" 'Well, of course I did n't know; so I was inquiring. I thought it might belong to that Henry what 's-his-name — Longfellow,' said Bill.

" 'Longfellow!' said both of them in a breath.

" 'We saw that name in the house. We went into the house,' said Bill.

" 'Why, that 's the name of a poet,' said Eva, talking kinder than ever. 'The colored folks were using that room for their meetings. They were studying about him.'

" 'And we use the garden. They have a Chau-tau-qua,' said Nellie, looking at Bill, with the dimples in her cheeks, and speaking plain and kind, like a school-teacher to a good boy. Bill looked down again and began digging in the socket of the hoe-blade with the piece of steel he broke jail with. I was going to say something to keep the talk going till Bill came to. But just then I put my hand in my pocket and felt the potatoes I had taken. So I did n't think of anything.

" 'Is he going to fix your hoe for you, Nellie?' said the older one.

" 'Well, I did n't think to speak of it,' she said, smiling in a way that let him down easy. That put Bill on his own side of the fence, and he brightened up.

" 'I can soon fix that,' he said. 'The best way is to burn the wood out of the socket in the forge. Then we 'll taper down the end of the handle with the hoof-rasp, burn her in to get the taper to fit, and rivet her.'

"They invited us into the open hallway, giving me a rocking-chair and Bill a low stool. Then they went into one of the rooms off the open hallway and shut the door. Sometimes we could hear their voices; they were talking something over. Bill and I sat looking out of the other end of the hallway into the oak-grove.

Some wild-looking pigs were running about looking for acorns.

"After a while the girls came out and took us to the shop. Eva unlocked the door and followed us in.

" 'I wish you would use the second forge,' she said. 'And you will be careful not to touch anything on the first anvil, won't you? I would rather keep them that way,' she said, pointing to the other anvil.

"Bill stood looking at the A of the branding-iron on the anvil and the O in the jaws of the tongs. He stooped to pick up the leather apron, but suddenly stopped himself.

" 'How about the shoeing-kit? Can I use anything in that?'

" 'It 's just the job on the anvil that I mean,' she replied. 'And now, Nellie, you had better open the shop for him so that he can see better.'

"Nellie turned some wooden buttons along the wall, and let the light in with a bang and a clatter as the long board windows fell out on their hinges and made window-shelves hanging on chains toward the street. When Bill had kindled the fire and blowed it up, the older sister went away. Nellie stood in the door watching us. And pretty soon Bill was talking to her free and easy, amusing himself with her like he did with anybody that stood and watched him work.

" 'That 's a pretty good show-window you have got,' said he. 'You ought to have it filled with swingletree hooks and yoke-rings and such. Then you could keep store.'

" 'I did keep store,' she said. 'I sold out all that father left.'

" 'Have pretty good custom?' asked Bill, banking the fire and sprinkling it from the cooling-tub.

" 'Quite fair. I sold to pretty near every farmer that came along.'

" 'Quite fair, eh?' said Bill, taking a look at her as he wiped the rust off the tongs. 'Well, I should n't wonder if you could.' "

Finerty shifted his pipe contemplatively to the other side of his mouth. "Th' felly Bill was a divil wid th' ladies, I 'm thinkin'."

CHAPTER XI

"I T was n't that," replied Stumpy, "so much as that he was cock-of-the-walk when he got the hammer in his hand. Nellie answered him, 'Yes,' looking at him in a way that I could see she was getting on to his style. 'Yes,' she said; 'Eva used to call it my jewelry-shop.'

"Bill took the hoe out of the fire and knocked the wood out of the socket. He banked the fire again and went to work on the handle. As he was putting the rivet in, a farmer stopped with an ox-team and leaned in at the window, watching him work.

"'Howdy, blacksmith? Got the place goin' again?'

"'We 're doing a little work,' said Bill.

"'Well, I 've got a plow-p'int here for ye to do,' said the farmer, swinging up a plow-point that he was carrying with a piece of twine.

"'Does the soil scour in these parts?' asked Bill.

" 'Yes, siree. She does in this sandy country. But further south she wads up on the moldin'-board like chewin'-gum; she sticks like beeswax. They have to use the scraper. Here she scours—but she wears out the p'ints mighty fast.'

" 'Well, it's an ill wind that does n't blow any good,' said Bill, heaving on the bellows till she blew up red. When he had finished the hoe he laid it on the shelf and took up the plow-point, looking it over. 'Yes—I could shape it up for you,' he said, hesitating and looking at Nellie.

" 'That's all right; do it if you want to,' she said, seeing what was bothering him. And as Bill drew it red from the fire she came and stood close, watching him work. Bill welded a wing on the plow, hammered an edge on it, soused it in the cooling-tub, and swung it up on the shelf.

" 'How's that?' he said.

" 'Jest about right; good as new,' said the farmer. 'I'll be needin' ye to make a knife-coulter for me before long to bu'st some tough soil.' He laid down forty cents and drove away. Bill walked back into the shop, leaving the money where the farmer laid it.

"While he was untying the knots of his apron-strings, he saw a crooked piece of iron on the floor and picked it up. As he studied it over Nellie came and stood before him, smiling.

" 'Well, what do you think of it?' she asked.

" 'I was just trying to think,' he answered.

" 'That 's some of my blacksmithing. Can you guess what it was going to be?'

" '*Yours?*' said Bill, studying it harder than ever. 'Was it going to be a—a—a hook for a clothes-line?'

" 'No; it was going to be an eye-bolt for a yoke. When I was keeping the jewelry-shop I sold a big eye-bolt, and then I found I should n't have sold it. It belonged to that yoke over there that father had just made. Finally, I did n't have anything left but the yoke, and I could n't sell that without the ironwork on it. I just made that for practice. If I could have done that, I would have made one with a ring on it. You would n't believe how hard I worked on that. It made me disgusted with myself. I thought I knew how.'

" 'You could n't weld it. I see. And you turned it up too short, anyhow. I guess you 'd better try to make another one. Take that length of rod-iron over there and put it in the fire so that it heats up about a foot from the end. I 'll blow the fire.'

"She measured off the distance with her

9

knuckles and marked it off with the chalk. Then she put it in the fire, and stood holding the long rod while Bill worked the bellows.

" '*Heat,*' said Bill, suddenly, grabbing up the sledge and the tongs.

"She laid it across the hot chisel and Bill cut it off, holding the piece he wanted in the tongs.

" 'Good job,' said Bill, putting the short piece in the fire and blowing up again.

" 'I got along that far before,' said Nellie. 'But the hot end fell down and burned a hole in my shoe.' She put her foot forward and showed him.

" 'That 's because you did n't have the right kind of a helper,' said Bill. 'All that 's necessary to be a blacksmith is to have a good helper and then tell him what you want. For instance: suppose you wanted me to make a ring out of this.' He drew it out at welding-heat and began making the sparks fly. She watched him as he bent it into a circle, welded the ends together, and then trued it up on the horn as the red was fading. He swished it around in the water and handed it to her.

" 'Now,' said Bill, 'all you would have to do would be to hold that and tell me you wanted an eye-bolt to put it on.'

" 'Can't you finish the one I started?' said

she, slipping the big iron ring on her wrist like a bracelet.

" 'All it needs is a little alteration,' said Bill.

"He straightened it out like it was before she began and gave it a longer turn-up. Then he put it back in the fire for the weld.

" 'Stand ready with the jewelry,' said Bill. He held the sparking-iron toward her, and she slipped the ring onto the hook. Bill slapped the bolt onto the anvil and closed the eye. He let it sizzle in the tub again and handed it to her.

" 'What next?' said Bill.

" 'Now,' she said, 'I want you to put it in that hole in the yoke and rivet it on with a washer. I 'll get you the washer.'

"Bill brought the yoke to the anvil and put on the ironwork. When it was done he stood the yoke on end and turned it round for her to look it over.

" 'Is it all right?' he asked.

" 'Very good. It is better than I thought we could do. Now, if you will put it over there on the window-shelf I will do the rest myself.'

" 'The rest? What 's that?' said Bill.

" 'Why, sell it. Is n't that a part of the trade?' She looked at him with the dimples in her cheeks again and her eyes sparkling with deviltry. Bill threw the yoke across his neck and carried it to the shelf. He put the bows in it and stood it up outside the window.

"As he walked back to the anvil he picked up half a horseshoe. 'Then if you was running a shop,' he said, 'I suppose you would know what to do with this.'

" 'Whenever the helper is n't busy striking,' said she, 'he ought to turn all old horseshoes into swingletree hooks and such things.'

" 'And the boss should always be willing to let him practise—seeing it would n't be much loss if he spoiled it,' said Bill, putting it in the fire. She had been carrying out the joke as well as Bill did, but now she burst out laughing. But Bill kept on solemnly with his apprentice-ship.

"He gathered up a lot of old horseshoes and laid them on the forge, telling me to take the bellows. Pretty soon he had the hammer going at a great rate and the hot hooks dropping from the anvil. Nellie cooled one off and examined it. And when he had about a dozen made, Eva came and looked in at the door.

" 'Dinner 's ready, Nellie,' she called out.

" 'Dinner 's ready,' said Nellie.

"She turned and searched for something at the back of the shop.

" 'Here 's the soap,' she said, laying it on the

anvil where Bill had just been hitting, and bringing him to a stop. 'And you will have to wash in the cooling-tub, because the bucket has fallen to pieces.'

"Bill hung his apron on the horn and spluttered and splashed in the tub, making lather on his face and then handing me the soap over his head.

" 'We can put that bucket together again,' said Bill, straightening up suddenly and stopping to talk to her with the foam on his face.

" 'But not now,' she said. 'Dinner 's ready.'

"Bill had got rid of his ammunition-pouch without letting her see it when he took off his coat, rolling it up inside. As he unrolled the coat to put it on, he turned his back to her so that she would not see, and slipped the pouch into a corner, with the revolver pushed in deep and out of sight. I managed to be a little late in following them, so that I could get rid of the potatoes I had in my pocket.

"When we were almost to the house Nellie happened to think that we had forgotten the forty cents, and Bill went to fetch it. When he got back to the house Eva was standing at the head of the table, with the chairs pulled out. She motioned Bill to a seat.

" 'You can sit down there, Mr.—but I believe we have forgotten to ask your name.'

" 'My name 's Alonzo. That 's my first name. And my second name is Dalton. And my helper's name is Sidney Marr; but I call him perfessor. And he 's Stumpy for short.'

" 'Our name is Dixon. And I suppose you have heard our first names. She 's Miss Nellie and I 'm Eva. Now help yourselves, because you must be hungry. Nellie seems to have found plenty for you to do.' Eva sat down and poured the tea.

"Her mentioning the work reminded Bill of the forty cents. He took it out of his pocket and laid it in the middle of the table, and Nellie told about all that we had been doing. She looked at Bill now and then in an amused way, as if she expected him to keep up his joking. But, as Bill used to say, 'A man is shy in another man's corner.' When he was at the forge with his sleeves rolled up he would have given the glad hand to the Prince of Wales. But now, in the girls' cottage, he felt like company. He would glance at Eva once in a while, and then keep his eyes on the plate, saying little.

" 'Yes, we have been letting the shop stand idle,' said Eva, as we finished dinner and pushed our chairs back. 'Nellie and I never knew how much it was a part of us till the anvil stopped ringing. And we can't decide to give up being blacksmiths, as you might say.'

" 'Well, trades is born and raised in folks,' said Bill. 'I suppose I 'd be mighty lonesome and lost if I got where I could n't smell the iron once in a while. How 's farming round here? Do most of them own their own land?'

" 'Quite a number of them,' said Eva. 'A good many of the old settlers are only good to sit around the depot and go fishing, just as they did before the war, letting their land out. They are like me with the shop. They are neither fixed to run it themselves nor to hire it run.'

" 'Why don't you follow their plan—run it on shares?' said Bill.

" 'Why, I would be very glad to do it with *you*, if you cared to try it that way,' said Eva. 'But I was thinking you might not like it, for it might take you some time to get the work to coming again.'

" 'If it did n't come, I 'd take the chances. All I need is the tools. I 'd take it a month; and then if you did n't like it that way I would move on,' said Bill.

" 'I know a job now,' suddenly exclaimed Nellie, rising from her chair and looking at her sister. 'He can shoe Will Upton's mare if *any-body* can—which they say they can't. And then we would have Colonel Upton's trade.' She turned to Bill and explained. 'Will Upton 's back on vacation from West Point, where he 's learning to be a general. Everybody said, when he first intended to break the black mare, that it would be a case of her breaking him— and goodness knows they both need it. But she was the high-spirited kind that Will likes, and they fought it out till he got her broke. She 's gentle now, except that she won't let a blacksmith touch her.'

" 'Did the blacksmith try hard?' asked Bill.

" 'Why, down at Wilton she pretty near broke up the shop. She finally went out back-ward through the side of it. Ephraim tried her, too.'

" 'Did he fasten her head up?'

" 'I should say he did. He put the stake-rope round her.neck and threw it over a rafter and drew her up till you 'd think he was going to hang her. She stood on her hind legs and waltzed around, and pretty near pulled the shop down. Do you suppose you could make her keep her legs still long enough to get shoes on her?'

" 'Well, if it was my job I 'd go at it, any-way,' said Bill.

" 'Then I 'll go and see him about it. I saw him at the depot waiting for some one. He 'll give the job to me.' She put on the pink bonnet, tied a quick knot under her chin, and hurried away.

" 'And now,' said Eva, pausing as she cleared up the dinner dishes, 'we will have to decide where you are going to sleep.'

· " 'We can put up at the shop and call it home,' answered Bill.

" 'Oh, no; you would n't want to be sleeping with your work all the time—you would n't have any home at all then. I was thinking the old house would be better—that is, if you do not object to having the colored folks use the front room once a week. The kitchen is in good condition, and you could fix it up to suit yourself. And if you were over there, we would n't be likely to lose so much out of the garden. But I must tell you that the society sings a great deal on that evening.'

" 'I like singing first-rate,' said Bill. 'I 'll put some bunks for me and my helper in the kitchen, and live there. They can have the other part.'

"Eva had got the dishes off, and now she stood, with the corners of the table-cloth in her hands, looking at the forty cents that Bill had laid in the middle of it.

" 'Had n't you better take up your money, Mr. Dalton? I want to get the table-cloth off.'

"Bill took it up and laid twenty cents down again. 'We 'll start working on shares now,' he said.

" 'I am afraid you are rather liberal,' said Eva. 'However, we will say that we divide that way—which will include your board and washing. And the house-rent costs you nothing.'

" 'It 's a bargain, then,' said Bill. 'There she is now with the horse. She is a beauty.'

"When we reached the shop, Nellie had the mare at the door, patting her neck and trying to coax her in. But the black mare had her ears perked and her head down, sniffing the air as if she smelled trouble.

" 'What 's her name?' asked Bill.

" 'Lady,' answered Nellie. 'Will says he don't think you can manage her. But he will come over after a while to see.'

" 'Whoa, Lady,' said Bill, patting her neck. 'We won't take her inside. Her getting the best of blacksmith-shops has spoiled her. We 'll tackle her in the open.'

"He drove a big staple in the side of the shop and clinched it. Then he tied her to it tight and short, giving her hardly two inches

of halter, so that her nose was almost against
the board. Then he put his hand on her shoulder, and she made no objections. But he no
more than began to pass his hand down to her
hoof than she started the trouble. It was her
signal for fight. She slammed round from one
side to another, with Bill sticking to her shoulder and slapping her back whenever she
crowded him to the wall. He caught her fore
leg when she had it raised and clung to it tight,
bending it up with all his muscle, so that it
looked as if he was as strong as she was. At
that she plunged backward, with fight in her
eye, and jerked the board clean off the side of
the shop, pulling the nails top and bottom.
Then she whisked away in the open, with the
board fastened tight to her head by its middle.
There was as fine a wrestling-match as you
would want to see between a horse and a board.

"Bill did n't go after her. He sat down the
same as if he was waiting for a piece of iron
to heat.

" 'Now, Lady,' he said, 'we will see who is
going to have their way this time.' For he
knew that the staple was clinched and the knot
tight.

"She reared and plunged and whirled. And
every time she turned the board went with her,

as if it knew what Bill wanted it to do, and it slapped her broadside and stuck her with the nails. She raged back and forth, bucking and tossing her head, but she could n't outrun the board; she whirled this way and that, and she could n't outdodge it; and when she brought herself up short on her haunches, the board slapped round and came against her like a collision. The worse she got, the more the board beat her. After a while she stood stock-still, with her tail between her legs and her haunches trembling. She had made such a fight that now she was afraid of herself.

" 'The beauty of it is,' said Bill, 'that a horse has only one spirit to break.' He rose from where he was sitting and went to her, taking his time about it, and giving her plenty of chance to change her mind and run from him, if she wanted to. But she stood waiting for him to come to the rescue; and her fine eyes were looking for him. He patted her and talked to her. Then he ran his hand down her leg. She let him raise her hoof without moving. As he pounded her hoof with a stone, to see whether she would stand for shoeing, she rolled her eyes around at him in a way that seemed to say: 'I wonder if this wise man can get me out of trouble.' Bill cobbled her with the stone, giving her a chance to have another round with the board, if she wanted it; then he took it off her head and led her back to the shop. He put the board in the side of the shop where it belonged, but he only drove one nail top and bottom, so that it would pull off easy; and he tied her the same as before.

"He shod her without trouble. In fact, she seemed to think he was doing her a favor, from the anxious way she watched him. And in less than an hour she was staked out on the prairie, eating grass contentedly, with four shoes on her feet.

"When Will Upton came to the shop and saw her grazing he thought the trouble had not begun yet.

" 'Well, old man,' said he to Bill, 'you 're in for trouble. I thought I 'd come and take a hand in it.'

" 'What trouble?' says Bill, turning the bucket round on the anvil, and working the hoop over the loose staves. 'Wait till I get this fixed. If I stop now she 'll fall to pieces.'

"When he had the staves bound tight, he walked out to the horse, motioning Upton to follow. 'There,' he said, picking up a hind hoof, 'I made them light for saddle-work; I suppose those are about the weight you want, ain't they?' He went around Lady and showed all four.

"Will Upton stood speechless for about a minute.

" 'Did n't she object?' he asked.

" 'Considerable,' said Bill. 'But we over-ruled her objections.'

" 'How did you shoe her?'

" 'First one leg and then the other, same as always. Ain't that the way they do it in these parts?'

" 'Have a cigar,' said Upton, taking a cigar-case from the jacket of his fatigue-uniform, which Bill said was called that because it was so tight that it made him tired. Bill took a cigar and began rubbing a match on his pants; but they were too greasy to strike a light on. He picked up one of Lady's hoofs and struck a light on the new shoe.

" 'Have a light,' said Bill, handing the match to Upton.

" 'Say, old man, you 're a regular. That 's what you are—a regular. Take another smoke for to-night. And if you ever want a recom-mend as farrier just ask me. How much does it come to?'

" 'Two-fifty even,' says Bill.

"And that was all Upton ever learned of

how it was done. As Bill used to say, 'A man has to work so hard for the credit he does n't get, he can't afford to throw away any that comes easy.'

"We went into the shop again, and started making things for Nellie's jewelry-shop.

" 'Well, Bill,' says I, 'the girls have n't quite got the upper hand of you the way they had a while back—on that Longfellow business.'

" 'A man is shy in another man's corner,' said Bill.

" 'Or a woman's corner,' said I.

"Bill did n't say anything to that, but found some hammering to do."

The story was abruptly stopped by a screech from Number Twenty-six, which did not whistle until it was almost at the chutes. Finerty, hearing it so ominously near, popped off his bucket and out of the door. He was in a hurry to "make connections."

CHAPTER XII

HILE the evening was thus being spent, the thirteen arrivals of the morning, who had now sought haven at the "White Elephant," were having a series of misfortunes.

The "White Elephant," bedroom and bar, was crowded to its utmost capacity long before dark, the plethora of patronage being due to a combination of circumstances. Too many of these human birds of passage had been drawn that winter to a promising field at New Orleans, so that they had overstocked the city. Their appeals to the public had become such an old story that it was the worst possible place for a vagrant to "work." Many of them therefore deemed it advisable to make the pilgrimage North earlier in the season than instinct would otherwise have prompted them. The arrival of spring, as officially scheduled, had made them too optimistic. At Memphis they made the discovery that spring was late, and that it was phenomenally chilly. And so, with the forbidding North before them, and the unwelcoming South behind, and with the cold driving them to shelter as they halted between, the "White Elephant" had a congestion of vagrancy which was hourly growing greater.

The box-car crew, seeing the state of affairs, engaged their lodgings early, laying down each his five cents—five cents which each had got in his own characteristic way: Pap Smith, by personifying fallen gentility; Rochester Red, by exhibiting the loss of a finger, with remarks upon the fatalities of shingle-mills (the truth being that he had been bereft of it in his own profession of traveling); and the printer, by putting himself in evidence at the "Avalanche" and starting a conversation on Walt Whitman.

The "White Elephant" lodgings, like others of their ilk, consisted of a series of bunks built scaffold-wise from floor to ceiling—a sort of apartment-bed five stories in height and covering the wall.

Rough side-boards were nailed around each story; and the length of it was subdivided into beds, or boxes, by like boards. Here, with two

10

in a bed, some fifty or sixty guests could lay themselves away overnight as on shelves, the cheap price for this necessity of life being made possible to the proprietor by the fact that extra nickels would go for luxuries over the bar. For as men of better repute buy drinks in order to have dinner from a free-lunch counter, the vagrants' saloon carries the scheme to the point of having sleeping-counters which are all but free.

With the unusually heavy patronage, the apartment-bed, which had not been given the attention by the building inspector that a structure of so much responsibility would warrant, suddenly collapsed. With a thunderous crash the lodging-room of the "White Elephant" was converted into a pile of debris, boards and boarders. And the suddenly awakened occupants had hardly separated themselves from the lumber and taken stock of scratches and bruises when they were routed forth by the fire department, which had been called in the excitement caused by the fallen stovepipe. The box-car crew, after searching each other out by the white lint on their clothing, held council on a street corner; and after they had counted noses by the cold, green light of a drug-store that had been lighted early, they turned, by common consent, and wended their way through back streets to the police station.

Pap Smith dipped the pen into the ink-well and began to inscribe his necessary name, with a large flourish, on the station register, preliminary to a free bed on the floor. But the station-keeper softly stayed his hand. The station floor was fully occupied by guests sleeping on the "soft side of a newspaper." And the sergeant, refusing to engage in conversation with Pap Smith, who had hoped thereby to absorb some of the station warmth, simply said, "Get out of here." Thus again they found themselves on a cold street corner, excluded from the only caravansaries possible to their imagination.

"This is hell," said Rochester Red.

The others, with turned-up collars and the fastening of a stray button here and there, stood about in dumb endurance, neither assenting nor denying.

"The *sand-house!*" said Pap Smith, in a hoarse whisper, suddenly laying his forefinger on Rochester's shoulder, as the idea occurred to him. This suggestion needed no expounding. They saw visions of a beaming, egg-shaped railroad stove. The company came to attention at once. With Rochester and the old man in the lead, and the printer marking time in the rear, they trailed back to the levee; some withdrawn turtle-like into their clothing, some holding their hands in bottomless pockets, and all of them seeing promise ahead in the fact that they had a scraping acquaintance with the host of the sand-house.

"The sand-house, is it?" queried Finerty, when he had finished coaling up Number Seven. He held the lantern before each face in turn, making inspection.

"It 's aisy to see yees have been in a wreck. The sand-house, is it? And what worruk are yez going to do to pay for the lodgin'? Sure I have no ingine for yees to coal up now." The fore-man of the chutes took a moment of deep thought, with his arms akimbo and the lantern at his hip. Suddenly he said, "Can anny av yez sing or dance or tell a shtory?"

"He can sing," volunteered the printer, in-dicating the obvious form of Big George.

"Then let 's hear how ye can," said Finerty.

Big George, urged forward by several hands pressing at his back, stood forth at the head of the company. He placed his hands behind his back, and held up his head like a dog baying. With his eyes turned upward, as if his hungry nature were contemplating the skyful of cold stars and the thin, pale slice of moon, he tried his throat. And having found his voice, he gave forth "The Boston Burglar" in his sweetest nasal intonations:

"Oh, lissen now a-hand I will tell
About the fa-hate that once befell
    In Bosti-i-in long ago;
They brought him o'er the stormy brie—e-en,
Within a dungeon cell to pi-e-e-en,
A-hand that's the fate that once befell
    The Bostin Burgul—ler-r-r."

"Sure ye can sing. But yez ought to learn the words to 'Ballyhooly'; 't is betther nor that. Can anny av yez dance?"

A besotted hulk whose remainder of brains was given over to the delusion that he was light on his feet shambled heavily forward. He was immediately intercepted by Rochester Red, who spurned him back with a shove and a warning, and himself cast about till he found a suitable footing on the weighing-platform under the chutes. Sweeping about with his feet right and left to clear away any small obstruction, he began a preliminary tapping of clog-steps. Then, with a sudden clap of his hands, he fell into a jig.

Finerty held the lantern close to his feet, and watched the movements critically.

"'T is th' right way," he commented. "'T is none av yer naygur wadin' about an' shcrapin' the flure. Heel an' toe it is."

Several times he raised his lantern to inspect the deportment of the waist-line and shoulders and the conduct of the arms and hands. Finally he set the lantern close to the dancer's feet and sat down, the light snapping from his eyes. The rest of the crew stood about, watching the illumined pair of feet. It seemed but half a man dancing, the upper part of his body being in the total eclipse of the blackness beneath the chutes. And the seeming lack of weight upon them, as they went through the variations, made it seem all the more like a mere pair of legs disporting themselves in the light of the lantern. Finerty's smile grew broader as the repertoire of steps was exhibited to him. He gave no other sign of approbation, except to repeat at every change, "Heel an' toe it is." With a finale of clog, jig, and breakdown, the tramp slapped his foot down with a weight that jarred the beam of the scales and walked off.

"I see yez can do that," said Finerty, arising. "I 'm thinkin' I might let ye into th' sand-house."

Again he took a spell of thought.

"Can anny av yez play th' mouth-accordeen or th' jooce-ha-r-rp?"

To this there were two affirmative replies.

"Thin come alawng—I 'll give yees a thry for th' night." And he led the way to the sand-house.

"There 't is for ye," he said, unlocking the hasp and ushering them into the company of the radiant egg-shaped stove. "I 'll be back whin I 'm needin' ye to do it." And he departed.

The occupants spent some time in mutual discomfort as they settled down in the small available space, using each other for pillow or support in experimental ways of sleeping that no sooner proved comfortable to some than they became unsatisfactory to others. After many changes which ended in everybody's dissatisfaction, a number of them decided to climb up and sleep on the side of the sand-pile. But the slope was too steep to give them a resting-place, and they did not dare to throw any superfluity out of its proper place when they saw that it would go into the dirt and coal on the floor. This constituency slid down by degrees to the bottom in spite of their efforts, and they finally contented themselves with sitting on the edge of the board that bounded its base, and leaning back against the warm and comfortably fitting material as in an easy-chair.

Only Stumpy had been successful in making a bed of it. He climbed up higher, drove his wooden leg deep into the sand, and lay back full length, with his arms behind his head. This arrangement relieved the situation and solved the problem. But just as comfort had become unanimous, with no objectionable knees and elbows, Finerty returned.

He had a bucket in his hand. Stepping carefully between them, he forded his way to the coal-box in the far corner and let down the lid. He sprinkled it with sand, picked his way back to the entrance, turned the bucket upside down, and sat upon it.

" 'T is as good a shtage as ye 'd want," he remarked. Then he brought forth the short-stemmed clay pipe, which he filled with the scrapings from his pocket and carefully packed. As he threw his head back to avoid the flames of the match so close to his face, he caught sight of the one-legged member and stopped puffing long enough to remark: "An' 't will be th' wan-legged bye in th' gallery."

From another pocket he produced a long, wide nickel-plated mouth-organ.

"'T is this side ye are to play on," said he, addressing Big George, and indicating the particular side with his forefinger. "'T is the side wid th' rid paint on it for you—an' mind ye don't be turnin' it over an' playin' on me *own* side; 't is the wan I kape for mesilf. 'T was a naygur sp'iled me last wan wid carelessness. An' be sure ye mind what I 'm tellin' ye, or 't is out in th' cold wid yez.

"We will now have a sawng, folleyed by jiggin' an' reelin' be Misther Rochester."

Stumpy got little sleep that night. The features of that program would be a weariness to tell, for Finerty conducted two performances and would have insisted on a third had not his mind reverted to the story again. But while Stumpy was coming to it—for Pap Smith continually interrupted him to know the first part —Finerty looked at his watch and immediately jumped up.

"I have me worruk to do," he said. "Whin I come back we 'll wait f'r th' jiggin' an' reelin' till we 've had th' shtory."

When he came back the sand-house was heavy with sleep, and the wrecks of humanity were strewn upon the sand. So the chance for the story was gone.

CHAPTER XIII

INERTY awoke in the parlor at "three-tin P.M.," and got up instantly. When he had gone through the simple operation of putting on his trousers, he proceeded sleepily to the kitchen and immediately sat down at the table, resting his elbows on it, and surveying the table-cloth in heavy contemplation of being fed. Mrs. Finerty made herself busy at once; and when she had the meal before him she sat down to watch him eat.

"Well, Michael, I have learned something th' day that I niver knew befure."

"What is 't?"

"'T is called ivvolution; 't is about animals. An' there was a caller this morning—some one that ye know."

"Was it Dinnis?"

"'T was not him. I hear he has now gone away on a case again. If 't was n't for that I 'd have ye go to th' station an' thry to see him again. An' th' nixt time ye 'll not be goin' out widout yer black tie on an' yer shoes shined. Ye can't tell whin ye 'll be took up again for a juryman or a pall-bearer, an' be morthifyin' me. A man w'u'd be a haythen intirely if 't was n't for some wan opposin' him an' handin' him a clane shirt. No, 't was n't Dinnis; but I 'll tell ye who 't was. I was out in th' yard dhrivin' th' goat away from th' corner av th' house; for he has come *through*, Michael.'' Mrs. Finerty pointed to the corner of the kitchen, where an opening like a rat-hole led to outer day—a result of the goat having discovered that a foundation-beam of the kitchen was friable with age and temptingly easy to gnaw. ''I knew he w'u'd be comin' through, wid ye puttin' it off all th' time. Ye should have, annyway, nailed a tin can over th' place. Whiniver his mind w'u'd be empty, wid nothin' to do, he w'u'd think av th' corner av th' house again; an' I c'u'd not be kapin' me eye on him *all* th' time. Now ye will have to be findin' more tools nor th' hatchet. I 'm thinkin', if I knew the likes av th' blackshmith ye are tellin' about, I w'u'd have him make a muzzle for th' goat. 'T is a pity a man like him should be a murd'rer whin there is so *manny* things in th' worruld to be fixed.''

"D'ye mane 't was th' goat that called?" asked Finerty.

"No; th' idee! I was shtandin' lookin' at th' hole whin I seen th' goat put his head down an' shtart off, the way I knew at wanst there was some one comin'.''

"He is th' fine watch-goat," interpolated Finerty.

"Yis; but he is not like a dog, that w'u'd have some sinse or judgment. I mind th' goat me father had in th' ould counthry. An' there was a high shtone wall about me father's place. An' th' goat w'u'd be doin' nothin' but walkin' on top av th' wall, back and forth, like th' guardeen av a pinitintiary. He was th' fine watch-goat for ye. An' whin th' front dure w'u'd be open he w'u'd go up-shtairs to th' front room an' be rummagin' in th' girls' things. I mind me father tied a sthring from his front legs till his hind wans so that he c'u'd not be shteppin' up. An' from that on he w'u'd go up th' shtairs sideways.''

"Was it that ye learned about animals?" remarked Finerty. "Sure I knew that befure.''

"'T was n't that. I saw th' goat shtart off wid his head down, an' I looked up. An' there goin' out av th' gate again was a dacint ould man, genteel wid age an' th' white whiskers av him. So I wint and commanded th' goat to be lavin' him alone. An' he says to me that he was goin' past, an' c'u'd I shpare him a dhrink av wather? I gave him a dhrink in th' flowery cup, an' he shtood dhrinkin' an' shmackin' his lips an' sayin' 't was th' finest wather he iver tasted, an' did we dig th' well oursilves? An' whin he was handin' th' cup back he shtopped suddenly an' says: 'Am I mistaken, or are ye Mrs. Finerty? I was thinkin' ye looked familiar to me,' says he. 'I know yer husband. He has been very kind to me.' "

"Had he a pimple on th' top av his head?" inquired Finerty.

"I was n't lookin' that close at him," replied Mrs. Finerty. "But he *might* 'a' had."

" 'T is th' wan they call Pap Smith. Would n't it bate ye that he should happen to come here? But th' likes av thim are all over."

"Yis; 't was th' ould man that is shtoppin' wid th' thramps. 'T is a pity, Michael, for he comes av fine people an' has seen his day himsilf—if 't was n't for th' palpitation. 'T is bad to have th' likes av that come on whiniver ye exert yersilf. An' him that rosy wid health. But 't is n't th' healthy fat, Michael."

"No wan is kapin' him wid th' thramps if he

don't like th' place," replied Finerty. "An'
what is it about th' ivvolution?"

"I was goin' to tell if ye 'd not be intherruptin' me. We were shpakin' av th' well, an'
him tellin' me av th' different layers av geol-
ogy in th' ground; for he is eddicated, an' must
be always improvin' his mind at th' public li-
braries."

"Whin 't is a rainy day," remarked Finerty.

"Befure long we were talkin' about th' bukes
an' eddication, shtartin', in th' way I can't tell,
from me sayin' somethin' to th' goat. ''T is
quare about animals,' says he. 'Did ye iver
hear av ivvolution?' says he. 'For 't was a
man named Darwin invinted it.' "

"What is 't?" inquired Michael.

"Well, 't is like this," answered Mrs. Finerty. "''T is that animals changes thimsilves,
like, accordin' to th' neighborhood they 're in.
But it takes a long time, an' ye can't see thim do
it; for nature is slow about makin' thim over.
'T is like as if an elephant was to be moved to
th' north pole, where 't is all shnow an' ice.
An' mabby in a long time he w'u'd be gettin' th'
likes av an ice-pick on th' ind av his thrunk for
to be burrowin' in th' icebergs an' makin' his
way about."

"An' ye 're *belavin'* it?" remarked Michael.

"''T is not that I w'u'd be belavin' it. But Agnes says 't is *thrue*. 'T is a worrud in th' bukes, an' 't is like *that*. Ye don't suppose I 'd be takin' the worrud av ivery wan, only for that. An' whilst we were talkin' I saw the likes av a big rid bug shtickin' out av a paper in his pocket. 'T was a lobster. He took it out to be showin' me th' curiosity av it—'t was some friends av his had given it to him. An' d' ye know, Michael, th' lobster was both heads an' no tails. An' I says to him, 'How is that? Is it the heads av two lobsters?'

"'Yis,' says he; ''t is that; at laste I 'm thinkin' 't is that,' says he. An' wid that he was minded to tell me more about th' ivvolution. 'Have ye iver noticed,' says he, 'how a crab does be walkin' backwards most av th' time? Well,' says he, 'accordin' to th' laws av nature, 't will only be a matther av time till they 'll be gettin' heads on th' other ind to be seein' where they 're goin'. 'T is that makes ivvolution,' says he. 'An',' says he, 'th' lobster I have was probably but two halves; but I 'm not sure av that,' says he; 'for I fell down an' might 'a' broke it in two, for they 're awful tender acrost th' bellies. It might have been wan av th' early samples, although I w'u'd n't have ye think it is,' says he. 'An' 't is bound

to come in time, accordin' to ivvolution. Nature,' says he, 'is a wonderful thing whin ye
come to shtudy it.' An' he showed me th' curiosity av it. But I w'u'd not want to be atin' it.
I am not much to ate th' insides av annything.''

"Pass me th' butther," said Michael. "An'
ye *belavin'* it!''

" 'T is not that I 'd be such a fool," she replied, "except that Agnes says 't is thrue. An'
't is th' survival av th' fittenest. 'T is *like*
that, an' all th' t'achers say 't is *thrue*. 'T is
only that I belave.''

Michael took another potato and peeled it
slowly, cut it up and buttered it, and ate it solemnly.

"Were ye sayin' Agnes says 't is thrue, an'
that 't is in th' bukes?''

" 'T is that I was tellin' ye.''

Michael took another potato. "Well," he remarked, "if Agnes says 't is thrue I have no
doubt av it. But at th' same time I don't belave it.''

"Annyway," said Mrs. Finerty, "he is that
well eddicated. An' ye must n't be puttin' him
out, Michael, till th' cold is pasht. 'T w'u'd be
a shame. Th' rist av thim, he was tellin' me,
are only jist thramps, except th' poor wan-
legged bye an' th' rid-haired wan that has th'

dancin' in him an' is no more good for worrukin' than a piper. An' some av th' others that has n't got th' advantage av good sinse, like ye, are jist thramps; but he says there is no harm in thim. 'T is little I w'u'd help bummers an' loafers. But wan w'u'd n't be denyin' th' fire to a human bein' on a cold night.''

"I 'm not mindin' havin' thim about; 't is company,'' replied Michael.

Being thus reminded of the story-teller at the sand-house, Mrs. Finerty at once asked for the latest instalment of the blacksmith's adventures; and Michael told her of his partnership with Nellie and Eva in the Texas town.

"An' th' two girls takin' up wid a murd'rer! What w'u'd they be thinkin' if they knew that!"

"He was n't tellin' thim that,'' replied Michael. "He was too sharp for that.''

"I 'm thinkin' 't is sthrange that th' wanlegged bye should be tellin' *ye* all about it— an' th' blackshmith so kind to him. 'T w'u'd be sthrange if he should be tellin' ye all, an' where the blackshmith wint—an' him not caught yet. Ye 'll have to be seein' Dinnis.''

"Th' felly Shtoompy is shtarted to tellin' it now,'' said Finerty; "an' there is no way for him but to be kapin' on this kind av weather.

11

An' Dinnis will be back befure Soonda', ye 're sayin'."

"Mabby he won't be tellin' ye all, even if he is shtarted," replied Mrs. Finerty. "If the blackshmith is not caught yet, he will be tellin' ye that he was caught or is dead, or mabby proved innocint or th' likes av that. He 'd not be tellin' on him."

"Well," said Finerty, "he is th' kind that ye can see w'u'd not be good at makin' *up* annything. An' th' way he 's shtarted he will have to tell it like 't is thrue—wid ivery little part av it. He 'll have to kape up wid th' thruth, for he is th' innocint wan that has little lyin' in him."

"Lave him take his time, Michael; an' make him go on till th' ind. Then ye can tell. An' Dinnis w'u'd be th' wan that can tell."

Finerty put on the soft head-piece, which, not being a "right an' lift hat," as he said, could be donned with no thought whatever; and with the big pail he went through the gate. But he had not gone far on the cinder-path when his wife called, as she leaned on the fence:

"Michael dear!"

"What is it ye want now?"

"Be careful. An' mind ye get him to tell it all to ye."

CHAPTER XIV

HE tramps began to straggle into the sand-house early, among the first being Pap Smith, who preëmpted the most comfortable location. Stumpy arrived early, having received a peremptory command to that effect from the fiery Rochester, who had found that any delay of the story would have to be filled by himself with the "jiggin' an' reelin'." Stumpy had scarcely taken account of the last arrival from his station on the heights when Finerty came in and sat on the upturned bucket. Finerty turned his eyes several times in the direction of Pap Smith, as if he intended making some personal allusions. But he evidently changed his mind, for when the pipe was in operation he ignored both the diplomat and the dancer, and went directly at the story.

"An' so ye got settled down, like?"

"As I was saying," began Stumpy, "on the

163

afternoon of our first day in the blacksmith-shop we had no job in sight. So we fixed up the kitchen of the old house while Nellie watched the shop. She hung the new swingletree hooks outside of her 'jewelry-store,' and stood behind the counter watching for farmers to go by. We built a bunk in the corner of the kitchen, and Bill made a bench outside that we could use for a wash-stand in the morning, and sit on evenings and smell the flowers in the garden. Bill found a lantern in the shop, and he hung a wire from a hook in the middle of the ceiling, so that we could use the lantern for a chandelier. Eva gave us some blankets and an empty tick which Bill got filled with hay at the feed-store. We took two of the Chautauqua chairs out of the front room, and then we had a home of our own.

"During the afternoon Nellie sold a hook for ten cents, and she called Bill to point another plow. That brought us three dollars for the afternoon—counting what we got for shoeing Lady. That night Bill laid the money in the middle of the supper-table, and after supper we divided with the girls; and every night after that we settled in the same way. Bill and I kept our money in partnership, buying anything that either of us needed.

"In a few days I was learning to measure my blows with the sledge, and when to go from the bellows to the anvil without being told. Whenever there was a chance between jobs Bill would let me practise making hooks out of old shoes. At first they would turn out all shapes and sizes; but once in a while I would turn out one that was fit to sell. When a farmer came along and bought one of my hooks and stopped to see me pounding a piece of red iron—as if I was a blacksmith—I felt mighty proud, and would pound away as if I knew the trade. But a good deal of Bill's work was of a kind where I would only be in the road; so I would have to sit idle. We both wished that I could have the use of the first anvil to practise on.

"After a couple of weeks we got the use of it through a piece of good luck—or bad luck, whichever you might call it. One hot morning, when I had sprinkled the shop from the cooling-tub, and we were sitting down, taking it comfortable,—for there is n't a better place in summer than a blacksmith-shop with a dirt floor when it is wet down,—Mrs. Gulley appeared at the door trying to steer a stubborn pig into the shop. The pig's head was wedged into a big tin can that came back to his shoulders. The can was jammed out of shape, and was fitted on his head as tight as if a blacksmith had shrunk it on. As the pig could not see where he was going, she navigated him by the tail, which she gripped with one hand; and with the other she clung to a rope that was tied around him behind his fore legs. The pig came to a sudden stop outside the door, and stood as if he was thinking inside the can.''

"Mabby," remarked Finerty, "the pig was thinkin' he was worrukin' nights."

"As I was saying, he stopped, and then he made a sudden dash sideways, as if he decided to go in another direction; but Mrs. Gulley gave a strong heave on his tail that changed his direction and brought him into the shop. She gave the rope a turn around Bill's vise, wiped the sweat from her forehead on the corner of her apron, and took a deep breath.

" 'How-do, Blacksmith?' she said. 'I jest wonder if you can git my hog out of this here can. Is ther' any way that ye can cut tin?'

"At this the pig began grunting.

" 'Jest hear him grunting in there,' said Mrs. Gulley. 'He sounds like the base horn in the county-seat band. An' ther' ain't no use in tryin' to pull it off. We tried that.'

" 'How did he get it on so tight?' asked Bill.

" 'Well, I 'll tell ye jest how it come to be.'

She sat down on a box and rolled her hands up in her apron. 'Ye see, my brother out in the country had a lot of big sheep-dip cans that he had used all the tobacker juice outen; and I got him to bring me one in fer to set by the back door fer a swill-pail. Well, John Henry —he 's the hog—John Henry, whenever he breaks pen, makes a bee-line fer the swill-can. He could n't get his snout more 'n half-way to bottom by rights. But bein' as the can 's square—which it *was*—he could keep pushin' his head in and bulgin' out the sides till it was fit on the shape of his head, and awful tight. An' that way he could get his snout 'most to bottom. An' then when he would find that it was stuck on he would go rampagin' round till he shuck it off—an' then he would eat what he had spilled. Well, this here morning, while I was makin' some sal'ratus biscuit, John Henry broke pen again, and he e't his way down till it was on him tighter 'n ever. He went tearin' round with his head shet up in the dark, squealin' terrible. When I come to the door with my hands full of dough from the sal'ratus biscuit, he was domineerin' down the road with the can on his head. And he run hellity-larrup into a fence-post. Of course that druv it clean over his head and bent it; that 's what made it fit tight like that. He broke down two of my apple saplin's. An' that 's how he got in that fool fix. An' I forgot to tell, he broke the door of the school-house, crackin' it. Do you think you kin black-smith it off 'n him someways?'

"Bill started to cut it off with the tin-shears; but the hog would not stand to be worked on. A hog is a hard thing to hold—especially a Texas razor-back. Mrs. Gulley held him by the tail and a hind leg, and I caught him by the fore legs; but that only gave him the idea of getting away. Whenever he felt the shears on his head, he would plunge about and knock Bill's legs from under him.

" 'I 'll fix him,' said Bill. He went and got the ox-yoke. He took out the bows and slipped one of them up around the hog's chest and put the yoke on him that way. The hog was a tight fit, so that he spread the bows some; but by squeezing the ends together we managed to get them through the holes in the beam and put the pegs in. Bill put an iron stake through one of the holes at the other end, and drove it into the ground. As Bill went to get another stake to drive in the other hole, the hog broke away from us and started to run. But as he could only run in a circle, he went round and round the stake, with the beam on him—like a blind horse running away on a pug-mill.

" 'Lawdy suz!' says Mrs. Gulley, 'I suppose John Henry thinks he is going somewheres. But he ain't.'

"When Bill had got another stake he slipped it into the second hole, and then he hit it a belt with the sledge that stopped the hog on the spot. Then he could n't move in any direction, for, as Bill said, he had him 'nailed.'

" 'That 'll transfixiate John Henry, I guess,' said Bill. 'But take hold of his tail and his legs again, to make sure that he can't pull out while I go at him.'

"The pig squealed and trumpeted inside the can.

" 'It hurts his pride awful,' said Mrs. Gulley. 'He sounds like a brass band gone crazy.'

"Miss Eva and Miss Nellie came running to find what the trouble was. When Bill had got the can off, and was trying to draw the bow-pins, John Henry got his legs away from me, and gave a jump that lifted the yoke off the inner stake. He started running round the circle again, and he went so swift that when the beam came round and struck the other stake, it pried both of them out of the ground, and let him loose, with the yoke on him. He ran about the shop, swinging the timber around; and whenever he turned he played crack-the-whip with it, knocking things over. As Mrs. Gulley was heading him off at the door, he banged it against the base of the first anvil and knocked off the A. That brought him to a stop long enough for Bill to get a stake into the bow-hole again and nail him to the spot. This time Bill got the bow off; and John Henry bolted through the door and ran out on the prairie, freed from the tin can.

"The two girls were standing in the doorway laughing. Bill was scratching his head, and looking down at the fallen letter. And as Bill raised his eyes and looked serious at Miss Eva, she took in what was troubling him. She picked up the A, took the O out of the jaws of the tongs, and laid them on the anvil.

" 'Don't you want to finish the branding-iron, Alonzo?' she said.

" 'Just as you say about it, Miss Eva,' said Bill.

" 'I guess you were hardly to blame—seeing how it happened,' said Eva. 'And I suppose, after all, that father would not want to see his job unfinished—although I could hardly make up my mind to disturb it. But Hendricks was

inquiring for it yesterday. The other letter is
H. Make it A. O. H.'

"Bill finished the branding-iron that morning. And that was how I happened to get the
first anvil to practise on.

"One evening, about a week after that, Bill
quit work early and went over to town. He
brought home a looking-glass and a white shirt.
When we fixed up our house we put up a row
of hooks for clothes, and pretty soon we bought
plenty of blue shirts and some extra clothes.
Bill said at the time that they were all we would
need. This evening, when he brought in the
fancy stuff, he laid it down on the bunk without
asking me how I liked it, or making any remarks—not a word. He hung up the looking-
glass, with a shelf under it, and he put up a
separate hook beside the glass to hang the
white shirt on. I could see he was n't going
to let it associate with the common clothes.
Then we went to supper. When we came back
from the girls' house I went and sat out on our
bench, smelling the flowers and waiting for
Bill to come out, too; for it was Thursday evening, and the Afro-Americans would soon be
coming to have their Chautauqua in our front
room. They studied about poetry and geol-
ogy and such things, and they mixed it up with

a good deal of fine singing. So every Thursday night Bill and I would sit out on the bench together in the evening, smelling the garden and enjoying the singing.

"I waited quite a while, but Bill did not come out. Then I heard him spluttering and splashing in the bucket at the back door, and I wondered what he could be giving himself an extra wash for. And pretty soon he came round the corner of the kitchen, dressed up, with the white shirt on. And he picked a red flower out of the garden and put it in the buttonhole of his coat.

" 'You can listen to the singing,' he said, stopping and looking down at me a while before he went away. Then he went over to the girls' house. After a while I saw him sitting on the front of the porch with both of them. Later on, when I looked again, there seemed to be only one; but it had grown dusk, so that I could n't see which one it was. I sat and listened to the singing. Bill did not come home till meeting was over and I had gone to bed.

"Every Thursday evening after that he would do the same. One evening, when we had come home from supper, he found that the girls had forgot to bring his shirt back from the wash. So he went over and got it, and went back dressed up in it, as if he was calling on strangers. When I would look over that way, in the dusk, I could see that sometimes he was sitting with both of them, and sometimes one or the other. I could n't tell which he went to see; and sometimes I wondered if they knew and how they decided. And every time he went he would come to a stop where I was sitting on the bench, and look at me serious and say, 'You can listen to the singing.' I could always see that he felt responsible about turning his back on me for some one else and leaving me alone like that. But that was all he would ever say about it.

"I kept coming on at the trade. Before long I could make a swingletree hook, and knew how to go ahead and make things ready on most of the regular work that came in. If it was a loose tire I could take it off the wheel, and when Bill had it made smaller I could build a circular fire back of the shop and expand it and help put it on. If it was a horse that came in I could cut the nails and take off the shoes, and when Bill had the new ones fitted and put on I could rasp the hoofs and finish. And if it was a piece of welding or shaping I could strike where Bill tapped. As I was always busy, and as every job came out right without any trouble, I began to think that, from having such a good chance, it would not be long before I would be a blacksmith.

"One evening, when we were sitting on the bench looking at the garden, I said, 'Well, Bill, ain't I coming on pretty well?'

" 'Good as could be expected. Stick to me four or five years, perfessor, and I 'll have you started to being a mechanic.'

" 'Started!' said I.

" 'Yes; started to thinking for yourself.'

" 'Don't I think now?' said I.

" 'Good as could be expected for a man that never had any trade at all. If you 'd been a watchmaker or something you 'd get along faster at this.'

" 'What good would that do me shoeing horses?' said I.

" 'Well, I 'll explain. When I first told you to take off a shoe you put the horse's hind hoof between your legs instead of in your lap. Then, because I corrected you on that, you started putting the front legs in your lap instead of between your legs. You had watched me take off and put on dozens of shoes and never seen me. You had to be told. Now, it 's pretty much the same all round in everything, till you 've got to be a mechanic. If you 'd been a mechanic already you 'd 'a' had that trick stolen and studied out the reason for it before I could have showed you.' "

Finerty took out his pipe at this and remarked: "Th' felly Bill was turnin' on ye, was n't he? He was n't goin' to give away his thrade like ye thought."

"Turn on *me!*" exclaimed Stumpy, rising as if he intended to straighten up bodily on the leg that was anchored in the sand. "Bill would never turn on *me*. He was always square, Bill was."

"Don't let me be shtoppin' ye," said Finerty, seeing that the story might come to an untimely end. And Stumpy continued.

CHAPTER XV

" 'UT I ought to get along faster than most of them, because you are willing to show me all the tricks,' I said to Bill.

" ' 'Bein' a mechanic,' says he, 'ain't knowin' a certain number of tricks; it 's bein' a certain kind of a man. After you 've learned to be a mechanic you 'll soon be a blacksmith.'

" 'I don't exactly understand what you mean,' I said.

" 'Well,' said Bill, 'when I 'm setting an iron axle so the wheels will track, I tap it with the hammer and say, "Hit her there," don't I?'

" 'Yes.'

" 'Well, that 's bein' a mechanic; it 's thinkin'.'

"Bill sat quiet for a while. I guess he was thinking. Then he said: 'The best thing that ever happened to me was being put at the trade

176

in a shop where they did n't want me to learn anything—although I did n't look at it that way at the time. And when I found that out I watched them like a hawk, and I kept thinking about everything they did. I had the satisfaction, as you might say, of stealing it. And the result was that when I had learned what the common every-day ones called the trade, I kept going ahead and thinking and trying to get the best of things, because I had had so much practice. I had so much practice getting the best of men that, when I came to dealing with things themselves, and on my own hook, I had the habit of watching them sharp and prying secrets out of them. Things don't tell you anything. You 'll find that all you learn from them you 've got to steal. What was your father?'

" 'He was a cooper,' said I.

" 'Maybe that will help some; but it 's for you to do the thinkin' and the askin'. You 've got the anvil to practise on now; and I 'm there all the time to steal the trade from.'

"The next day Bill went away to Wilton to look over a printing-press and fix it. Before he left he gave me a tire to cut down and try to fit on the old wheel that was leaning against the front of the shop; and he said, 'Whenever

I am gone be sure and keep busy. When you
see a farmer coming along get a piece of red
iron on the anvil, and, whatever you do, make
a noise. And don't tell anybody you 're just
learning. When anybody brings a job in tell
them you 're so busy that they can't get it till
to-morrow. Then when I come back I 'll do
it all. But, whatever you do, make a noise
once in a while. The way to be a blacksmith is
to start being one.'

"After Bill fixed the printing-press and they
found he understood machinery, he got a call
to go to another part of the county and tamp
the flues in a leaky boiler. While he was there
he took a look at the engine. He reset the ec-
centric and fixed the valve so that she would
work with less steam. He was particular to
explain the reason for it, so that the boss would
see that he knew what he was doing. That way
he got a reputation, and before long he was
gone a day or two out of every week; and whenever he was going he would set me at a job.
'Whatever you do,' he would say, 'keep the
place busy. If you run out of work, unmake a
hook and make it over; you can always do it
better.'

"Being left alone that way and having farmers call me 'blacksmith' was what put me to

learning for myself. The jobs I took in seemed to be my own—although I could n't do them. And the next day, instead of expecting to be shown, I would find myself stealing the trade from Bill. And the moment I would pick up an idea of my own he would notice it; and I would see him smiling to himself.

"When Will Upton went back to West Point he brought Lady into the shop, and offered to sell her to Bill. He said he would rather know that she was in his hands than to leave her with somebody that she could n't get along with. Bill and the girls bought her in partnership. We kept her in the corner of the shop, and we all made a pet of her. With the girls bringing her bread and cookies and Bill talking to her when he was n't working, she got to be one of the family. He gave her lessons in trotting with an old sulky that he fixed up like new; and sometimes he would take the girls out riding, and show them how he had got her speeded up.

"Finally a peculiar thing happened. One Saturday afternoon we went blackberrying out in the country along the railroad tracks. We took Lady along; for there was a farmer up that way who owed Bill money, and they had bargained to settle it by giving Lady a vacation, and letting her take it out in grass with a mea-

sure of corn every day. When we got out to
the berry-patch, Bill left us beside the tracks
and took Lady along a path through the thick
woods to the farm. When he came back we all
went a little farther up the tracks, and found
a thicker patch of berries growing along a rail
fence. We had a great deal of fun seeing who
could get his pail filled first. I found a bush
loaded with berries inside a clump of briers,
where they were too far to reach. So I climbed
in, not minding the scratching; and, while I
was picking away as fast as I could on my secret bush, I heard Eva scream.''

"Ye *did!*" exclaimed Finerty, half rising
from his upturned bucket, and staring at
Stumpy. "Th' *divil!*"

CHAPTER XVI

"AS I was saying," continued Stumpy, "I heard Eva screaming. I jumped out of the bush and saw her running up the bank to the tracks. She was calling out, 'William, William!' I jumped along as fast as I could to her.

"Bill jumped out of a bush at the same time and got to her first.

" 'Oh, William,' she said, 'I saw a snake!'

"Bill went where she pointed and killed the snake; and after the snake was dead, all but its tail, she began to call him Alonzo again. He had to go and pick berries with her because she was afraid.

"I was so surprised to hear her call him his right name, and I was so worried for fear it was me that had called him that some time when I was n't thinking, that I could n't pick berries as fast as the rest of them. When they were all through I had n't my pail half filled. The girls and Bill made great fun of me for being beat, laughing and joking. And on the way home she called him Alonzo the same as ever.

"That night Bill did n't say anything about it; so the next morning, when we were at work, I began to think he had n't noticed it, and I decided I had better tell him.

" 'Bill,' said I, 'did you take notice what Eva called you yesterday?'

" 'That was when the snake scared her,' said he, not seeming to think much about it. 'She knows my name.'

"With that he went to hammering so hard that I could n't talk any more about it. When the shoe was done he threw it down and started another, working the bellows himself, with his hand on his hip, the way he always did when he was thinking. Suddenly he said: 'Don't call me that damn name any more, perfessor. I don't like that Alonzo, anyway; I 'm sick of it.'

" 'But you 've got to stick to it now,' I said.

" 'Yes, when anybody 's around; but when I 'm eating at my own table I 'm going to be myself.'

"After that the girls always called him by

his right name when I was around and no one else was. I wondered what kind of a story he had fixed up to make it seem all right to them. I started to ask Bill about it several times; but it seemed, whenever I would start that subject, he would have a mighty noisy job to do on the anvil. And after a few times I saw that it was n't all a happen-so, and I could n't help sort of half feeling that maybe Bill did n't need me for a partner as much as he used to; so I made up my mind to tend to my own business on that subject.

"It was a couple of weeks after that when luck first started to go against Bill. In the afternoon he left me running the place while he went to buy a new hat and another white shirt at the store opposite the depot. When he came back I could see that something was wrong. I saw it the minute he stepped through the door. He slapped his new hat down on the work-bench, and stood glaring at a pile of horse-shoes as if he was going to make them hot by looking at them.

" 'What 's the matter, Bill?' said I.

" 'We 're set back—clean back to Arkansaw.'

"He punched the wrinkles out of his hat and sat down on the shoeing-kit.

" 'You remember,' said he, 'the time I went up to the roundhouse at Texarkana, and came back with a dollar? Well, I was just now standing on the depot platform, watching the train come in. When she had come to a stop, some one suddenly slapped me on the back, saying, ''Here 's the fellow now.'' I turned round so quick I pretty near went out of my shoes; and I felt it shooting through me to knock him down. It 's a good thing I thought quick enough to hold myself back, for it was the engineer holding his hand out to me and grinning. He was motioning to the fireman and the baggage-master and saying, ''Here 's the fellow that fixed my petticoat-pipe. He 's the boy that done it.''

" 'Then I knew who he was. You see, that time when I went over to the roundhouse at Texarkana to see whether there was an engine getting ready to pull out, the master mechanic was arguing with the engineer. The engineer claimed his engine did n't make steam right, and he wanted some one else called out for the run. But there was n't anybody else.

" 'I got to talking to them about her not making steam. I climbed up on the boiler and looked down the smoke-stack,—sticking my blamed nose into things the way I have n't any business to,—and I told them I thought it would be a good scheme to close up the end of the exhaust a little so that she would puff harder and make better suction in the petticoat-pipe. "It 'll blow up her fire better," says I. The master mechanic said it was a good idea; and, as they were short of machinists on account of the strike, he gave me the job. I did it in quick time, because you and me was in a hurry to pull out of the town, and I wanted to get the engine in shape so that we would have something to go on. And that was how I got the dollar. Well, the engineer saw me just now, and was glad to see me. I wanted to tell him to shut up about it, but that would have been suspicious; so I had to let him go on. Why, Stumpy, when you and I was put off that train at the tank, I could have spoken to that engineer, and he would have given us a ride if he had to put us on top of the cab. He was the same fellow. But I did n't do it because I did n't want any one to have any trace of where I was going. And now this has gone and happened. I got away from him as quick as I could to make him forget it; and when I left he was telling everybody around the depot how easy I doctored her up, and talking about the petticoat-pipe.'

" 'Well, what are you mad about that for?'
said I.

" 'What for? Why, they 've got me connected up with Texarkana now; and we *left*
that place because it was n't far enough away,
did n't we? Pretty soon we might as well have
our shop in New Orleans. A couple of more
jumps like that will put us there.'

"But before long Bill began to look pleased.
He sat twirling the new hat round on his finger
as if he was winding up the smile on his face.
Suddenly the wrinkles came round his eyes,
and he said: 'Say, perfessor, the job was *all
right*. She 's been making steam ever since.'

"Then the hat began to go slower, till finally
it run down, and Bill sat looking serious again.
He pitched into the work and did more that
day than usual. That night he made his
Thursday call on the girls on Tuesday. He
came home late with the old man's Winchester,
and hung it over the bunk; and the next day he
took it to the shop and gave it an overhauling.

"Lately, when I looked back and thought how
Bill used to be, it seemed to me that some sort
of a change had come over him. He was the
same to me and other folks, but he was n't the
same to himself; he acted more serious and responsible. He used to be the kind that when-

ever there was trouble he would go at it like a job of work; but he would n't worry much about it beforehand. He was always a man that did a good deal of thinking at his work, but now it seemed that it was n't always the work that he was thinking about. And now that he was keeping the Winchester over the bed and the revolver always handy, I began to think he was losing his nerve from thinking things over too much.

"One day I said to him, 'Bill, we 're pretty well fixed now. Everything 's come out right, after all—and nothing to worry about.'

" 'Yes; it 's all right—if it lasts.'

" 'There is n't any reason to think it won 't,' said I.

" 'And no knowing that it will,' said he.

" 'Well,' said I, 'when they pretty near had you, you used to say you would take your chances. Now there ain 't so many chances. You did n't look at things this way a while back.'

" 'Maybe so. But those days it was a case of alive or dead and only me to bother myself about. Now I 'd rather be alivê. That 's different.'

"Sometimes, when I would sit out in the garden Thursday evenings, waiting for Bill to come home, I would get to thinking of how I used to live; and it seemed years ago. The summer had gone on, one day about like another, and Thursday nights coming regular, with me sitting up waiting for Bill. And when I thought about how I used to live, it seemed to me as if it was n't me at all that used to go around without a home and with nothing to do. It seemed as if it was somebody else. With coming and going regular and always knowing what was going to happen next, it did n't seem to me at all as if it could all depend on not getting caught at it. And sometimes I would think that Bill had nearly forgot they were after him —except always in the morning, when he would strap on his revolver under his pants where it would n't show.

"Along toward the end of summer Bill sent away to St. Louis for some machinist tools and some spelter for fixing a broken casting. He went to the depot a number of times to see whether they had come. The third time he came back to the shop without them I thought, from the way he looked and acted, that he was disappointed at not getting them. He looked about the shop in a half-alive, downcast sort of way, and then sat down on the handle of the shoeing-kit, leaning over as if he was tired out. It was the first time I ever saw Bill look as if he had clean given up.

" 'What 's the matter, Bill? Are you sick?' I asked.

" 'Stumpy, luck 's started to go against us.'

" 'Maybe you 're just sick from worrying,' I said.

" 'We 're connected up with Memphis and New Orleans now, if I ain't mistaken. The Land Company excursion just went through. I saw Cap Berry, of the *Creole Belle*, looking out of one of the car windows; I 'm pretty sure he saw me.'

" 'Do you suppose he recognized you?'

" 'I think so. When I came out of the express-room onto the platform, I had to walk around the train to get home. I looked up at a window and I saw a man's eye just letting go of me; that was the way it seemed. When I took a second look I saw it was the captain, sitting and looking straight ahead as if he did not see me. It all happened as quick as a wink; but it went through me that he had been looking at me; and of course he knows I 'm wanted.'

" 'I don't think he saw you,' I said.

" 'Think not?' he said, looking up quick and hopeful.

"He sat on the shoeing-kit studying, as if he had an idea he could think it out. Then he said: 'I would like to know, one way or the other. I will go and ask Eva.'

"After a while I went and looked out of the door, wondering what was keeping him. I saw Miss Eva coming across the prairie to the shop. I waited in the door for her, watching how pretty she walked. One time I heard Will Upton say she was 'the jaunty cadet,' and now I could see what he meant. She had on her black dress, neat and slim, with the red ribbon in her dark hair; and she was coming on like a soldier, with her eyes straight ahead, as if she had particular business that she was coming straight to do.

" 'I want you to go out and get Lady,' she said. 'Tell the farmer we need her, and that he need not bother about the two weeks' pasture that he still owes us.' And when she saw me taking off my apron and getting ready she went back to the house without another word.

"I walked up the tracks and turned into the path that Bill followed when he left us black-berrying. The farm was in a clearing, a mile or so back in the woods, where there was no road. When the farmer had given me a lift on Lady's back and let down the bars, he started to

explain where I could find another road home;
but he had got no farther than to point the way
when Lady pricked up her ears with a whinny
and sprang away without waiting for explana-
tions. I tried to bring her round toward the
path; but she kept on straight through the
woods, running under low branches, as if she
did not care whether there was any one on her
back or not. It kept me ducking and dodging;
and I had so many narrow escapes from being
knocked off, that finally I lay down, with my
arms around her neck, and gave all my attention to hanging on. Sometimes a branch would
give my coat such a brushing that it would
nearly pull it off.

"When we had gone along like that for a
while she struck a road and turned into it.
Here she let out another link in her throttle—
as Bill would say—and stretched out as if she
was running a race. I held fast, hoping I
could stay on till she made her station; for it
was plain that she was headed for some place
in particular and she would n't be stopped. And
I hoped that it was the blacksmith-shop, and
that maybe her hurry was all on account of
Eva's bread and cookies. I tried to pull her
up, but she only went faster on a stiff rein. I
was bouncing so that every time I went up I

expected to come down and find that she had gone on and left me while I was in the air. So I dropped the bridle entirely, and watched out for myself, with a good grip on her mane. Once in a while she would let out a whinny like an express-train whistling for the cross-roads. People would hear us thumping along, and they would stand in front of farm-houses to see what was coming; and farmers would stop their plows to watch us go.

"Suddenly she dodged into another road, and we had n't gone far before I saw it was the road that went through town. I tried to haul her round to another road that would take us in by a back way; for I did n't want to go down the main street riding like that. I kept pulling on one rein and hanging on at the same time, but she went straight on. I guess I was the worst but the swiftest rider that ever went through that town — not excepting cow-boys. At the other end of town she jumped into the cross-road to the left; and a few more bounds brought us to the wagon-trail, where she ran right into the door of the shop and stood before Bill at the anvil.

" 'You must have made good time, perfessor,' said Bill, patting her on the neck as I rolled off. 'You did n't need to be in such a hurry as all that.'

" 'I did n't hurry her up at all,' said I, sitting down on the shoeing-kit to rest. 'But Miss Eva seemed to think I ought to get her quick. What did she say about the captain?'

" 'She says I 've got to go—right away.'

" 'And when are you going to start?' I asked him.

"Bill put a piece of rod in the fire, banked it up, and then stood blowing it and thinking the matter over.

" 'Oh, I guess there is n't any particular hurry,' he said, taking his time about it. And when the rod was heated he went to work on it, whistling and pounding it round the horn to the tune of 'The Campbells are Coming.'

" 'You seem to be taking things mighty cheerful to what you was a while back,' said I.

" 'Oh, well, if there 's going to be trouble I guess I can take care of my end when the time comes—that is, if it does come. I guess it 's just a notion of Eva's that the captain saw me and that there is any danger. Anyway, it 's time for me to leave here when I have to.'

"He went ahead and finished the eye-bolt, whistling. I had n't seen him as cheerful as that since the time he was hiding in the wharf-boat putting the ferrule on my leg. He took up a tire and got inside of it, telling me to hold it level on the anvil while he gaged it.

13

"He was just turning round on his heel running the gage-wheel round the inside of the tire, when Mrs. Gulley appeared at the door. She motioned to him, jerking her crooked finger quick toward her face.

" 'Mr. Dalton,' she said, 'I 'm going to tell you something—something that 's going to happen. I hearn that Lant Williams telling it to my boy Dent. I put my ear to the keyhole to hear what they was sayin', because that no-account Lant Williams got my boy into danger oncet before—that was the time they got up the possey to go out after the train-robbers. He ain't no good for anything but that and to hang around the whisky-saloon; an', anyway, if there 'd been five hundred in it, or only five cents, my boy Dent 'd 'a' had to spend it all there. So when I hearn what they was talkin' about I stood at the keyhole, with the dough on my hands,—for I was jest mixin' some sal 'ratus biscuit,—an' when I hearn what it was I made up my mind that I would come an' tell; an' I 've left my dough a-settin'. You fixed my hog for me jest for friendship, an' I says to myself that between you and Lant there 's mighty quick choosin'. An' I 've seen how you take care of them two girls that 's always been good neighbors to me—an' so—'

" 'When are they comin'?' says Bill; for he had dropped his hammer and was getting ready all the time she was talking.

" 'Law suz!' says Mrs. Gulley; 'ef you knew it already ther' was n't no use me comin' to tell. I thought I would do you a mighty favor. But they 're gettin' up the possey. Somebody 's telegrafted something about you, and they 're going to get you to-night. Thet Lant don't like you, nohow, and he is going to get part of the money; but they 're going to wait and get you in bed, because they know you kin put up a fight an' have got the old man's gun. An' I says to myself, "I 'm jest goin' to tell him, an' my boy Dent won't be puttin' hisself in no sech thing." '

"Just then Eva came to the door of the shop. Bill stood by the anvil, hitching up his revolver-belt. Mrs. Gulley started telling her, and explaining about the saleratus biscuit. She had n't got half to the point when Eva hurried across the shop and took Lady by the bit.

" 'William,' she said, 'go and get your things together—and take the rifle. I 'll put something in the saddle-bags and have Lady on the other side of the hill. Meet me there. And hurry.'

"Then she turned to me and said, 'Keep the anvil sounding while he is doing it.'

"She stood in the door with Lady and hurried Bill up while he was getting his apron off and his sleeves rolled down; and she did n't forget to speak and smile to Mrs. Gulley, saying she would call on her and tell her how much obliged she was. When she saw that Bill was out of the shop and headed for the old house, she went marching away with Lady.

"I took out the rod-iron that Bill had left in the fire, and went to work on it, bending it one way and then another, hitting once on the iron and twice on the anvil.

"After it turned black and stiff I kept clattering away on it, and kept thinking things over. What was I going to do there when Bill was gone? Without him I could n't do much more than make a noise. And it would n't be long until the noise I was making would n't be of any more use. The rod fell on the floor, and I stood looking out of the window. But I kept busy bouncing the hammer on the anvil —imitating work. I wished Miss Eva had given Bill a chance to talk to me and say whether I would ever meet him anywhere again. I kept tolling away on cold iron till the place began to sound solemn and empty; and I felt as useless as a clock that is striking the wrong hour. I could imagine Lant Williams and the rest of them sitting in the saloon listening to it and thinking Bill was working.

"And I said to myself: 'When the posse comes to get Bill in bed, what will they say to me?' I saw I could n't get along in that town any more, so I made up my mind I had better leave, too. After I thought I had given Bill a start I dropped the hammer, and went to the girls' house. When I got to the back door of the kitchen, I looked up the steep little hill through the oak-trees, and saw Miss Eva standing on top of the hill. I went up, too. There was Bill rocking away about a mile to the southwest—headed for the Territory. We stood and watched him till Lady went over a distant slope like a black speck on the blue sky. Then Lady disappeared on the other side like a coal suddenly going out. And Bill was gone.

"Then Eva turned to me and spoke. 'The posse can take up their part of the job whenever they see fit to try it now,' she said.

" 'They 'll need to have swift horses,' said I. 'That Lady can go.'

" 'If they get too hot on his trail they 'll hear later on about William catching the posse. I told him to shoot to the end,' she said. And

I could see by the look in her eye that she would handle a rifle herself if she was along with Bill.

"'I guess he might as well make a fight,' says I. 'For it 's a sure case against him.'

"'William was very sorry he could n't say good-by to you,' she said, speaking in a milder way. She wiped a tear from the corner of her eye with her handkerchief stretched over the end of her finger. 'He hopes,' she said, 'that some day he will come across you—and us—again.'

"'Miss Eva,' said I, 'I 've been thinking I had better get out of here myself.'

"'I 've been thinking so, too,' she replied. 'If you 're once gone they won't take much trouble to get you. But you can't take the train here. You will have to walk out of town and get on somewhere else. I 'll put you up a lunch.'

"She went down to the kitchen; and I stood a while looking off and thinking where I would go to. After a little while I went down the hill and stood at the kitchen door. Nellie was sitting at the table holding a handkerchief to her eyes. Eva was tying a string round the lunch. She handed it to me with a lot of paper money on top.

" 'Here 's twenty dollars that William left for you. We wish it was ten times as much,' she said. 'And we hope that you will have good luck—wherever you go.'

" 'I wish the same to you, Miss Eva, and to Miss Nellie,' said I.

"As Nellie came to say good-by I saw that her eyes were red. I shook hands with both the girls and started off.

"As I looked back they were both sitting on the kitchen steps. Nellie was holding the handkerchief to her eyes and sobbing. Eva had her arm around Nellie, and sat looking straight at the side of the hill and thinking. Nellie was a tender-hearted girl. Eva was true-hearted, too, and fine-tempered—like steel.

"I stopped at the old house and took some clothes, and started down the tracks to Wilton. I walked the railroad tracks all afternoon. As my shadow got longer and longer I began to look ahead wherever the road curved round a hill, expecting that the next turn would bring me in sight of the town. And after I had done that a good many times I began to feel surer that the next turn would bring me to it, for I had walked so long that I was tired out. And I was so thirsty that I would have given my lunch for a cup of water. The more I was disappointed coming round a curve, or out of a cut, the surer I felt that the next turn would bring me in sight of the end. But finally I had disappointed myself so much that I walked along expecting to be disappointed. And I said to myself: 'It 's been so far back since I ought to have got to the town that there 's no telling how far it may be yet.' And the farther I went the less hope I had of getting there —I was so tired out and down-hearted.

"As it grew on toward dusk the frogs began to croak and the crickets to whir in the low places; and I expected to be caught out in the night with all the lonesome things. Off to the right of the tracks I saw a big blasted tree, with nothing on its crooked black branches but hundreds of crows. And they were all cawing. I began to walk faster. I had n't got used to such things yet, because it was my first day from home.

"Around the next curve I came across the prettiest sight I ever saw in my life. There was a broad slope of plowed field that broke off against the red sky. And walking along the ridge was a string of negro men and women with hoes on their shoulders—all walking along in a black file against the red sunset. I had never seen anything that struck me or stayed in my mind like that did. And now I knew that I was getting to the town.

"Before long I came to it, and sat down, tired out, on the depot platform. The station-master's little girl brought me a cup of water from the kitchen where they lived, at one end of the depot.

"I sat there resting and thinking about the beautiful sight I had seen, and wondering why it seemed so beautiful. Pretty soon it struck me why I was so taken with it. It was because they were going home. And I did n't have any home. And I was tired and lonesome and pretty near sick—and I wondered how Bill was feeling. As I looked back and tried to imagine Eva and Nellie and Bill, it all seemed years ago —for now everything was changed. It seemed like a dream."

As the sound of a bell came from a distance down the tracks, Finerty arose, scratching his head. "I 'll have to tell that to me wife," he said. "An' now yez can all shlape—which ye are already doin'," he added, looking about on the slumbering vagrants. Pap Smith was having symptoms of snoring. "An' I 'll not be wakin' ye whin I come again, Shtoompy; I have now all I can hold at wanst." And Finerty departed.

CHAPTER XVII

NE of the problems of Finerty's way of life was what to do with "Sunday night off." Once a week, when everybody had gone to sleep, and he could not, his world was put out of joint; and it usually left him sitting outside the kitchen door contemplating his day of darkness until it became an elephant on his hands. He would smoke his solitary pipe until he had philosophically digested "th' way av th' worruld" up to date; then he would find some excuse to putter about the kitchen, or even take a tour of inspection around the outside of the house, with a light in his hand. He had even been seen in the small garden—which was strongly fortified against the goat—looking the posies over with the bull's-eye lantern. It was under such circumstances that he one night put the elbow of stovepipe on the kitchen chimney—an arrangement which would have

made it draw excellently had the wind not changed after he had it done. Whenever Mrs. Finerty started up from her pillow at night in expectation of burglars, her first waking thought would be the day of the week. If it were Sunday night she would compose herself with the knowledge that it was Michael fixing something.

In this struggle that he had with one seventh of his time was the secret of Finerty's instant willingness to have a "par-r-ty" whenever Agnes suggested it; for, owing to the peculiar disposal of his days, the affair would have to be on Sunday night if Finerty himself was to be "invited." A party which had been under consideration for a long time always brought about a disagreement.

"I will have no more a Soonda' night," Mrs. Finerty would declare. "Th' lasht wan we had, th' Shmiths were talkin' about us, an' makin' thimsilves out to be *betther*. An' I will *not* give her th' satisfaction." And there the arrangements would always come to a deadlock. But on the fourth day of the murder story things shaped themselves favorably, and Mrs. Finerty saw her way to a compromise.

On that day Mrs. Finerty sat in the kitchen, erect and prim, looking straight before her, with her hands clasped—or, rather, with each hand clasping the wrist of the other. She was waiting for the time to be fulfilled when Michael should awake. When, finally, he appeared at the door of the middle room, and turned with his usual promptness to his seat at the table, she arose and went to the "safe," whence she produced an envelop.

"Ye have a letther," she said, laying it before him. Then she stepped back and remained at a formal distance. Michael gave the envelop skeptic examination, front and back; and being convinced that it was his own, he left the table and sat on the step of the middle room. He gave a workmanlike hitch to each of his sleeves, and went to work very deliberately, opening the end of the envelop by pinching and tearing with his thumb-nail. Taking out a slip of blue paper and a white sheet, he looked them over, upside down and right side up.

"Humph—th' divil!" he remarked.

"Why don't ye rade it out?" said Mrs. Finerty.

Michael smoothed out the blue slip on his thigh; and then, taking up the communication proper, he "read it out." It sounded to Mrs. Finerty as follows:

MISTHER MICHAEL FINERTY.

Dear Misther Finerty: I take me pin in hand t' inclose th' inclosed—which Jawn w'u'd have me tind f'r him. He has got th' vouchers cashed, an' will be expectin' ye at th' nixt meetin' av th' precin't. Wid manny thanks f'r yer neuthral shtand in th' matter av th' namination, he raymains yours thruly,

MRS. EX-ALDERMAN HOGAN.

"What dooes it mane, that she sh'u'd be writin' till ye?" asked Mrs. Finerty.

"'T is a check. Don't ye know what that manes?" replied Michael.

"'T is f'r th' jury-work!" exclaimed Mrs. Finerty. She took the blue check off his knee and examined it. "Ye 'll have t' be takin' it t' th' bank, Michael; for they 'll not be changin' that at the grocery."

"Don't be thryin' it; f'r 't is no good till I have signed me signater on it. I 'll have time t' do it Soonda'."

She stood in the middle of the kitchen, holding it, while Michael sat on the door-step re-reading the letter and taking in its information.

"An' here I am shtandin' *holdin'* it," said Mrs. Finerty, suddenly. She hurried to the "safe," and from an upper corner she took down an earthen fruit-jar. Having carefully removed the loose pieces of sealing-wax from the top and laid them in order on the table, she took off the lid and deposited the check on top of the eleven dollars and forty cents; then she readjusted the pieces of wax and replaced the jar in the "safe."

"I 'm thinkin' if I kape on makin' money as aisy as that I will *do* it. I will sind her t' th' college." And after a period of thought he concluded: "Whin I get me nixt month's pay I *will* do it. We will have eighty-wan dollars an' forty cints. An' what is twinty?"

"'T will surprise th' Dugans," soliloquized Mrs. Finerty.

Michael took his seat at the table; and when his wife had put his meal before him she sat down opposite. "Agnes has been wantin' a par-r-ty this long time," she offered.

"Well, I don't mind havin' it Soonda' night," replied Michael.

"Ye 'll not be havin' it th' Soonda', Michael." And having considered her own ultimatum, she added: "Not excipt 't is afther twelve o'clock. There 'll not be wan shtep befure that."

"Sure 't is airly enough. I 'm not all awake befure twelve P.M.," replied Finerty, sorting his potatoes over philosophically. "And if anny should get here a bit airlier—which they will—we can shpind th' time tellin' shtories. 'T will be no harm in that.''

"And," added Mrs. Finerty, emphasizing every word, "if I hear wan worrud av Mrs. Shmith sayin' we had dancin' on Soonda', I will *in-form* her av her *ig-nor-ance.* I 'll have Agnes write invitations th' morrow."

"We 'll have a dancin'-match, an' get ould Jerry t' fiddle. 'T will do me good t' show young Barney his aquils. I 'll back th' rid-headed wan against him."

"What—th' *thramp!*" said Mrs. Finerty. "W'u'd ye have him come t' a par-r-ty?"

"He 'll not *come* to it—but only for to be enthertainin' th' rest. An' ye can hand him a bite in the kitchen." But this was not to be encompassed until much argument had accustomed her to the idea.

And Dennis, who was away on his usual quest of a criminal, would be back at the station in time to be invited. He would be informed of Stumpy's knowledge of the five-hundred-dollar murderer. There was no telling what might happen.

And now the story—which had escaped her in the excitement caused by the check—being thus brought to Mrs. Finerty's mind, she de-

manded to know the end of it. When Michael
had recounted last night's developments of the
tale, she insisted that he should keep on even
after he declared that he knew no more.

" 'T is that comes from not guardin' yer tem-
per, Michael. An' d' ye know," she said re-
flectively, "if 't was only a shtory, an' it could
be *med up* that th' blackshmith did n't do it,
afther all, 't is th' way I w'u'd want it to be.
But 't is only in shtories that it can be. An'
't is too late now; 't w'u'd all have to be different. It sh'u'd be a warnin' t' anny man."

She put the green-plaid shawl over her head,
and accompanied him to work, turning over
plans for the party. As Michael stepped over
to the chutes she looked into the sand-house,
and seeing Stumpy, she was on the point of
ordering him to tell her the rest. But at that
moment Rochester Red appeared, and she has-
tily departed.

Finerty came into the sand-house earlier that
night, accompanied by his faithful dinner-pail.
He sat down to eat his meal in the very eyes
of the tramps, for he wanted to get the story
started early and bring it to a possible end.
He paused to start it before he bit his sandwich.

"An' what did ye do whin ye wint away
from that town?"

"Well," said Stumpy, "Bill wandered around the Territory a while; but he did n't like the country, so he—"

"How do *ye* know what he did, whin ye was n't with him?" interrogated Finerty.

"Why, I heard about it afterward; if it was n't for that I would n't know any more about him. I 'm telling things just as they happened—I 'm telling it straight. I can't go ahead and then tell it backwards."

"No; don't be tellin' it to me backwards," said Finerty. "I see how 't is."

CHAPTER XVIII

"AS I was saying," continued Stumpy, "after he had been in the Territory a while he did n't like it very well, and he kept going from place to place on Lady, always riding south. One Sunday morning he arrived at a little town in the middle of Texas. There did n't seem to be anything but horses in the town—and not many of them. There were a lot of buggies and saddle-horses in front of a little white church, and there was a row of cow-ponies along the hitching-rack at the post-office, which was next to a saloon. In a place like that a cow-boy can always tell who 's in town by looking at the hitching-rack the same as a city directory. Bill stopped Lady and sat looking them over, thinking to himself that he would n't trade Lady for the whole outfit. There was a sleepy sort of a short-coupled bay, and a red-and-white pinto, and a stocky buckskin, and a

little black stallion. Bill tied Lady at the end
of the rack next to the buckskin; but just as
he turned away the buckskin grunted and laid
his ears back ugly, as if Lady had no business
there. At that Lady gave a grunt herself, and
shot out one of her legs, giving the buckskin
a jolt on the flank. But as Lady was tied too
near to get full swing, she only landed with the
side of her leg, not doing any great damage.
Bill saw that it would n't do to take chances,
so he untied her again.

" 'Come on, Lady,' says Bill; 'you and me
will go up among the religious horses.' There
was a choir singing in the church, so Bill tied
her next to a Roman-nose, settled-down sort of
a buggy-horse, and went in and took a back seat
in the church to hear the singing. Bill liked
that singing better than any he had ever heard;
it was done by boys all in white gowns. So he
sat listening to the sermon. After a while the
boys all marched away, singing, through a
door back of the pulpit, with their voices dying
away in the distance where you could n't
see them, and sounding like angels. Bill sat
till they had gone so far he could n't hear them
at all. And when it was done, almost every
one had left the church but Bill, and was going
away in carriages and on horseback. He got

on Lady and went down to the post-office again.
This time he tried Lady at the other end of
the rack, and when he saw that she did n't fight
with the stallion he went into the saloon—for
there was n't any place else to go.

"In the saloon he got to talking with a stockman who was looking to hire a sheep-herder.

" 'I 'm looking for somebody that won't go
mooning around when he is left alone a month
or two, and that won't get so lazy that when
a norther comes he can't wake up and hustle
them back and hold them together; I want
somebody that 's got a little action in him, but
don't need something happening *all* the time
without going crazy. The last one I had was
that kind, and now he is up in the crazy-pen
at the county seat. It 's the second time I have
had that kind of luck. Suppose you take the
job and try it a while. You don't look like
the soft kind. Try it, if you ain't working.'

" 'Where is it?' asked Bill.

" 'About twenty miles out here. I 'll send
you out good chuck every month, and make
it pleasant. It 's a small bunch, so that you
will have to take a shack alone. But you 're
sure to see a range-rider every couple of weeks,
anyway—for there 's only nineteen thousand
acres, wire-fenced for cattle. You 'll see a steer

once in a while, anyway, for a change. And, besides that, the scab 's on the range now, and you will have to do some dipping—so that will give you a change and keep you busy now and then. It ain't as bad as some jobs.'

"Bill stood thinking it over.

"'Oh, Maggie,' said the stockman, 'come here.' A collie that was lying back in a dark corner got up and came to him. She was a beautiful dog, all curves and neat, thick hair. 'Shake hands with the gentleman, Maggie,' said the stockman. She raised her foot to Bill, and he gave it a shake, for he had a great eye for a dog—'most any kind of a dog. 'I 'll let you take her,' said the stockman. 'The fellow that 's out there temporary has a dog of his own. Maggie 's a good partner. Look at the faith in her,' said the stockman, laying his hand on her forehead while she looked up with her brown eyes in a way that Bill declared he could see she knew what he was saying. 'If there 's much trouble, that dog 'll show you a trick or two. She knows a few,' said the stockman. 'Have a drink on me.'

"When Bill had thought it over, the idea struck him all of a heap. Month after month he had been going from one place to another, only to move along when he got there, for fear that

it was the place he might be caught in. It
had all been doubt and uncertainty day after
day, with no settlement of it when he went to
bed or when he got up. There was no looking
ahead with any satisfaction, but just wander-
ing around; and as for the monotony of sheep-
herding, he knew nothing could be more monotonous than what *he* was doing. And as
for being away from people, he was already
cut off from all the rest of the world, and was
only an actor and a somebody else. And he
made up his mind that there were worse things
than going and living with animals—cows and
sheep and Lady and Maggie. And he saw that
being out there, like the only person in the
world, there would be no one to bother him
if he had killed a dozen men. When Bill
thought of it he began to feel rested already,
with the idea of being out where there would
be no object in staying anywhere but just there,
and knowing that it was certain to be the same
as long as he did stay there. It was like taking
a vacation from being a murderer. And after
a while maybe the world would forget about
him. It began to rest him right on the spot—
like when your nerves suddenly let down with
a jerk and show you how they have been strung
up. I say it struck Bill of a heap—and he took

the job. They had a few more drinks and went away together on horseback. And before they went the man had pointed Bill out to Maggie and explained, and she was frisking round him like she understood.

"Next morning Bill was riding out to the ranch on Lady, behind a wagon that was loaded with a hogshead sawed in two, some barrels of petroleum, and food supplies for six weeks— hog and hominy and white flour and molasses and pepper-sauce. Bill did n't want the pepper-sauce, but the man made him take it. 'Texas sheep-herders always get to wanting pepper-sauce, and you will, too,' he said. And Maggie sat in the tail of the wagon watching him come along. About that time some one had got up the idea of dipping the sheep in petroleum instead of the tobacco cure. Bill's boss had told him about it, asking him if he minded trying the oil. And Bill said that he was used to getting his hands on oily machinery, and he guessed he would rather use it than to be messing round in a vat of tobacco juice; so it was satisfactory to both of them. When they got out to the place the man on the wagon found that the herder had already moved the sheep to the new shack and corral away from the infected pasture. Everything was ready, so that when they were dipped they could be turned out on clean grass. And all the sheep were baaing in the pen; and they all turned and stared at Bill with a thousand eyes, the way sheep do. The other herder was already dipping some and sending them, dripping with tobacco juice, up the stile and over the rails of the corral.

"The fellow that was there was to stay a couple of days and help Bill get the flock in shape —so the wagon went away and left the two of them. The fellow's name was Jonas, and he was one of the sociable kind that Bill took a shine to.

" 'Well, partner,' said he, 'have you decided to turn Baptis'? How are you on church, anyway,—ever go to any?'

" 'Sometimes,' said Bill. 'I dropped into that white church in town.'

" 'Well, that won't do—that 's Episcopal. Out here we 're dead set on regeneration by immersion. This oil dip ain't accordin' to my religion that I 've been used to. But I ain't so narrow but what I can try it. The perfessors say it 's a cure.' He kicked the fire out from under his tobacco-caldron and bailed the dip out into the hogshead. Then he went at emptying his dipping-tank. Bill got a pail and

helped him take the dip out and put the petroleum in. Then they went at the flock. And it
was n't long till Bill found out he did n't like
a sheep, and that they were n't his style. He
never did like any sort of a martyr person that
was always swallowing down their sufferings
and looking sorry and good about other people's badness to them. He 'd rather have them
fight than complain,—and a sheep is just the
other way around. He lifted up a ewe to souse
her in the dip, and she let out a trembling bawl
that made Bill feel cruel. And when he put
her in, she rolled up her eyeballs and shut her
bleat off, as if she had made up her mind to
stand it and let him abuse her more, and she
would give right up to it and look to heaven for
support. Bill picked up another and another,
and they did the same; and somehow their
eyes chastised him till it made him mad. And
he felt like giving them an extra souse—seeing
they were so good at putting up with suffering.

" 'That 's the way to do it!' said Jonas, as
Bill kept sending them over the stile. 'The
clean to the right, and the unclean to the left—
the righteous and the unrighteous.'

" 'You talk as if you was used to being God,'
remarked Bill.

" 'Well, I have been—considerable. And

by the time you 've been out here long enough, you 'll feel that way, too; for you won't see anything like yourself. I ain't following the flock now. But I 've had the universe on my hands in my day—and all that was contained therein. It 's a big responsibility. How do you like sheep, take 'em one at a time?'

" 'I can't say that I exactly take to them,' said Bill. 'They ain't an animal that I would sit up nights to talk to.'

" 'Yes,' said Jonas; 'there ain't much in their eyes, except the stony stare. And they can't wag their tail like a dog. Many a time I 've been glad that there was an animal that could talk with his tail. They 're an unmanly beast that ain't of this world at all. And if they see a good chance to die they 'll lay right down and wait for kingdom come. They 're a mackerel-eyed martyr from their Hebrew noses to their helpless tail.'

" 'You don't like them, either?' said Bill.

" 'Not one at a time—and still less in a bunch. They 're all right, though, for a piece of the landscape on a sunny day. They do say that they 're the beast that stands for the human race in the Scriptures,' said Jonas, who was a great hand to talk religion. 'And I 'll be dinged if I hain't seen Christians just like them.'

''With that, he picked up a ram and plunged him in the dip, holding him by a horn. 'It does seem,' he went on, 'that when the Almighty Creator arranged that man must get bread by the sweat of his brow, he also fixed it up so that he would have to get clothes at the risk of his intellect. And many a one 's lost *hisn* sitting out watching the clothes grow for people. The last one here got so bad he was writing poetry all over the shack.'

'' 'If they ever took me up for crazy,' said Bill, 'I 'd make them prove it. I saw a trial in a town up here, and I thought to myself that if it was me I 'd make the jurors prove that they were sane. I think they 'd have a hard time doing it.'

'' 'It is a sort of majority vote, and nothing else,' said Jonas. 'It 's a kind of circumstantial evidence.'

'' 'Circumstantial evidence!' said Bill. 'What do you think of that?'

'' 'Say, partner,' said Jonas, 'it makes me die laughing. Last spring I was out here at lambing-time, running them a few days alone when the other one mislaid his mind. The preacher's mother, from up North, came out in a carriage to see what it was like. Just when they drove up I was drying off a new-born with the back of a butcher knife—starting him out comfortable and cozy, same as always. Just when she was stepping out of the carriage she seen me, and threw up both her hands and yelled, "Oh!" and fainted back so that they had to catch her.

" 'She said afterward that she thought I was killing the dear little lamb. And, somehow, she could n't get it out of her head that I was a brute, anyway. That 's circumstantial evidence for ye, hey?'

"Bill and the herder talked and dipped, and by night they had the flock all run through the vat. And the next morning the herder ate breakfast and got ready to leave.

" 'So you won't herd—if you can help it,' said Bill, as he was going away.

" 'Not me—thank you,' said Jonas. 'Although I 'm a natural at it. You don't catch me shippin' in a shack for the land of Nowhere. When I 'm marooned I 'll take it on the water —where I can see the hills heave up and down, anyway. I 'm a Baptist. So long, partner— don't fall out with yerself.'

" 'Good-by,' said Bill.

CHAPTER XIX

"BILL herded sheep for four weeks, and then a man came out and brought him some more chuck, saying, 'How-do?' and 'How are you getting along?' and 'Good-by.' Bill kept on herding sheep again, and in four weeks more the man came out and brought him some chuck and said, 'Hello!' And when he had said 'Good-by' Bill started to herding sheep and looking ahead to when the man would come out again. The man brought him his wages, too; and every few days, when Bill was lonesome, he would look the money over, and think how useless it was—for out there it was n't good to spend or to give away, or to send to the heathen. Bill said afterward—and I don't know how true it is, but he ought to know because he took enough lessons in it—that a person can't change his own mind. He says they only think they can, and that when they want it changed they have to look at something different or go somewhere or see another person, and it is that that changes it. And he said that when a person got the idea that the mind can change itself, and that he can outflank his own wits, it's because he was never put in a place where he could really try it.

"One morning, when he was getting breakfast on the fire-hole, he noticed that the handle of the coffee-pot was loose. He did n't have anything to fix it with, so he knocked it off entirely, for he would rather see no handle at all than a loose one. That reminded him of the sailors' 'monkey,' that did n't have any handle to it, and made him think of Tiffin. After that, as sure as he would start breakfast the coffee-pot would remind him of Tiffin and the bloody shirt they made him look at when they arrested him. And he would have Tiffin for breakfast.

"Another day some little thing would remind him of something else, and then it would keep up. The days were all alike; and so, after a while, he would know just what the next day would be like and all that it would remind him of beforehand. The days got to be cut and dried, and time was a sort of a machine turning them all out alike. In the morning, when he grazed the sheep in a bunch on the plain, the clouds would be grazing in bunches on the sky. Then at noon the clouds would be higher and laying along in streaks, as if a whitewash-brush had been wiped on the sky—the lines of cloud all in rank and file. And about the time they did that the sheep would stop for noon and string along in broken files, as each sheep would stand with his head drooping in the shadow of a sheep ahead—and another sheep standing in his. It seemed to him as if the sheep and the clouds were only imitations of each other, and there was n't any variety at all. He got tired of being out always in the middle of things—as if he was the only man on earth stuck out there in the dead center of it all. It seemed to him as if he was sentenced to walk and walk toward the edge of the horizon and never get any nearer to it. So there was nothing to do but stand out like a pin on a sun-dial until his shadow got short enough before him to turn round and graze back. And all afternoon he would follow his shadow home again. There was n't any sound in the world but bleating and baaing and bawling that sounded like complaint and melancholy—and never a word that meant anything. He got so that he hated the sound of them. Every day was alike, with the sky above and the plain beneath; and after a while they penned him in and at the same time would n't have anything to do with him. Sometimes he thought he would rather be back in the cell again, where he could at least touch the low ceiling and feel it and be friendly with it. And the birds that flew in the sky—but would never come to him— was n't half as good as a spider he knew that would drop down in his cell and amuse him. The scenery prisoned him in the same, even if it was bigger—for it was only around *him*. And at night, when the darkness took it all away, the stars would come out like a big example on a black slate. They would n't let his mind alone, and at the same time *they* would n't have anything to do with him. And that was the way it went, day after day and night after night. And all through it at regular times was Tiffin and the bloody shirt, till he could n't think of anything else. The fellow that was there before him had an old physical geography, and Bill found it under the bunk. He carried it out herding with him to change his mind. He studied about clouds, and he found that in the morning the sheep were scattered in bunches like certain kinds of cloud, and at noon they were strung along like others. And it was n't long till the book was playing the same trick on him as everything else. But he carried it along and looked for new places in it.

"There were a good many cattle on the range, but they were scattered out few and far between. One day Bill saved a cow that was bogged in a watering-hole. In that country the black soil is deep as any post-hole, and tough and clinging. It was the kind that the old farmer in Upton had told Bill about; it would n't even slide from the polished slant of a plow, but packed on it like gum so that a plowman would have to stop and cut it off with the scraper. And it would pack up on wagon-wheels till the tires and felloes were all swollen up with it. Where it is trampled at watering-holes the cattle sink deep; and if they stand too long, with their small hoofs and great weight, it sometimes gets a hold on them that tests their strength. Then if they lose their footing and fall down it has them trapped.

"After Bill saved the cow he felt good all day, walking along and thinking how he had saved a life. Besides that, it was a change for him, and gave him something to do; so after that he managed to herd the sheep past a watering-hole whenever he could and save a cow and do a good turn for somebody. If it had n't

15

been for that and for talking to Maggie and for
having the company of Lady, Bill could n't
have stood it, as much as he wanted to stay
there. He used to sink in pretty deep himself sometimes, but there was n't any danger
in that; it does n't get the best of a man as
it does with a cow. For some weeks there
came a drought and some of the watering-
holes that were too far from their spring became bogs. The little stream that fed them was
drunk by the sun and licked up by the breezes
from the Gulf. But the cattle that were used
to watering there would keep coming as long
as there was a little seepage in the middle, for
they have their regular habits and grazing-
grounds. In that way the shallow watering-
holes got to be nothing more than hoof-marked
muck.

"One morning Bill got out of his bunk feeling down-hearted and guilty. When he had
made the coffee, thinking of Tiffin and the
bloody shirt, and had made some hot bread and
eaten it, he went around to the corral to let the
sheep out for the day. They all turned their
faces to him, the same as always, and looked at
him with a thousand eyes, staring at him as if
he was a wonderful being, expected to do wonderful things. He leaned on the rail of the

corral and looked into all their inhuman eyes, wondering what the meaning of them could be. They always looked at him like strangers, and they were getting to be greater strangers the longer he knew them. A ram stamped his foot as if he was impatient with Bill, and stared at him like one of the just and righteous; and then it seemed to Bill that all of them were waiting for him to speak and say, 'Guilty' or 'Not guilty.' He let down the bars and stood till they had all filed out. Then he went out for the day again, thinking that *that* day he would have to find a cow to save.

"Toward noon he came across a cream-colored heifer that was stuck in one of the small holes. It was a beautiful heifer with big gentle eyes; although the fact was that before she got into that hole she would have fought a horse and a cow-boy if they got her into the notion. Bill looked her over and he made up his mind, from her depth and condition, that there was enough strength in her to pull out if he put her in the way of getting up. He went in and roused her to make an effort, but she only strained weakly, without making any headway at rising. The next time Bill helped her she got part way up, but fell back again. He had a notion to leave her till the next day, and then,

if she was still living, come to help her with
Lady and a rope. But he wanted to get her
out. He had set a good many free just with
his own strength, and he always claimed that
lifting was science as much as strength. He
had plenty of both, and the more he failed the
more determined he was. At each lift he went
deeper into the muck, till finally it filled his
shoes and came half-way to his knees; but he
did n't mind that, for it was nothing serious.
He pulled his feet out and stood a while to give
himself and the cow a rest, and then he went
at it with one big effort. He got her to struggling, and pretty soon she was coming up. He
gathered all his power in his back and Bill and
the heifer made the big effort shoulder to
shoulder.

"He got her to her feet, leaning against her
to steady her. But just as she got up she made
a lunge forward; and not getting her legs
out, she lost her balance and fell over again on
top of Bill. And there he was, sitting with
the cow across his lap and his bent legs buried
to the knees by her weight.

"It was n't a minute before he saw he
could n't get out of there with his own strength.
The worst of his fix was n't that his legs were
so deep, or that the weight of a cow was on

them—for he could have lifted a cow with the
right way of going at it. But he was wedged
down in such a way that he could get no pur-
chase. He made a few strong efforts, but
he could feel that all the power he put into
his legs had n't any leverage. And when he
found that he could n't even make a start at
dislodging them, he made up his mind that he
would not waste his strength in struggling—
the way a cow does. He went to work to dig
himself loose with his hands, thinking that if
he could only sink down till his legs were
straighter he would have an advantage. The
sticky, tough dirt clung to his hands and
packed on till each finger was big and heavy.
It seemed that the dirt was protecting itself
against him, and fighting to hold him. When
he got a little gutter dug around him, the water oozed into it. Then his big, blunt fingers
would only slip and slide, and he could n't dig
at all. He would wipe them off on the cow
and try again, and it would be the same. The
mud would fill in, and he could only make a
puddle.

"Maggie sat on the bank, looking at him.
Sometimes she seemed to understand and real-
ize the fix he was in, for she would whine and
run about the black hole. Then she would sit

down and look at him as if she would like to
speak. This bothered him, and he sent her out
on errands to the sheep. It seemed strange to
Bill to be exercising his power on the sheep
that way, when he could n't help himself. But
it gave him something to do, and he sent her
out several times.

"He could only sit there and look about on
the scenery he was tired of, and keep on waiting—which he was even more tired of. He
hoped he would get out for an hour, and then
he hoped another hour—and he got tired of
even hoping. That afternoon he did not get
hungry. Anyway, his lunch was lying out of
reach, wrapped in the slicker where he had laid
it down at the edge of the watering-hole. He
found there was a sort of comfort in feeling
that the cow was in the same fix he was; and
somehow it gave him a friendly feeling toward
the cow. She lay there quiet, and Bill sat looking into her eyes and hardly knowing what
he thought, but just waiting and feeling the
live, warm cow. He wondered how long it
would be before she would die and he would
lose her. He did n't hope and he did n't feel
desperate, but just sat there like a convict. He
had been through a good deal, and now it came
over him that if this was the kind of a world
it was, he did n't much care.

"Late in the afternoon he began to feel hungry. Near him was a small bone. With this he managed to scrape toward him a longer bone from the skeleton of a cow that had been bogged there the season before. With this bone he could barely touch his dinner. By careful working he upset the package so that it tumbled a few inches nearer. He shoved it with the bone, one side and then another, until he could reach it with his fingers. After dinner he felt stronger and he tried to rouse the heifer. When she made no effort he pounded her with the bone. She only looked round at him, and Bill laid the bone down.

"After a while Bill reached out to his slicker and got the book that was wrapped in it. He laid it on the cow and turned the pages over, thinking it might take his mind for a while. But the reading in it was like talking to some person that only thought of himself and his learning and did n't think or care what became of him. He liked the company of the heifer better, so he threw it aside, and folded his arms on her, leaning his head against her side.

"At last night came on to bother him again —and it was a clear, deep sky filled with stars. At night Bill usually sat in front of the shack, looking at the fire-hole to keep his mind at home, and speaking to Maggie. He did n't like the stars. But now he was in a fix where he could hardly help looking at them. It was as if they had got him at last where he could n't get away. He folded his arms on the cow again, and put his face against her warm side, with his eyes shut, and waited for sleep. And after a long time the breathing of the cow helped him to forget and put him to sleep.

"In the morning he woke up with a start. It was just past dawn. Maggie sat watching him; when he moved she stood up and set her tail going and tried to show how glad she was. The sheep were still in sight, where she had kept them bunched until he should go along. A buzzard was sailing high above him, circling round and round to signal the other buzzards that there was carrion below. And before long another buzzard arrived and took up the wheeling round and round. He had sunk a little during the night, and the cow had sunk with him. She lay with her neck stretched out and one eye was in the mud; but the other eye was open, and Bill could see that it had a glazed stare. Pretty soon her flesh felt different to him—and then Bill felt bad, and had a different kind of loneliness. It was like losing a friend.

"A buzzard lit near by and sat looking at them.

"He reached for the thigh-bone. 'Hike out of here, you hunch-backed scavenger!'—and he threw the bone straight and swift. The buzzard flapped up in the air and landed on the same spot again, jumping over the bone as it passed. Bill looked around for something else to throw, and there was nothing in reach but the mud. Bill and the buzzard sat looking at each other, and waiting.

"Then the sun rose higher and got hot on his head, for he had laid his hat at the edge of the hole when he went to work. He made up his mind that if the buzzards came to the cow while he was there, he would tear them to pieces.

"He looked around toward his hat and saw a yearling bull coming across the range toward the watering-hole. The idea jumped into his head that if he had hold of the bull's tail it would be the way of getting out. He knew he had enough strength in his arms, if he had hold of something on a straightaway pull. He rubbed his hands quick and hard on the cow to get them dry and clean. He turned his body around as far as he could twist—which was n't far—and tried reaching out behind him. When he found that one of his hands would reach no farther back than his own shoulder his heart went down again, for he was afraid he would get hold only with one hand. The other arm would go out full length, and the little pool was only three feet away. It all depended on which way the bull would turn when he was through drinking. He crouched down low, with his hands at his breast, and waited.

"The bull was one of the kind that had probably never seen a man except on horseback; anyway, it paid no attention to him, as he sat twisted and bent, but walked straight in and drank all the seepage in the little pool. Its head was so near Bill that he could smell its sweet breath as it breathed deep and blew from its nostrils. And as it pulled itself from the mire he saw that it was going to keep straight on and go out of the other side, which would bring its tail past him. He was crouching low with all his power coiled up inside of him ready for a quick reach and a grab, and he saw that he was only going to get it with one hand. But as he was about to spring, the bull whisked its tail straight into his hands, and he clenched it just above the tuft of hair. The bull made a lunge to start suddenly away, but the mire held its feet, and that saved Bill from having the tail jerked out of his hands. The bull had to pull out slow, and Bill put the power into his hands and arms. He pulled straight out from under the cow.

"As the bull got to the edge of the bog the tail went out of his hands with a jerk, and Bill lay with his head on the grass. He had come out easier than he expected. As he tried to get up he found that his legs were asleep. He was helpless and without feeling from the hips down—as much as if he had been paralyzed. He propped himself up with one hand and worked his legs up and down, grasping them by the knees. He slapped and kneaded them, and then rolled on the ground. And when they were almost done prickling he kicked them up in the air until he got them working so that he could rise on them.

"As he stood up and moved about he felt dizzy, and his head was so dull and numb-feeling that he thumped it with his knuckles, as if he was testing it. It sounded as if it was filled with water; and when he moved it suddenly it seemed to stir up the settlings at the bottom, and he could see the specks floating before his eyes. It sounded so dull and strange that he thumped it again and listened—just as if he was knocking on his skull to see if his brains was home. And it seemed to him that they were sleeping, and he could only get them half awake. He decided that it was on account of the sun beating down on his head, and the don't-care way he had got his mind into and then gone to sleep on. Maggie capered round him, barking, and she jumped against him so hard it almost threw him over. He picked up his hat and went across the range to his shack, jerking his head once in a while the way a horse tosses his mane, and thumping his head to see if it felt the same. At the shack he held his head in the cool spring, and this cleared his brains a good deal. Then he got himself a meal with lots of coffee, and this pulled him together still more. After he sat a while he patted Maggie on the head and they started out to get the sheep together. As he walked back across the range he felt still better, and then he got to thinking of the fine way he had got out of that place, and how he had got the best of things. He saw the bull again, and then he smiled and began to be pleased with himself and have great satisfaction—the same as when he had done a good job.

"When he had got the sheep together he made up his mind that when the month was up, and the man came out again, he would give notice and quit the herding; he felt as if he would like to get out where he could kick his

mind up the same as he had his legs, and get
the life back into it. He took his revolver out
and looked it over. He put an old long-horn
skull up in a mesquite bush, and then stood off
and put a round of lead into it; and then he
smiled again to think how he had learned to
do that kind of a job. His mind had entirely
changed about having some one always trying
to catch him, and now he was looking ahead
to the time when they would think they had
him, and he would take the tool from his belt,
and beat them at the job. And as he thought
it over he wanted to quit right away and get at
it. He brought the sheep in earlier that evening, and had them behind the bars before sundown. As the last lamb trotted in he lit the
four red coyote-lanterns and put them on their
poles at the corners of the pen. Then he went
round to the front of the shack, lit the fire-
hole before the door, and put on his supper.
The sun was going down as red as a coyote-
lantern. Far off to the right was the line of
trees along the San Gabriel; it seemed to Bill
as if they were a black procession winding
across the prairie and following the red sun
away from that monotonous, lonesome place.
Presently the sun went down over the edge of
the world and took all the bright clouds after

it; and then the line of trees filed away and
left only the darkness behind. And the night
came down and drew nearer and hemmed him
in. His work had tired him, and he had no
appetite. His brain was heavy again, and he
sat with his head between his hands, thinking
of Tiffin and of Eva and Nellie and me, and of
all that he had gone through. The hominy
boiled over. He set it aside, drank a cup of
coffee, and then went and sat in the door of
the shack, drawing farther away from the
night. Maggie followed him and sat down beside him, and they stayed there together watching the dark. He had dipped the sheep again
a week before, and some of the petroleum was
near the door. He poured some of it on the
fire and watched it blaze up and chase the
night back from his fire-hole. As he sat watching it he spoke to Maggie as she sat down again,
and she started up her tail, beating it on the
ground. The embers died away in the fire-hole
and buried themselves in the night. He kept
on sitting there, with Maggie resting her chin
on his thigh and dreaming with her eyes half
closed as he stroked her head. He rested his
chin in his palm, thinking of Eva and Nellie.
And then he would think of Tiffin again, and
sit with his eyes open to the dark, and his ears

open to the howl of a coyote that sounded as
if it was complaining of its hunger to the night.
The stars were out, all hung up in their places
in the sky, and he found they had his mind
again. He started up, thinking he would go
into the shack and bar the door against the
night and the stars. As he rose and spoke to
Maggie he noticed that the edge of the shack
cast a faint shadow, as if the rising moon was
coming out over the edge of a cloud. Then the
ground turned brighter, as if the moon had
suddenly leaped up into the sky. It startled
him to have such a foolish thought. And
while he was looking and doubting, the light
upon the ground looked redder and flowed with
smoke-shadows, as if the moon had—*caught
fire*. For one instant he stood holding his
breath, with his eyes on the shadows and his
two fists doubled up before him. And suddenly there was a chorus of bleats and ba-a-as
that burst out as if they had been let out of a
door, and there was a lull and a bigger glow of
red, and then the ba-a-as all together again,
and the trembling cries of lambs, as if the lid
had been taken off a hell of infants. That 's
what Bill said it was like—and that 's the way
he said it.

"Bill jumped from behind the shack, and as

he looked round the corner he gave a yell and swore everything he could think of—as if he was trying to cuss himself straight into perdition. It was the petroleum burning the flock— caught from a coyote-lantern that had fallen from a pole. The woolly, oily backs smoked and flamed and stunk, and the fire was going from sheep to sheep. The corral was burning, and the shed had caught and was helping it spread.

"Bill's wits came back to his head with a leap. He ran and made an opening in the far side of the pen, kicking and tearing the rails off like a madman. He made a grab for an old wether and dragged her out on the prairie, calling, 'She-e-e-p! She-e-e-p!' Some of the sheep followed the other out of the opening; and soon he had more of the flock following as he backed along with his fingers in the wool of the wether. It looked as if he could save part of the flock. But those that had just caught fire crowded along behind until they were all in a scared mass; and the wind blew the flames of the corral forward over the backs of the others. Bill pulled the wether and stumbled and fell; and as he went down on his back he saw some of the smoking sheep crowding toward him and crying all at once. And as he scrambled to his feet he turned and struck out for the darkness.

"What it was that came over him he did n't know; it seemed that all his troubles had been unloaded on him at once, and the furies were after him for revenge. He did n't look back, for his very soul was turned against the place, and he had to get away from it and out of sight of it. And as he ran he could see it all as plain as if he had an eye behind—and there were the sheep pursuing him with brands of fire.

"The burning of the pen and sheds caught the dry grass. A line of prairie fire took up the chase and threw his long shadow before him. And the long legs of his shadow, stepping so high before him, and then coming down in his own tracks again, seemed like a thing mocking him and making fun of the little speed his own legs were making. He had stopped yelling, but he could still hear his own strange voice inside his dull head, and the trembling bleats of the little lambs were echoing in his brain.

"He did not stop till he had splashed through the San Gabriel and run up a high bank; and then he only looked back a moment. The grass was burning its last in a fringe of flame along the creek. Spots of smoldering fire were sprinkled on the black prairie about

16

the corral, as if an army had camped out for the night. The sheep had not followed him as far as he imagined—it was the prairie fire; but this made no difference to his feelings. He felt as if something was haunting his back, and that he must get away from there; and he again took up the flight. Near the road he came to Lady, where he had staked her out. He jerked out the stake, gathered up the rope quickly to the length of a bridle, jumped on her, and struck out along the road. It was a wild ride he had—the hardest run that Lady ever made. Bill leaned forward, with one arm ahead as he held to her mane, and the other arm working like a pump-handle at every bound, as he held the stake and tangled coil of rope. Lady stretched and doubled along the road. When they came to a turn in the road she was going so fast that she sat and slid; but she turned on her heel and sprang away to the left, with her nostrils opened wider as she put on the speed—as if she knew that Bill wanted her to go. On and on they flew toward the rising moon—and it seemed to Bill as if he was a lunatic trying to catch it. He could still hear the bleating in his mind, and the chorus bursting out again, like the organ in the church with the trembling stop pulled out. And the dread was still behind him like a fury chasing him on.

"After a while he saw a white cottage far down the road, shining in the moonlight between the orchard trees. He could see the yellow gleaming of pumpkins stored in the crotches of the trees before the house. He whacked his hand on Lady's neck, and she went wild with travel—and then the cottage came nearer, faster and faster.

"As he reached the house he tugged madly at the rope to stop her—for he wanted to get to where there were people and hear human voices once again. She went on her haunches again, stopping so short that she unseated him; and he made a flight through the air, holding tight to the stake and followed by flourishing coils of rope.

"Bill struck on his head and shoulders. And right there he got what he was looking for— to forget the sheep and the lambs and Tiffin and the bloody shirt. It knocked him senseless. And Lady had got her blood up, so that she kept on down the road, scared more and more by the stake that was tumbling and jumping along behind her and cutting capers at the end of the rope.

"When Bill came to, his eyes half opened on

a ceiling. It seemed to him as if the world was being all made over new; for first he saw only the whiteness of the ceiling, and then he began to know length and breadth, and he knew it was solid. When things took form around him he began to *feel* that they were solid, and pretty soon the pillow became so hard that it hurt a sore place on the back of his head, and he rolled it sideways on the feathers.

"Suddenly he heard a call, 'She-e-e-p! She-e-e-p!'

"It was screeched in a squeaky voice, and brought him to his live senses, as if some one had touched a nerve. Then he knew that it had been going on for some time, and it was this that brought him awake; and he sat up to listen. It was the squeaking of a pump in the yard.

"The gushing of the water and the rusty screeching of the handle reminded him of his own voice calling the hateful word, and he lay back to endure it till it stopped. When it was over he looked about him curiously. He was in a strange room in a small house; his bed was by a window looking out on a yard, with the blinds half open. Then he remembered and knew it must be the white house where the pumpkins were in the trees. In the next room he heard voices; now and then he caught a word; once he heard some one plainly say, 'Sheep.' He listened hard, but could not get the drift of the talk. There was the deep grumble of men's voices and the chatter of a woman. Presently he heard the chairs screech all at once as they pushed them back and arose. They went out on the porch. Their voices rose louder as they took leave of some one, and out there he could hear the plainer.

" 'Yes, Mr. Haskins; Luke wanted to go down the road and leave me with that man, and him likely to come to at any time, and no telling what he might do. I smelled sheep on him right away when Luke found him in the ditch, and now I *know* he is crazy.'

" 'That 's right,' said Haskins. 'He would n't have left the bunch running loose and come down here in that shape if he was n't gone wrong.'

" 'When was it you saw them last?' inquired the other man.

" 'Just now, when I was coming down here —about a couple of hours ago.'

" 'How long do you suppose they might have been straying?'

" 'Well, they might have been out a month,

and they might have been out a day. There were only a thousand or so—a small bunch if that was all there was of them to start with. They were up at the north end of the San Gabriel range, near where they put in the wire last fall. The dog looked hungry and pretty much disgusted; but I did n't bother about them; I 'm no sheep-man. It would n't hurt if the coyotes did take off a few; it would be better for cattle. I tell you, Luke, you better stay with her and keep an eye on him. She 's right about it: he might do damage.' They talked it all over again, and then the visitor said good-by.

"Bill imagined himself getting up and saying, 'My sheep caught fire and burned up. They ran after me and scared me, and I got on a horse and came away so fast I could n't stay on her back.'

"That thing of coming so far down the road on such a run, and getting in the ditch with a lump on the back of his head, was what he saw would be hard to explain away. If he told them the simple truth, it would only convince them that he was what they thought he was— crazy. He thought he would just get up and try to act as sane as possible, and put on his clothes and go away. But he could n't make up a story, and they would want to know. The only way out of it, then, was for him to get up and say he was much obliged and that he was going on his way; and then, if they tried to prevent him, to get the upper hand of them. But he did n't want to make trouble for them or scare the woman that had been so kind to him. It was a conundrum for Bill. He thought he would take a little time to consider it so that he would do the right thing. He rearranged the bedclothes, placed himself in the position in which he awoke, and shut his eyes, not quite closing them, but looking at the ceiling through his lashes. He thought that maybe, in order to get out easy, it would be good for him to pretend the unharmed sheep were his own, and make up a tale to fit that. And then he fell to thinking and wondering how the sheep got out there—a bunch the size of his own, and in his range, and with the herder gone, the same as he was from his. He could n't get that out of his mind.

"While he was thinking the door opened, and he pretended to be insensible, with his eyes opened so that he saw as if it was twilight. A woman worked around busily in the corner of the room. Then she came and stood at the foot of his bed, looking at him. She brushed a fly off his nose and went out. After that Bill lay very quiet and kept his eyes closed, for fear she might suddenly look in. He hated the idea of being taken for a lunatic, and he hated worse to be *pretending* he was sane—and he could n't come to a conclusion. After a while his head got to swimming round again and he went to sleep.

"When he awoke it was night. There was a lamp burning in the corner of the room. A man was sitting in the middle of the room, beside a small center-table, his sombrero lying by the lamp. He was a giant of a fellow, and sat with his head bowed and his hands in his lap, with the fingers locked and his thumbs sticking up.

"The chair was a flimsy white affair with long, slender legs—a sort of parlor ornament. The fellow sat on it with only one hip and with his legs crossed. The chair caught him in the middle of the back, and Bill could see that it was uncomfortable; for he shifted to the other hip, crossed his legs in the opposite way, and tried to settle himself again, using a good deal of care, as if he was afraid the chair might break.

"Bill lay with his eyes half opened, looking him over. The man's belt had a holster, but there was no revolver in it. Bill looked to the table to see if it was there. It was n't there or anywhere else in sight. That struck Bill as being strange; so he lay with his eyes on the empty holster, thinking it over. When the man shifted again he saw that the gun was at the opposite side of the belt from where the holster was. It was a patent snaffle. That interested Bill and he lay studying it. He saw that with the snaffle the gun could be slipped out sideways past a steel spring and brought up to shoot without the motion of drawing; or the gun could be simply tipped up on a swivel and fired from the belt directly, in the time it takes to jerk the wrist. It struck him as a good thing for a constable or a detective, but he did n't fancy it for himself. He wondered whether the man was a constable or a sheriff or a detective. He had seen one like it on a sheriff in one of the northern counties; but, as the fellow had the holster too, it looked to Bill as if he did all-round work, and had just taken a fancy to this. Maybe he was only a cow-boy. He lay quiet, and breathed as if it was something he had to tend to and must do quietly.

"After a time his watcher became sleepy. His head would fall slowly; he would wilt down gradually so that it would look as if he would fall over; but just as he was almost gone he would catch himself with a limp jerk and get his balance again. Then he would begin to wilt away again. At last, when he had nearly toppled over, he arose, pushed the chair aside, and sat down in the corner with his knees almost in his armpits. His heavy breathing became a snore, and finally Bill heard him gasp at times as if he was drowning in the depths of his own sleep.

"It struck Bill that this was the proper time for him to leave. He sat up carefully and looked about. He took his coat and trousers from the foot-board of the bed. His revolver was gone from the holster, but his money was in his pocket. He found his shoes and hat, and when he had everything gathered under his arm and was ready to go he stopped a moment and looked at the man. He took the fellow's revolver, pressing the spring so that it slipped out of the snaffle without as much as touching him; for they had hidden his revolver and he thought it was fair trade. Then he dropped out of the open window and hurried across the yard and down the road, where he got into the ditch behind some tall weeds and dressed himself. Then he ran on down the road, looking back now and then, ready to drop in the weeds in case the fellow came after him with his own revolver. He had hardly gone half a mile when he came across Lady. The stake had caught in a mesquite bush and tethered her. He loosened the stake, and this time he arranged his riding-gear with more care, using the iron stake as a bit and making a rope headpiece with reins knotted at the horse's withers. He patted Lady on the neck and spoke to her; then he got on and rode back, skirting round as he came to the cottage, and then striking the road and loping along back to the San Gabriel ranch again. It was a queer bridle, but a good one; the iron stake was sticking out, fierce-looking, from the corners of Lady's mouth, like the feelers of a big insect.''

Finerty, who had been listening attentively to Stumpy's narrative, raised his hand and exclaimed: ''Back to th' *place* again! D'ye know, 'twas what I thought he'd be doin'—to find if he was crazy or not.''

CHAPTER XX

"T HAT would make a fine story—
if it was told right," remarked
Stumpy. "I 'll bet, if he had
been going back for that, he
would have been anxious to see
whose mark was on that stray
flock. But the fact is, Bill was n't going out
there for that. He was just going back 'to stick
his blame nose in things'—the way Bill used to
blame himself for. And besides that, he was
going out the same as he would make a horse go
back and look at a piece of paper that it had got
scared at. He had got kind of ashamed of himself for letting himself go like that, and he did
n't feel satisfied to leave until he had gone out
and done it right; and he wanted to find about
those sheep, thinking he might do a favor to
some other herder that had bad luck. It was
against his nature every step, for the bleating
of the lambs had gone into him deep; but after
he had made up his mind to make himself do it,

252

he did n't mind it so much. And he felt so good to be out in the world again and free from herding that he was n't even afraid of the stars now.

"The sky was covered with cloud like a blanket all tatters and tears, and as it drifted along the moon would sail past the holes in the depths of blue. He followed along the road, riding Lady at a lope, till he came to a gate at the corner of the range, and then he struck out across the open. The shadows lay over the prairie in so misleading a way that he lost his bearings. He wanted to find a shack somewhere to lay down in till morning, for it felt like rain. Presently the moon shone out and showed him an old shed in the distance—one that had been infected and abandoned some seasons back. This would set him right; so he rode toward it, keeping in view the open side, that looked dark and deep like a cave, and was easy to see. When he got near it he could see the fringe of old pelts and the rams' skulls with crooked horns all hung up round the edge of roof in the moonlight. Then he knew where he was, and he turned to the northeast. He had not gone far when he suddenly rode in among the sheep."

" 'T was his own sheep, I 'm thinkin'. He

had been out av his mind!'' exclaimed Finerty.

"Naw," replied Stumpy, with a tinge of disgust at Finerty's pertinacity; "they were just a stray flock. I might as well tell you right now about them. The herder had been struck by lightning and the sheep had grazed along for over a hundred miles. They found the herder afterward sitting under a pecan-tree, where he had gone to get out of the rain. That has happened many a time—or something else. As I was saying, Bill suddenly heard a bleat and rode in among a bunch of sheep. A dog barked and snarled and ran back and forth among them, somewhere ahead. Bill threw himself from the horse, grabbed a sheep, and looked her over curiously. But it was so dim moonlight that he could not see any marks or make them out. They were like his own sheep —and everybody else's sheep. He dropped the sheep and ran toward the dog, pulling Lady after him. The collie stood holding her ground, growling and snarling; but as he came closer she backed away and raised an awful yapping to scare him off.

" 'Come, dog; come, dog,' said Bill, stooping down and patting his knee to coax her. Then she went through strange antics, running about and wagging half her body, as if she would like to trust him, but always keeping her distance. And she acted it out with all kinds of contortions, fawning round on the air and twisting and walking sideways, and acting humble and friendly, and snarling and showing her teeth whenever he ran toward her. And the way she did it pained Bill and touched his heart.''

''I 'm thinkin', if he *was* goin' out there to find was he crazy, he w'u'd 'a' been in a divil av a shtate av mind in that place. 'T w'u'd 'a' been a botheration av a fix to be in,'' put in Finerty.

''But ain't I telling you Bill did n't think he was crazy? He was n't any duffer like that. If Bill had been crazy he would n't 'a' let on,'' insisted Stumpy.

''We 'll not argy about it,'' said Finerty.

''As I was saying,'' continued Stumpy, ''when Bill got a glimpse of her in the moonlight he saw that she ran about with the slouchy gait of a hyena, as if she was half starved and weak in the hind quarters; and when Bill coaxed and spoke kind to her, she would run about with her head twisted round and held down humble so that she would almost step on it. Sometimes she tried to speak like a dog does—mouthing a whine out and rolling her head. And the more Bill coaxed, the more she capered and writhed and wagged her body and snarled and whined and kept her distance—as if she was in pain with wanting a friend, and not being able to trust him. She just as much as said: 'I am a good dog, but I must n't trust people like you.' And then she would waste all her affection on the ground and the air. Bill felt so bad for her that he could have cried. Since he had been chased round so much, he liked dogs and horses more and more, because they are a friend that sticks to you and trusts you, and can be depended on. When he saw how she acted Bill knew just how she felt, and it made him feel bad to see an animal that way.

"He began to see that he might coax her all night—but he kept on trying to make his voice sound more friendly. He wanted to convince her, and it bothered him that he could n't. Then he sat down on the prairie, with his head on his hand, and felt bad. While he sat there he noticed that it was growing black in the north; and the prairie was turning so dark that he could not see his way. Then it began to sprinkle in a scattering way—big, heavy drops that hardly had the life to be called rain. I don't suppose Bill ever cried for himself— he was n't the kind that could. But I know he used to feel bad in his own way. Once in a while a drop would spatter on his neck, but he sat there and did n't care—just as if it was a natural thing for him to do.

"Suddenly the wind rose, and it came in a drench. He jumped to his feet and began to be anxious about the animals around him. The distance was growing blacker, and he could see a downpour coming that would soak their heavy wool and bear the weak ones to the ground and chill them.

"He grabbed the stake from Lady's mouth and jabbed it into the ground to hold her fast. Then he ran about, stirring up the sheep and calling them together in hope of getting them to the old shed. The dog began to help him. She scurried about and chased them together till they crowded round him. The rain came in a cloudburst, with pitch-darkness, so that he could see nothing. He stood still, unable to help them. He could feel their fat forms, wet and woolly, crowding about and moving against his legs. He just stood there—how long he did not know—calling, 'She-e-e-p, sh-e-e-p, sh-e-e-p!' Everything had gone out of his mind but the idea of saving the sheep, and it seemed to Bill as if he and the storm were put out there to fight it out. And

17

all he could do was to stand and roar out his call.

"After a time the cloud came to an end, and a chilling breeze began to clean up the sky after it in a clear strip that came closer and spread and began to shed the moonlight around him again. The sheep were all huddled about; many of them lying helpless on the ground, chilled and spiritless, and weighted down with the rain. He went about, pulling the flock in shape. One by one, he set the fat forms on their pipe-stem legs, picking one up again when it went down, and holding it till it would stand alone. Then he would leave it to set up another. And some of them were so spiritless that they would be down before he could get the rest up, and he was afraid he could never get them all in shape. The dog worked with him, poking them with her nose and getting many to rise alone. The two of them worked that way till they were all up and he had them móving toward the old shed, away from the chilling wind. He walked along, dragging a ram by the horn, with the dog hurrying about, managing the stragglers. Bill said it was a queer sight to look and see the heavy, fat ones all being taken care of by an animal that was staggering with starvation. The dog, you see, had been sticking to them so much that she had n't time to go away and forage for herself.

"Bill went along that way, stopping now and then to pick up one that was weak-spirited and feeble-minded enough to give over, and finally he got them all into harbor. As he was driving the last ones in, he heard the dog whining again, and looking about, he saw her setting up a show of being friends with him. And the instant he called her, she crawled to him on her belly and crouched before him. Bill took hold of her, and then sat down with her head in his hands, and patted her, saying, 'Good dog! good dog!' And while he sat there he began to have a feeling of satisfaction. He had lost a flock—but he had saved another. Now he felt that he could leave that place right—and he felt free of it, and contented with himself again.

"In the cool air of the morning Bill began to smell things that reminded him of something to eat—ham and eggs and bread and butter, and especially coffee. He was so hungry that he could almost smell the ghost of a breakfast in the air. And then, as the appetite came to him, he thought of the dog. He put his fingers in her long hair and felt her ribs and stomach.

" 'Poor dog; you 're hungry,' said Bill.

"Suddenly something came over him, and

he stood up, looking at the sheep, and especially at a fat one that was snuffling as it breathed. He grabbed a ram's skull from under the eaves of the shed, and stood for an instant aiming the battered horns above the round white head. Then it came down, skull on skull—and the fat one was meat. He pulled out his knife, and when he had opened it he dropped to his knees. But he paused and stood up again.

" 'What in hell did I do that for?' he said. He stood there, thinking it all over, and looking at what was before him: the half-starved dog, the fat carcass, and the empty skull. He closed his knife and put it away.

" 'No, girl,' he said to the dog. 'I 'd rather have you dead than be a different kind of a dog from what you are. You could have killed a sheep yourself. I won't make you a sheep-killer.'

"He found a rusty bit in the manure of the place, and with it and the rope he made a good bridle. He threw the carcass across the horse's withers, patted the collie's head again, telling her good-by, and mounted. As he looked back she was sitting before the shed, fluttering her tail and looking for an invitation to follow him. But as she started to come he ordered her back.

"On a fence by the road there sat a row of buzzards. They did not move as he reined up and stopped before them—they just sat there and stunk and had their lawful rights. He cast down the sheep before them; they stooped down in the air, with hanging talons; and when Bill saw that the sheep was where it would never tempt the dog, he spoke to Lady and gave her the rein. At a farm-house he had breakfast. The woman gave him a wash-basin before a cracked looking-glass. He washed his hands of the smell of sheep, splashed his face in the cool water, and combed his hair and brushed it down smooth. And when he had eaten he told exactly what had happened, and made arrangements to have the man go out and feed the dog and tend to the sheep. With a package of provisions tied to the strings of a new saddle, he touched Lady with the quirt, and then bade good-by to that part of the country and to sheep. He rode south, intending to work his way along to San Antonio—and maybe Galveston."

"D' ye know," remarked Finerty, "I was thinkin' all th' time mabby th' felly Bill was crazy, or w'u'd get to thinkin' mabby he was crazy."

"Well, I suppose it could have happened

that way with some. But it was n't that way
with Bill. You would n't catch Bill getting
a loose head on his shoulders—although I 've
seen his feelings worked up at times. And he
was a square partner, Bill was.''

"Be *hivins!*" exclaimed Finerty, grabbing
out his alarming watch, "'t is time f'r Number Twinty-four!" And as he walked across
the tracks he soliloquized: "I am gettin' awful intherested to be nearly late. I 'll have him
tell th' lavin's av it this night.''

CHAPTER XXI

N this auspicious Sunday Michael arose at the usual hour in the afternoon. When they heard his footsteps in the middle room, Mrs. Finerty and Agnes scurried about, hustling things into the bottom of the "safe"; for while the party was ostensibly a mutual affair, in celebration of Agnes's going away to college, each had planned to take the other with some sort of surprise. Agnes had thought to pay tribute to her father in a most fashionable manner: she would have a "shower." At an opportune moment the pulling of a string would open a box above the door, and then a windfall of socks, blue, pink, and green, would heap honors upon his head. And this all required so much secrecy that when Finerty sat down to be fed, neither Agnes nor Mrs. Finerty mentioned such a thing as a party at all; and, strange to say, even Finerty did not broach the subject.

"Go on, Michael; we are now ready," said Mrs. Finerty, seating herself before him at the table.

"Go on wid *what?*" said Finerty.

"Why, wid th' shtory."

"Oh, wid th' shtory,"—as if he had forgotten it entirely. He set forth the facts of the blacksmith's adventures as far as Stumpy had passed them down to him from the sand-pile. Then he suddenly stopped.

"Kape on, Michael," said Mrs. Finerty.

"'T is all I know."

"Aw, go on, pa-a-a-a," coaxed Agnes.

"I will not. 'T is all there is av it."

"An' no *ind* to it?" said Mrs. Finerty. "D' ye know how it kem out? I 'm that afraid something might *happen* t' him."

"How do I know, whin th' ind is n't *in* th' shtory? Ye can hear th' lavin's av it from Shtoompy to-night. If ye won't let us be movin' a fut befure twelve, we must be doin' *something*. D' ye say Dinnis won't be to it?"

"He is n't back to th' station yet, Michael." Mrs. Finerty said this in evident disappointment. Although he was a rather far-fetched relative who had seldom crossed their threshold, she had hoped to have his official presence to honor her before the Dugans. And, besides, there was no telling how the story might turn out, and what might happen when Dennis should hear it. She was already beginning to wish that the blacksmith had escaped to some far-away country and made his peace with the church and reformed.

As the time for the party drew near, Mrs. Finerty, in her best "allapacky," and Agnes, done up in white and tied about with an extravagance of pink sash, turned their attention to Michael, who had been making such poor headway with his toilet that he was beginning to find fault with the ways of man. They went at him front and rear. Michael stood making a face at the ceiling while Mrs. Finerty worked at his throat and got in the collar-button, which he declared he was not strong enough to force through her starching; and Agnes hurriedly sewed a button on behind to "kape th' suspinders down." Michael even stood docile— although he made several threats to reform the fashions—while Mrs. Finerty brought forth the beautiful "made" tie. And she, after observing the workings of the wire hook on it, hung it on the collar-button, and then set it straight with his shirt-front, as she would hang a picture. Finerty was "all done"; and now, in full panoply, he turned a critical eye on Mrs. Finerty, and then on his daughter.

"Agnes," he said, "take th' goom out av yer mouth. Ye mind me av th' goat."

About ten o'clock the guests began to appear. Among the first were the O'Hagans and the Raffertys, with Sadie O'Neill and her beau. And then Dugan, with his wife, in all the flesh and affluence of a merchant. Rochester Red, with the serious professional air of one who was to exhibit his acquirements, came and sat in the kitchen. Almost at the same time there appeared young Barney, who had within him a fixed determination to do some classic clog-stepping that would entirely annul the "soft-shoe work" and sand-jigging of the agile Rochester. The two competitors gave inspection, betimes, to the stove-board that was leaned against the kitchen wall beside a bag of sand that Finerty had brought home from the chutes. And at times they each had whispered conferences with Jerry the fiddler.

As the company gradually gathered about the walls of the middle room, Finerty sat with his visage set in the plaster of Paris of formality—so close was the watch he had to keep on himself in order not to violate any of his wife's sacred injunctions.

When, at last, the Rooneys, with their following, had arrived in a body and settled themselves in the hum of social intercourse, Mrs. Finerty, hurrying through the middle room, stopped short in surprise to see Pap Smith comporting himself in a corner, decently groomed, and talking on lofty topics with company manners,—acting, for all the world, as if he were an invited guest. Agnes herself had shown him a seat, being entirely taken in by the cheerful equanimity with which he arrived at the door. Michael and Mrs. Finerty held a consultation in the kitchen, and were entirely nonplussed for a social precedent in such a case.

"'T w'u'd be hard," said Finerty, "to be puttin' a man out that has come to th' house *sociable-like*."

"An' Dugan that intherested talkin' to him about th' business *out*-luke," remarked Mrs. Finerty. "An' th' ould man comin' back at him like he was used t' his bread butthered on both sides. I doubt if Dugan *knows* he 's a thramp."

"Then 't is not us will be tellin' him," said Finerty. "Ye can lave it to th' ould man. He has th' illigant nerve."

And now, everything being settled, Finerty went into the middle room to "take charge."

"Ladies an' gintlemin," he said, "wan av th' byes I have f'r to be enthertainin' ye has not come yet. An' bein' as 't is a little while befure we can shtart th' dancin' off,—for me wife won't be havin' it roonin' on Soonda' time,—we might as well be tellin' shtories. An' now, who is 't will begin?"

"Finerty, Finerty—I nominate Finerty," said Dugan.

"Yes, pa-a-a-a," put in Agnes. "Tell them about you and the general." This was seconded and passed unanimously.

CHAPTER XXII

"WELL," said Finerty, leaning over, with his elbows on his knees, "I don't mind thryin'. Mabby 't will make ye laugh. Ye see, 't was airly in th' dark av th' mornin', an' me sittin' on me bench befure the sand-house, when the *Creole Belle* comes down the river, wid the pilot borin' a long hole in the night wid his electricity machine. He was jerkin' a spot of daylight back and forth on the wather a mile at a joomp. He took a feel of the Memphis bluff, and then, wid wan sweep of his arm from Tinnissee to Arkansaw, he began pokin' in the low woods on the other side of the Mississippi. 'He must be careful,' says I, 'not to be runnin' his boat into the woods after the high wather.'

"'T was then the light lit on a sight that near made me lose me pipe in surprise. For there, shtandin' on the other side, in all his fine clothes, was me gineral. And there he was wavin' his silver sword and joompin' round in the shpot of light across the wather a mile away, like a picther man in a kittenyscope. And I c'u'd hardly believe me sinses that a man of his intilligince w'u'd be shtandin' all night on the very shpot I left him the afternoon befure. 'From the way he prances around,' says I, ''t is plain to be seen there is nothin' holdin' him.'

"When the *Creole Belle* had made the landin' ferninst me and tied up at the wharf-boat, I ran aboord of her and up intil the pilot-house. And I says to the pilot, 'W'u'd ye do me the favor to squirt yer light over into Arkansaw again? I want to find a man. Ye 'll know him by the silver sword and the fine millinery he 's wearin' on his head. And w'u'd ye kape it playin' on him till I row over and see what meanin' he 's thryin' to impart to me?'

" 'Who is he and what is he?' says the pilot.

" 'Sure 't is my gineral,' says I.

" 'Gineral of what? And does he think the *Creole Belle* is a ferry?' says he.

" 'He don't call himself a gineral of anything at all; he says he 's a mason. And sure he is an illigant wan, wid the gold hod-cushions on his shoulders. 'T is them he wears when he goes to bury a member of his union. There was

a car-load of the likes of him wint through,
goin' up North from where they had been down
below at a conclavity. An' 't was him that
marched by himself up the post-office bluff to
look away into Arkansaw, where he knows
some people, till the injine went away and left
him. An' he has n't a stitch till his back but
the sowldier clothes an' th' buckskin apron.'

'' ''Wid that, the pilot shtuck his beam out into
the night again and began shweepin' it up and
down the Arkansaw shore. And wanst I seen
the gineral go through it like the flight av a
glorified angel, shinin' up all at wanst and
goin' out suddent-like.

'' 'I think I have him located,' says the pilot,
pullin' th' shtring aisy and makin' the elec-
tricity crawl along be inches. Wid a little fine
jigglin' he put the shpot on him, and there was
the gineral shtandin', wid his hand in his chist,
like the statoo of the man discoverin' the Mississippi and shinin' like an altarpiece.

'' 'What do ye say he 's shtandin' out in the
night like that for, makin' a tabloo of himself?'
says the pilot.

'' 'Ye can search me,' says I. 'He wint
over there to drop in on the Widdy Biggs,
whose departed was a frind of his. Maybe the
widdy was not at home—but why he 's out like

that all night, I dunno. Will ye light the way for me while I go across and find out? An' if he moves away, will ye keep it on him?'

" 'That I will,' says the pilot. 'I 'll give him leave to move a mile, and I 'll only budge this four inches.'

" 'And ye might give me a wink of it, whin I 'm rowin' across, to let him see I 'm comin'.'

"And so he did; and the gineral did n't move a fut.

" 'Hello, gineral,' says I, as I pulled the boat up ferninst him. 'Was n't the widdy at home?'

" 'How d' ye suppose I know?' says he, in-sulted-like. ' 'T is a fine place ye put me on. I thought ye knew the counthry.'

" 'And so I do,' says I; 'and the deppo is right over there where I told ye.'

" 'And a roarin' mill-race betwixt me and it. Ye have put me on an *island*,' says he.

" 'It can't be; 't is impossible,' says I. Wid that, I walked along the wather edge of the low, spongy sand; and befure long I came till where I started from.

" ' 'T is a cut-off ye 're on', says I.

" 'And what 's a cut-off?' says he.

" ' 'T is what they call a cashay,'[1] says I.

[1] Caché.

" 'And what 's a cashay?' says he.

" ' 'T is an island,' says I; ' 't is a new island that 's just been discovered. And ye 're the wan that 's discovered it. 'T was made by the high wather.'

" 'I 'm sorry now I did n't wait for the ferry instid of thrustin' to the likes of ye. 'T is a fine sight I 've been makin' of mesilf, not to say annything about shtandin' up in the wet all night,' says he.

" 'Sure ye did look fine and ye did yerself credit,' says I; 'and I tould ye the truth that the ferry is n't runnin'. 'T is too wet in the woods for a boat to come over. Get into me shkiff and I 'll put ye on rale land.'

"And so we did.

" 'And are ye sure, now, this is land?' says he as he got out of the boat, jinglin' himself. 'I 'm thinkin' ye had better go wid me a piece, and then I 'll be sure.'

" 'That I will,' says I; 'I 'll go to the plantation itself wid ye if the road is out of wather yet.'

" 'Out of wather?' says he.

" 'Yis,' says I; ' 't is that way sometimes; and when the rise is goin' down ye 're like to find that 't is land where 't is wather, and wather where 't is land.'

18

"'Wid that, the light that had been kapin' us company took wan lape across the Mississippi and shut itself off; and then I heard him clankin' round amongst the trees wid his sword.

"'Don't be handlin' the trees,' says I; 'for I doubt if they 're dry yet. And don't be leanin' against them, or they 'll be comin' off on yer clothes.'

"'I 'm lookin' for a place to sit and rest meself,' says he.

"'Don't do that,' says I; 'for 't is mud. Ye 'd have to be roostin' in the high branches like a chicken. Ye 'd betther come out of the dark into the boat. We 'll give the sun time to come up. 'T is only dry here on the wather.'

"So he came aboord and we sat till 't was daylight. When 't was mornin' we found what was left of the road, and we went along, pullin' our feet out of the mud. The trees were all painted yellow wid it, just so high; and it was pillars of mud holdin' up the woods as far as ye c'u'd see, for the wather had been deeper nor a man's head. And a flock of gnats gathered round each of our bare faces, perchin' on the air as numerous as coarse shmoke and follyin' along ahead of us. The gineral wint along, shooin' at them wid the white feather on his hat.

" ' 'T is no use to do that,' says I; 'for they 're like a ghost: ye can pass a club through them and still they 'll be there.'

" 'I wish the dom things w'u'd get onto me where I c'u'd smash them, or go away intirely, wan of the two,' says he, gettin' vexed-like.

" ' 'T would be an improvement,' says I; 'but ye 'll find 't is their way. Whin a gnat gets a place for himself on the air ye can't knock him off of it, so ye might as well be savin' yer fine feather.'

" ' 'T is dom annoyin' they are,' says he.

" ' 'T is that,' says I. ' 'T is hard they are on the poor dumb farm-animals that can nay-ther shmoke a pipe nor cover themselves wid mud like a hog; and after the spring rise like this many a cattle is worrid till he dies of dis-thraction.'

"But still he went along, dustin' the air wid his feather and chuggin' at the heels and blowin' like a shteam-man till he was red in the face. We were goin' along like that when we come to a serious-minded sort of a mule shtandin' by the roadside. We shtopped be-fure him, waitin' for some look of recognition. But he kept on lookin' off the length of his nose and shtandin' careless-like, lettin' his ears hang any way at all. And divil a care had he that he was shtandin' in the prisince of a human bein'. And the mule reminded the gineral that he was very tired.

" "'Tis a pity the mule wasn't goin' our way,' says I. 'And, though ye 'd have no business a-ridin' him, I 'm thinkin', if ye 'd sit on his back, I 'd lead the two of yees along.'

"And so we did.

"And whin I saw, afther a while, how meek was the mule, I says: 'Gineral, 't will be no harm at all. Whin ye get to where ye 're goin' I 'll ride him back an' shtand him in th' thracks where we found him. 'T will be no harm done thin.' No more had I th' words out of me mouth than the mule shtopped short and began lettin' out a volley of kicks behind him, firing the mud off his hoofs so quick that befure ye c'u'd say Jack Robinson he had mud stickin' against all the trees in gobs that 'u'd fill a flower-pot. When the mule began usin' his feet to shtand on again, the gineral sat like a frozen man, lookin' at me in an unearthly way that I c'u'd see no sinse in at all.

" 'What 's ailin' ye, and why don't ye move or shpake? Do ye want to shtay on or do ye want to get off?' says I.

"'*Move!*' says he, rollin' his eyeballs, and never shtirrin'. 'D' ye know, man, I 'm thinkin',' says he—'I believe,' says he, 'that I 'm *shtuck* to the mule.'

"Wid that, he moved his arm and pulled the leg of his pants careful wid his fingers. And it lifted the hair of the mule like a porous plaster. I made a move to peel him off, but he yelled me back like an Indian.

" 'Don't pull a hair of him,' says he. ' 'T was that made him go off befure.'

" ' 'T is a kind of varnish,' says I, 'they put on the cattle in these parts, I 've heerd tell.'

" 'We 're glued together! Is it a thrick they have?' says he.

" ' 'T is put on him out of mercy,' says I, 'and dried medium hard so that th' insecks can't get their bills intil him. Wid that on him, the gnats don't know is he a mule or a bedstead. But 't is aisy to tell that the man who did the job was no painter, for ye can see 't is too thick an' tacky'—puttin' me finger on till it shtuck, and then pullin' it off and causin' the mule to make a feint wid his hind leg.

" 'Don't be thriflin' wid him. Let 's think what we 're goin' to do,' says he.

" 'There 's nothin' to be done at all but to git off and lave him, for a little varnish won't hold a sthrong man like ye. But let me give ye warnin', whin ye shtart, not to be gettin' off part at a time. Ye must be quicker nor he is,' says I.

" 'Hold him tight be th' halther,' says he; 'for if he should go annywheres he 'd be takin' me along wid him.' And as we had a quiet spell, breakin' the news till ourselves, and him bringin' his mind t' th' deed, I began to have me doubts of how th' mule w'u'd take annything like that.

" 'Ready, now; 't is goin' to hurt him,' says he, takin' a breath, like he was goin' to dive, an' knottin' his fists. He gave a fling to his legs, like a joompin'-jack; but he had no more than ripped loose half the legs of his pants whin the baste wint shtraight up from the ground wid a jolt that shlapped th' gineral back onto him tighter than ever. An' th' mule only kem down long enough to get his fore feet to earth so that he c'u'd shtart a boxin'-match wid th' air behind him. I held his head, like the butt of a Gatlin' gun, till he was through wid th' first round. Thin for wan inshtant he laid off workin' behind and kem down an' shtood wid his ears laid back like a jack-rabbit,

and his teeth grinnin' and the divil lookin' out
av his eye. Th' gineral was that set in th' face
that I c'u'd see his mad was up.

"'I 'll get off the dom mule this time, if I
have to scalp the back av him,' says he, shtrik-
in' his hand wid his own fisht.

"I seen him thry it, and I seen no more.
What happened till me, I dunno. But when I
kem to a shtop, afther rollin' in the mud, I sat
up, an' there I saw the mule lapin' away down
th' road, wid th' gineral shtickin' to him like
ye 'd see a monkey ridin' a greyhound in th'
circus.

"'I wonder is the mule goin' home till his
folks?' says I to meself. 'If he does, 't will be
a fine bird they 'll think they 've caught.' An'
to satisfy meself what harm 'd come to him,
I hurried along in the mule's footsteps.

"As they come to a rise in th' ground the
mule switched off th' road wid a jerk of his
tail, and shtepped over a five-barred gate into
th' barn-yard av a house wid white pillars on
th' porch. Whin I kem up and looked through
th' gate th' mule had shtopped himself in th'
middle of the barn-yard. A black dawg wid a
bay voice was sittin' down wid his nose pointed
up at th' shky, mournin' their arrival in an
indless voice. Wid that, a fine body of a wo-

man come hastenin' out, folleyed by a naygur mammy an' a fair-haired girl.

" 'Well, if it is n't Misther Ta-a-a-aggart!' says she, lookin' at him an' holdin' up her two hands, like givin' a blessin'. 'Well, Misther Ta-a-a-aggart!'

"The gineral saluted her wid th' white feather, an' thin laid his hat on th' buckskin apron befure him. I seen his lips move, but what he got out av him I dunno for the howlin' of the dawg.

" 'Will ye keep shtill and let a body have a word!' says she to the dawg. An' she led him away wid wan av the ears that was hangin' down his back.

" 'You, mammy, go and put the kettle on,' says she. 'An' you, Mary, to th' field and tell John we 'll need him t' go for a valise.' And as she was comin' back afther puttin' the dawg away, I lept over th' fince and went in.

" 'Well, Misther Ta-a-a-aggart,' she wint on again, 'I 'm that surprised! Dismount this instant and come in.'

"He sat pethrified to the mule, wid his eyes lookin' off that far ye 'd think he was expectin' something out av the shky.

" 'Excuse me, ma'am,' says I, 'but is it your mule?'

" 'Gracious me!' says she, h'istin' up her jeweled white hands again; ''t is "Rooshy." An' me that taken up I did n't notice it! I 'm so delighted!'

" 'I 'm glad to hear he 's yours,' says I; 'for maybe ye 'd have some influence wid him. An' ye 're no more surprised than we are, for 't was him showed us th' way. An' we might as well tell it till ye now—seein' ye 'll have to know it annyway,' says I, shtoppin' a while to break it till her aisy.

" 'What is it? Don't be kapin' me in suspinse,' says she. 'Has annything happened?'

" ' 'T is nothin' to speak av,' says I, 'except that your mule is a little shticky. An' we don't want to be dishmountin' too quick-like, seein' 't is your mule, for fear 't will hurt his hair.'

"She tuk it in wid a gasp. And the gineral kem to wid a blush. She put her finger till th' mule's shoulder, and he spurned her away wid a wiggle of his hide. Then she flusthered hither and thither, blamin' herself for it all, an' fidgetin' in th' air wid her fine hands.

" 'Calm yerself, calm yerself, Misthress Biggs,' says the gineral. ' 'T is no harm at all,' says he, forcin' the words out wid a smile that w'u'd pacify a lion.

" ' 'T is no use gettin' excited,' says I. 'But

if ye have somethin' that th' mule w'u'd like
to ate, 't w'u'd occupy his mind. An' have
ye also a rope?'

"I led thim away t' th' barn. An' there I
had the lucky idee. Temptin' the baste wid
a wisp of hay, I got him to put his head bechune the stanchion-beams where they lock
the cows' heads in t' milk thim; and I closed
the scantlin' behind his jaw, so that he
would n't be goin' away widout pullin' his
head from its socket. Thin I tied his leg to
himself and gave the gineral th' word. 'Now
ye can dishmount,' says I.

"The mule was that mad about it that he
brayed like a dhry poomp, hollerin' out wid
one breath, and hollerin' back into himsilf wid
the nixt. An' whin th' gineral had both legs
hangin' over wan side av th' mule, th' sate
av him let go and dhropped him intil the arms
of the widdy.

" 'Dear me, I 'm so relieved!' says she, faint-
like.

" ' 'T is a relief,' says I. 'An' I 'm glad
they 're parted.' Wid that, they both wint off
and left me, th' gineral walkin' wide be way
of not intherferin' wid himself. I took the
riggin' off the mule and departed. An' in
half an hour I was paddlin' me way back to

Tinnissee to sit down and have a rist in p'ace.

"'T was th' lasht I thought I 'd be hearin' av it. But 't was only the beginnin'. Wan mornin', whin I was sittin' on me binch befure th' sand-house, afther coalin' up Number Twinty-nine and puttin' the sand intil her, along comes Mary Ann McBride, that works bechune times for th' widdy. She had her arms filled wid groceries that she 'd be takin' over on th' ferry, an' she shtopped on th' levee waitin' to be coaxed into havin' a word wid the likes av me, an' watchin' for th' clue of a chanst.

"'Good mornin', Mary!' says I. 'An' how is th' mule gettin' alawng?'

"'Quite well, thank ye kindly,' says she. 'An' how is yersilf?'

"'I 've me health,' says I.

"''T is too bad,' says she, 'that a mule was n't some kind av a Christian animal, that he c'u'd appriciate all that 'll be done for him, an' him livin' among the cows, an' bein' shtall-fed all th' time. The widdy gives him credit for it all.'

"'For all av what?' says I.

"'Hush, they 're engaged—t' be *marrid!*' says she in a whisper. 'An' 't is nothin' all day but what 'll Misther Taggart have, an' what might he want. An' 't is atin' lettuce three times a day we are, because he likes th' green taste av thim.'

"Wid that, she sat down on the bench beside me, wid the baskets and bundles around her, while she w'u'd be waitin' for th' ferry, and she tould me it all, throttin' a bag av sugar on her knee.

" 'Afther ye left,' says she, 'an' it kem to th' widdy's ears that his citizen's clothes was thravelin' home alone on th' thrain, she got out the best suit that th' late Misther Biggs left behind him, and she made him put thim on, so that he 'd not be shtickin' to things. 'T was thin I saw she began to act more free an' home-like till him than iver—an' ye can't blame her at all, for 't is an illigant, well-to-do bachelor man he is, wid none to care for him but the widdies an' orphans. She c'u'd niver be done blamin' hersilf for the shp'ilin' av his regayly clothes. An' she wint at thim wid her buke av "Three Thousand Receipts," and she thried as manny as they w'u'd shtand, till she had thim ruined intirely. An' I says to mesilf, he 'll not be lavin' now for a while, for he has no clothes av his own, an' he 'd have no right to be goin' away in the relics av Misther Biggs. An' I c'u'd see he made up his mind till it, for he contented himself as tame as a marrid man.

" ' 'T was two nights afther that I was sittin' in the parlor so 's to be lettin' thim have th' porch t' thimsilves. An' I was hangin' me nose out av the front windy to get a whiff av the smudge fire that was builded to kape the gnats away. An' av coorse I c'u'd not help hearin' that they wor whisperin' saycrits, although I could n't tell for th' life av me what 't was they wor sayin'. But av a sudden I heerd her whimperin' an' snufflin' an' shtoppin' herself up wid her han'kerchief, and at that he gave a move that made the legs av his chair stutter on th' boards.

" ' "What is it that 's ailin' ye, Missus Biggs?" says he, soft-like.

" ' " 'T is nothin' at all—nothin' at all— 't will pass in a minute," says she. "'T is only that ye look so natural—ye look so *natural*," says she, all in a blurt. It escaped from her all at wanst, as she was takin' the han'kerchief from her mouth to say somethin' else. Wid that, he began shpakin' kind till her an' consolin' her on the shoulder. An' befure long she was cryin' on him comfortable-like, wid th' han'kerchief spread like a bib on his chist to not be s'ilin' the coat.

" 'I was that disthracted thryin' to get an eye
and an ear to the crack av th' shutter at wanst
—an', d' ye know, 't is onpossible. An' betwixt choosin' between thim, I made up me
mind there 'd be more to hear than to see. But
jist thin the big-throated hound saw the moon,
and began to ullagoo at it for the night. An'
I says to mesilf, "I will get him away from
there, so that he won't be intherruptin' me."
An' afther a minute I wint out on the porch
as bould an' accidental as ye plase, an' laid
hould av him for to haul him away. An' the
widdy says to me, flirtin' her han'kerchief be
way av usin' it, "That is right, Mary Ann;
take him away. He can see the moon behind
the barn as well as he can here."

" 'Whin I was through tyin' him at a distance wid a piece av clothes-line I kem through
the kitchen an' med me way aisy-like to th' parlor again, an' put me ear till th' shutter. For
a bit av a while there was no word at all; 't was
as quiet outside as forty wimmen kapin' shtill
at wanst. But widout kapin' me waitin' too
long she began chattin' away, wid her cryin' all
over, an' tellin' what they 'd put intil the hun-
dherd-acre field, an' what intil the tin-acre
patch, an' how they 'd change the house inside,
an' put in a closet for his regayly clothes.

Thin she kem to a shtoppin'-place. I put me eye to th' crack, an' they wor sittin' close together, an' holdin' on like two in a shwing. 'T was thin I knew that it had taken place,— what I had suspected.'

" ' 'T is the suspected always happens,' says I.

" 'Yis; but to think av it happenin' whin I was away wid that nuisance av a dawg! An' now 't is all over but gettin' ready. He 's goin' to take her away to Brighton Beach. Where that is, I dunno.'

" ' 'T is a place where ladies go in shwimmin',' says I.

" 'D' ye mane it!' says Mary Ann, not knowin' what to do wid her hands. 'Th' ide-e-e-a! She tould me that same, an' I thought she was jokin' me. She 's makin' a little allapacky shkirt that dooes n't come till her knees—an' barely that. T' think av it! 'T is little we know!'

"Wid that, th' ferry came, and Mary Ann hurrid away, lavin' a big orange beside me. I sat till it would be time to coal up Number Thirty and put th' sand intil her, shmokin' me pipe, and thinkin' av the ways av th' worruld.''

CHAPTER XXIII

HEN the applause at Finerty's effort had subsided, Stumpy arrived, and all eyes turned to the door as he punctuated his way across the kitchen and appeared at the door of the middle room. Agnes gave him a chair.

"An' now, ladies an' gintlemin," Finerty resumed, "we will have th' nixt shtory. 'T is a shtory av a blackshmith. The blackshmith was workin' on a boat in New Orleans, an' wan time he had a fight wid th' bo's'n av th' nixt boat. An' he w'u'd 'a' bate th' life out av him, too, only that th' bo's'n got away. An' he wint afther him that mad that th' captain had to be ordherin' th' crew, 'All hands on deck,' t' unload th' blackshmith off th' ship— wid th' shmith shakin' his fist back at the ship wid wan hand, an' makin' throuble for th' sail- ors wid th' other, an' sayin' he w'u'd make an anvil out av th' bo's'n's face whin he caught

him bein' sint out to th' grocery. Th' nixt
mornin' they found nothin' where th' bo's'n
had been shlapin' in th' galluses av th' boat
but th' torn pieces av th' bloody shirt av him.
An' th' marks av blood wint over th' side av
th' ship an' into th' river where he had been
put away to float off to the Gulf av Mexico.

"Th' polis got th' blackshmith. He had th'
felly's brass-handled knife in his pocket; an'
th' worst av it was, he had th' sailor's lucky
penny, that he w'u'd not 'a' taken a dollar for.
For 't was a quare wan, wid th' likes av three
legs shtamped on it, that th' sailor w'u'd not
'a' parted with for th' bad luck av it. Th'
blackshmith w'u'd have th' polis believe he
did n't know how it got into his pocket at all.
Whin they had him in jail for it he got away,
an' all th' newspapers hollerin' bloody murther. An' from that time he did nothin' but
bate out th' polis runnin' from here till there.
He med frinds wid Misther Sidney—'t is him
that 's been inthrojooced till ye over there—
an' he took him along. But, ye see, Misther
Sidney did n't belave he did it, because th'
blackshmith *tould* him so. Av coorse th' three-
legged penny proved it in th' way it could not
be different, but Misther Sidney—that has only
wan leg—thought he did n't, an' he shtuck by

19

him. But wan time they got parted, wid th'
blackshmith havin' to ride away shwift on a
black horse. An' now we will have Misther
Sidney, whose name is Shtoompy, tellin' some
more about it. But ye must n't be thinkin' he
had annything t' do wid th' murther.''

As Finerty sat down there was a murmur
among the guests; and Stumpy, being pro-
vided with the highest chair, began the story.

"Well, I ran across Bill, about a year afterward, in New Orleans, going up Royal Street.''

"Wha-a-at!'' exclaimed Mrs. Finerty. ''I
thought that was th' place he was thryin' to
kape away from.''

"Bill thought so, too,'' replied Stumpy.
"When I asked him what he came back there
for, he said he did n't know. But he had got so
tired of the prairie country that he felt home-
sick to hear the boats whistle and see the river
running by. And the more he traveled the
nearer he got to the river, till finally he found
himself right back in New Orleans again.
Anyway, Bill was the kind that the nearer
he got to trouble the less he worried about it.
So I guess he came back there to give his mind
a rest where he would n't be running away.
Bill and me kept ourselves along the French-
town levee, a mile or so south of where the

river-boats landed. And we only made ourselves sociable among the boats from foreign parts. Bill got a job now and then on a brig or a bark, blacksmithing or doing any kind of repair work, and keeping me for a partner the same as always. We got along pretty well that way.

"One evening, when we were passing a sailors' saloon, we noticed that there was a great deal of fun going on inside. And not having much amusement ourselves, being as we were afraid to go down town, we went in to see it. There was a bulldog making fun for twenty or thirty men. The fellow who owned the dog would put a rolled newspaper under the back of the dog's collar so that it stuck out over his head. Then the bulldog would throw himself around in a way that was surprising, jumping four or five feet in the air and twisting and rolling over on the floor until he knocked the newspaper out and got it in his mouth. Then he would wait for it to be done again. And the sailors, standing round in a circle, would laugh and roar and clap their hands on their legs to see the way he went at it.

"While we were being amused, a broad fellow, in an open shirt with a trapeze-lady tattooed on his breast-bone, clapped Bill on the back and hailed him hearty. Bill turned round of a sudden, and who was it but the bo's'n!''

"D' ye mane 't was Tiffin?" exclaimed Finerty, straightening up.

"Wha-at—th' *sailor!*" exclaimed Mrs. Finerty. "I thought ye had him kilt!"

"No; I only said it looked like he was killed. Bill was so surprised he could hardly believe it himself till he found how it had all happened. But he was n't as surprised as Tiffin was to come back and find they thought he was murdered. But Bill did n't let him know about it right away—for he would have to go and take oath before a lot of lawyers that he was n't dead.

"As I was saying, it was Tiffin. Bill just stared at him. And Tiffin, who was about half seas over with drink, stood holding his big, hairy hand out, and smiling in a cheap sort of way, the way a fellow does when he finds he has put himself forward with a man that ain't going to be friends with him. But Bill suddenly clapped hands with him, and took him by the shoulder as hearty as any sailor could expect.

" 'Well, I 'll be hanged—I 'll be blowed, Tiffin!' said Bill, not being able to get out what was in him.

" 'Ho-ho!' bellows Tiffin, getting more friendly than ever, 'I *thought* ye did n't know me right away. You was n't holding any grudge about the little tap I gave you with the monkey, was you? Why, the belt you gave me in the face was the best thing ever happened to me. Come along and have a drink on it.'

"Tiffin pulled a roll of money from his pocket and rolled away on his sea-legs toward the bar, with Bill holding him tight by the arm. And while the whisky was coming Bill kept putting one question after another that Tiffin did n't seem to get the drift of at all. The bo's'n would go off into stories about his voyages and the captain he used to sail with.

" 'They thought you was—' But Bill stopped himself suddenly, and swallowed back the word. For he saw that Tiffin did n't know anything about his being dead at all. And Bill thought it best not to say anything about it till he found what Tiffin had to say.

"Tiffin was very talkative. 'If ye did n't swamp me with questions maybe I could spin me yarn. An' where did you pick up the boy with the one mast?' said Tiffin, looking at me.

" 'He 's a partner of mine. He 'll drink with us—but he does n't talk much,' said Bill, giving me his meaning with a look.

Bill ordered a bottle of brandy in the middle of the table, and we sat down. Tiffin was pleased with that, and to find Bill so interested in him and so willing to listen to his yarns.

" 'Ho-ho!' he roared, slapping the table; 'I 've been ashore only two hours from Havre, an' here I 've met a chummy! We 'll have a *hell* of a time! It 's the first time I 've made this port since the night I shipped for Liverpool. And if it was n't for the belt I got in the face, I 'd 'a' stuck with that damn Yankee captain, Amos Cleft. And I 'd 'a' been shivering another voyage on a load of ice. She was loading with ice again.'

" 'And what did my hitting you have to do with it? Tell us how you came to leave,' said Bill.

" 'I 'll spin you the yarn,' said Tiffin, holding his head back and tossing down a glass of brandy without touching his lips. ' 'T was this way. That day I was painting on top of the galley, and it started to rain. I was mad. And I was right, too. Let me tell you about all I 'd been going through with before that, and *see* if I was n't right. When I first shipped on the *Lion* we cleared for Jamaica with a load of ice—shivering all the way. In the fo'c'sle it was like Labrador, and down in the cabin it was like being a corpse in a coffin. The only spell of comfort you could get was laying aloft—and Amos Cleft down below swearing out of Yankee cussedness that it was n't cold. He was that kind.

" 'Then we cleared for Buenos Ayres. There Cleft had a choice of cargoes, and he took hides. They offered him more money for taking the hides, and at first he was n't going to do it—seeing they wanted him to. He was that kind. But the captain's wife—and she was a fine little lady that did n't know how to take him except strokin' him with the fur, thinking he would get tame—she says, when she saw he was hesitating, "I don't believe I would take hides if I was you, Amos."

" 'So he took 'em. All you needed to start Cleft any way at all was to blow a head wind.

" 'Well, you know what a cargo of hides is. We no more than got them stowed in the *Lion* and cleared for New Orleans than she started to hatch worms. You could n't lay down for a rest in the fo'c'sle but what a worm would drop in your eye; you could n't go forward with stepping on worms; you could n't go up to the cross-trees but what a worm would be up there waitin' for ye. Well, I could 'a' put up with that—I 've gone through a good deal and put up with it, with a little grog. But when it come to pickin' a worm off yer salt-horse, and having a worm sittin' on the hard-tack ye was going to eat, it 'd make me mad. There was n't any *privacy* from the worms. I got so I hated every one of them. And then, when we got to New Orleans, she started taking on ice again.

" 'That was the way I was feeling at the time we was lying next to the *Betsy*, where you was working. I was drinking pretty steady, trying to drown them out of my mind; and sometimes I thought they was turning into snakes. That 's how I come to hit you the tap with the monkey—that and the rain coming down on my painting. And, as I was saying, there she was loading with ice again.

" 'Well, that night, after you hit me the belt, I woke up and found my nose had sprung a leak. I opened my bag and took out a shirt and held it to my face, thinking I could swab it up. But the shirt got soaked, and it was the only cotton one I had. And not wanting to bloody the galley and have the cook after me for sleeping there, I went and leaned over the labbard-rail and let it drip into the river on the offshore side. After a while I saw that if I let it run like that I 'd have meself bailed

out dry, and I 'd better go and find a drug-store
where they 'd have something to calk the leak.
But I did n't want to dirty the deck going
ashore, for we had been holystoning all day,
till it was white and clean. Blood 's hard to
get out, and I did n't want to sprinkle it clear
across decks and down the waist to the gang-
way. "I 'll be damned if I will!" says I. So
I went up the labbard and around the bows and
down the stabbard, holding my head overboard
all the way—up the fo'c'sle and all—and I went
ashore. And I did n't get a drop on deck but
what I leaked from the door of the galley to
the labbard-rail. The man at the drug-store
got it stopped, and he gave me a glass of whisky
to get me under sail again. Well, you know
how I am, Bill. The one glass put me on that
tack, and I put into a saloon. And the few I
had there got to rilin' up the grudges I had in
me bilge against Captain Cleft and the brig
Lion. And ye know how I am. If I start my
drinks with a joke, it keeps getting finer weather all the time; and if I start out with a
cloud on my mind, she turns into a black squall.
Whatever I start the drink with, it keeps putting on the same cargo right along. This time
I had my mad on to start—thinking of the ice
and the worms, and the ice again. I put out

of that groggery five or six times, always thinking I would make the brig *Lion* on the next
tack. But every time I would get to the corner my mind would blow a contrary wind, and
I 'd put back again. And there blew in my old
shipmate Simpson, who was having his last
grog before they weighed anchor for Liverpool with a cargo of cotton. An' he says to
me: "We 're short a hand; come to Liverpool
along with me." An' the whisky was complaining to me about the ice we were putting
on the *Lion,* and I says: "Articles or no articles,
I 'll be no bo's'n along with Amos Cleft."
So I went along and shipped. An' early the
next morning I was laying low behind the cap-
stan as we dropped down-river, and laughing
to myself as we showed our stern to Cleft and
his old iceberg.'

"Well," continued Stumpy, "when the
bo's'n had got through telling the story to Bill,
he tipped the bottle and poured down himself
another four fingers of brandy. He had emp-
tied half the bottle already—Bill drinking only
a little. While Tiffin was telling it Bill would
suddenly straighten up every once in a while
and seem on the point of saying something; but
he would stop himself and keep quiet and watch

Tiffin sharp. I could see that Bill was doing some lively thinking; and it was easy enough for me to figure out that Tiffin was going to be his prisoner, and that the bo's'n would have a harder time getting away from Bill than if any policeman got a hold of him. Bill told me afterward that he did n't know what tantrum the brandy might take inside of Tiffin, with the idea of leaving the saloon and going away to jail with him—and the bo's'n only two hours ashore, with all the money in his pocket. Bill thought at times that he would tell Tiffin what had happened, and then if he did n't want to go right along he would whip him senseless. But he wanted to take him in good shape so that he could tell a straight story. He did n't want to take any chances of fighting and getting the job miscarried.

" 'How did I get your three-legged piece in my pocket?' said Bill.

"Tiffin suddenly started up from his chair and leaned over. 'I *knew* ye had that piece!' he said, bringing his fist down on the table. 'I had to give a fellow in Liverpool a dollar for one just like it. But it 's my own I want. It 's my lucky piece. You can have the other one, Bill.' Tiffin laid the same kind of a coin on the table and held his hand out.

" 'But how did I get it?' said Bill.

" 'Why, you got it this way,' said Tiffin, feeling in his pocket. He took out a brass-handled knife. Then he picked up the coin and slipped it into the slot of the knife. 'That 's how you got it. It used to always stick in there; and many a time I nearly lost it that way. It was in there the time I lent you the knife. You see, I had to get myself another knife, too; and it ain't good like the old one. Give me my knife, too. You can have this one, Bill.' And Tiffin held his hand out again for the knife and the coin.

" 'Well, I 'm mighty sorry,' said Bill— 'I 'm *mighty* sorry to tell you that the police took your knife and coin. When they saw the blood on the shirt and leading over the rail they thought you was dead. And they took your things away from me, saying I had no right to them.'

"Tiffin began to look threatening. 'And that was my lucky coin. I have n't had good luck since I lost it. What right had *they* to take it?'—suddenly flaring up. 'I lent it to *you.*'

" 'That 's just what I say,' said Bill, banging his fist down on the table. 'They said you was dead. But you can make them give your

things back. And I 'd *do* it, too—I 'd *make*
'em!'

"'Me dead? I 'll show 'em I ain't dead!'
exclaimed Tiffin, banging down his fist just the
way Bill did.

"'That 's what I say,' said Bill, banging
his fist down again. 'And if they did n't give
it back to me I 'd make trouble.' And Bill
hit the table so hard it made it jump an inch.
'And we can take *this* along. It belongs to us,'
said Bill, putting the brandy in his pocket and
turning to go. 'Come 'long, chummy—I 'll
tell them who 's who.'

"That seemed to catch the bo's'n right. As
Bill said, he pulled Tiffin when he was ripe.

"I stumped along behind them down the
street. Sometimes Tiffin would look back and
call me the 'tender,' and laugh loud at the
joke. And Bill would laugh, too. They went
along with their arms locked tight, Tiffin rolling
along on his sea-legs, bumping into Bill like
a coal-scow in choppy weather, and singing
a sailor song over and over:

> "'I swam from Chesapeake Bay
> To the middle of the sea,
> Three men upon my back,
> And nothing hurt me.

> I met a shark on the way,
>   And I bunged up his left eye—
> Upon my word, 't is true;
>   An' what 'll ye lay it 's a lie?'

" 'We 'll show 'em what 's what, Tiffin,' said Bill.

" 'We 'll show 'em, we will,' said Tiffin.

> " 'I met a friend in the East
>   Who had no window-sashes;
> The sunbeams entered the room
>   And burned his wife to ashes.
> "Sweep out your mistress," said he;
>   "Bring wine to my friend and I"—
> Upon my word, 't is true;
>   An' what 'll ye lay it 's a lie?'

"At the police station Tiffin rolled up to the sergeant's desk and banged his fist down, demanding his knife and penny. While he was arguing and explaining what his property was like, Bill gave himself up in the captain's office, telling what had happened, and demanding that they hold Tiffin for a witness. When they found who Bill was, it did n't take them long to put him behind the bars again. And pretty soon they came scuffling along with Tiffin, and turned the key on him in the cell next to Bill's. After the police captain had talked to me, he made up his mind I did n't have much to do with it; and seeing I was a friend of Bill's, he let me visit in the corridor.

"I stayed there a while, looking into the cage at Bill, and then into the cage at Tiffin. Bill was sitting on a bench, contented and comfortable, and Tiffin was roaring and swearing and trying to shake the door down, like a monkey rattling a cage. And when the policeman came in and rapped him on the knuckles to make him keep still, it made the bo's'n madder than ever. But when he found he could n't break the place down, and that nobody paid any attention to him, he stopped raging and looked through the bars at Bill. For he thought Bill was his only friend, seeing he was in a cage, too, and not knowing how it came about. Tiffin had n't been told. He had made such a rumpus at the sergeant's desk when they did n't give him his property that they were going to jug him up a while, anyway, till he got polite and sober. So when the captain said he was wanted for a witness they threw him in quick.

" 'We ain't drunk—are we, Bill?' said Tiffin, looking through the bars.

" 'Of course we ain't,' said Bill.

" ''Course we ain't. Don't the lubbers know I 've been walking on the waves for two months past? An' how can they expect me to walk straight on this damn level place? Then why don't they give me the knife and the lucky piece and let me out?'

" 'They don't want you for being drunk. They think I killed you on the brig *Lion*.'

" 'Can't they see I 'm alive, Bill?'

" 'But they 've got you put down for dead in the book. And they won't rub it out till you prove who you are in court. The sooner you can prove that you are Tiffin that was bo's'n of the brig *Lion*, the sooner you 'll get out of here —along with the piece that 's brought us so much luck.'

"Tiffin put his forefinger on the lady on his breast-bone and said: 'I 'll show 'em it 's me, all right—I 'll show 'em it 's me. They can change their old log-book.' At that he grabbed his shirt up to his chin, and began pointing round on himself with his forefinger. 'There 's the stars on me stomach—the same as on the "three-star Hennessy." And here 's the anchor on me side. An' here on me back,' he said, running his thumb across it, 'is the spread-eagle, with the words under it in Latin —which I could never read backward in the looking-glass. I guess they can see *that*, can't they? Then we 'll go out and have a drink.'

"He blew a loud blast on his bo's'n's whistle. And when the keeper came to find what it was, Tiffin pulled up his shirt again and said: 'This is *me,*' slapping himself on the chest. 'I 'm Tiffin that was bo's'n on the brig *Lion.* Tell the captain to fix his log right and let us out of here.'

"But the guard, seeing that he was drunk, told him to shut up and walked away. Tiffin stood and watched him going as if he could n't believe it, and it was all a dream; then he thrust his arm into Bill's cell and said, 'Give us the bottle of "three-star," Bill. We 'll have a drink.'

" 'I 'm sorry to say I have n't got it,' said Bill. 'They took it away from me. They have that with the knife and piece.'

" 'They *did!*' said the bo's'n, with his eyes staring wide open. And when he had taken time to believe that it could be possible, he rammed his fist down somewhere inside of his belt and pulled out a roll of money. 'Never mind, Bill; don't get discouraged. I 've got money, an' I 'll show 'em. We 'll send the one-masted boy out to get us some. An' I 'd like to see them come into *my* cage and take it away from *me!*' He poked a bill out into the corridor to me. I picked the money up and threw

20

it back through the bars again. Then I turned away, for I did n't like to see him, and went and talked to Bill at the far corner of his cell.

"Pretty soon we heard the bo's'n muttering and preaching to himself.

" 'It 's the money that 's worrying him,' said Bill. 'You 'd better go and buy him something to keep him still. He won't be contented till he 's rid of it.'

"I stepped in front of the bo's'n's cell again, and he had his money all spread out on his bunk, looking it over, paper and silver and nickels. And he was talking to it. 'What good are you? Ye ain't *no* good. We 're marooned.' And he went on telling himself about being only two hours in port and cast away like that.

" 'I can go and get you something else. What would you like?' said I. At that he looked hopeful at me, and stood thinking. But he did n't seem to know the name of anything except drinks.

" 'Maybe I could go to the bakery and get something good to eat,' said I.

" 'What do they keep there?' he asked.

" 'They have cookies—and lady-fingers—and cream-puffs.'

" 'Which costs the most?' he asked.

" 'Cream-puffs,' said I.

" 'I 'll try some of them,' he said, throwing out a bill.

"He ate the two I brought him, and he took such a liking to them that he threw out more money and told me to get a dollar's worth. 'An' I 'll try some fingers. Is it a lady that sells 'em to ye?'

" 'Yes,' I says.

" 'Is she good-lookin'?'

" 'She is pretty good-looking,' says I.

" 'Tell her to keep the change. An' tell her they 're for Tiffin that come in on the *Grand Sachem* from Havre.'

"The bakery did n't have as many as he wanted, but I brought him a big bagful that had to be shoved hard to go between the bars. That kept him quiet for a while. But when he began to get used to the taste of them he got restless again. And when I went away for the night he was walking up and down like a caged gorilla, complaining about his lot, and foaming at the mouth with cream-puffs.

"They kept Bill and the bo's'n in there till the court had some time to spare; and then they held an inquest over Tiffin, and they came to the conclusion that the bo's'n of the brig *Lion* was alive. And that let them free. But the police took Bill right up again and held him for breaking jail; for he had no right to be resisting the law, they said, whether he was guilty or innocent.

"I stayed around New Orleans, making out the best I could, waiting for Bill to be free again. I tried a good many places to get a job in a blacksmith-shop. But when they found I had n't learned the trade they would look at my wooden leg, and that would be the end of it. I laid around the levee, and sometimes when I was hungry I would eat fruit that was thrown aside from the West Indies fruit-boats. And somewhere I drank some water that was n't healthy. I got to feeling tired out, and I would lay around on the cotton-bales, not caring to stir, and thinking I was lazy. And when I got so that I was too lazy to get up when a policeman told me to move on, they called the wagon and took me off to a hospital. They said I had some kind of a fever. I was out of my head quite a while. And when I did know what was going on, I did n't take much interest in myself, or seem to care what would become of me. But when I got so strong again that I could stand up on one leg, they gave me the other one and turned me loose.

"I went around to the police station to find

out about Bill, and they told me he was out and gone long ago. At the trial they only gave him a short sentence, calling the case off after they had held him a while to pay him for what he did to the police. The police did n't seem to have much against him. They told me he was a 'good one'—seeing he was innocent. And that was the last I ever heard of him to this minute. If Bill had known I was in the hospital he would have stuck by me. He was a square partner.''

CHAPTER XXIV

A Stumpy's narrative came to an end, the company, which had been none too quiet while he was telling it, broke out into a babel of comment. Mrs. Finerty and Agnes were all eyes and "oh's." "W'u'd n't that bate ye!" said Finerty to Dugan. "D' ye know, I was thinkin' all along that th' blackshmith was lyin' to him about not doin' it. An' I 'd think so yet, if 't was n't for what th' sailor bye kem back an' said."

Mrs. Finerty made herself heard above the chatter, and she repeated herself until they all quieted and gave her the precedence of conversation.

"What I w'u'd like to be knowin'," she said to Stumpy, "is th' *ind* av it. Which wan did he get marrid to—was it Eva or Nellie?"

"Why, I don't know as he ever got married at all," said Stumpy. "I don't suppose Bill got married. But he is working somewhere, and wondering what became of me. I came through Upton last September, and I went up to the place after dark to look around. The old house was caved in, and the garden was full of weeds. There were strange people around the girls' house, and the blacksmith-shop was empty. When I saw that I pulled out—for they would n't know there how the murder came out, and I was afraid Lant Williams and the rest would make trouble for me.''

"An' what d' ye suppose bekem av th' dog he had—an' th' black horse—an' what did th' bo's'n do afther that?"

"I don't know," said Stumpy, who was plainly at the end of his story. "I suppose the bo's'n 's in the same place he always was—out on the ocean somewhere."

" 'T is no use askin' him anny more. He has sthruck th' bumper," said Finerty. "An' if I was radin' th' likes av it in a buke I w'u'd not belave it—if 't was n't that ye can see 't is thrue."

The clock stopped further comment by twanging out the first stroke of twelve. Michael jumped up instantly, and Jerry the fiddler struck up a solo from Kerry—"The Oyster Girl." As Finerty hurried out through the kitchen door to get the box to be "callin' off on," Agnes pulled the string and, amid a volley of cheers, overwhelmed him with a shower of color that made him "think th' wall-paper was fallin' down,"—but which, on cool inspection, he found to be socks. Then hurriedly gathering them into the box which he had brought, he turned it on its side and mounted it.

"A-l-l-l take yer parthners for th' dance. Wan couple over there in th' coorner," called Finerty, taking immediate charge of the festivities in a manner that came from long practice in being "boss."

"Wan more couple over there.—Here, Dugan; 't is here ye 're needed.—Right over here is a place for ye, Barney; an' ye 'll find worse dancers nor Agnes.—Good fur ye, Rafferty, to be pickin' out Miss O'Neill!—Some wan lind a hand here, now."

Mrs. Finerty had taken her place where a set had been started by Dugan and Mrs. Halloran, and she stood with a vacant place before her. At this juncture Pap Smith came forward in all his equanimity and placed himself opposite, with a courtly bow, to which Mrs. Finerty returned a curtsey. All the sets were quickly filled but one. But as Finerty orated on the exigencies of the occasion, Stumpy gave over to the persuasions of the bouncing Mrs. Dugan, who led him forward with a twinkle in her eye and the assurance that she would "see him through." As Jerry shifted to the lancers the party started off, and soon the floor of the middle room was heaving and creaking like a ship, with Finerty in command.

"Sa*lute* yer parthners! Salute th' *coorners*! Balance, *all*-av-yez! First foor-av-yez, foorward *and* back! *Balance*, parthners! *All* promenade now."

As they all promenaded, Finerty stood on his box and gazed in rapture on what he had set in motion: Pap Smith, in courtly convoy of Mrs. Finerty; Dugan and Mrs. Halloran, fat and easy; Mrs. Dugan, beaming and marking time with Stumpy; Barney and Agnes, in mutual admiration, with Agnes the most resplendent of them all, and chewing her gum again, in rhythm with the fiddle. Finerty paused so long that they overdid it, and he had to call them all to time: "*Shtop* promenadin'! La-a-a-dies, change! Gr-r-r-rand sashay! Alleman' *lift!*"

The jollification being thus thrown wide open by Finerty at the stroke of the clock, the glory of it went on through unnoticeable hours with "jiggin' an' reelin' an' singin'."

The refreshments were a grand success, especially with the hungry Rochester in the kitchen, who ate all the cold meat and then sat in ignorant hope that there might be boiled potatoes and pie. Nothing marred the function, except an accident in the second quadrille. Pap Smith was "balancing" in dangerous proximity to the steps of the middle room, when he went too far back and tumbled into the kitchen. Mrs. Finerty was given such a shock that she ran forward with her hands clasped.

"Are ye hurted, Misther Shmith?"

Mr. Smith promptly arose and bowed. "I just thought I 'd drop out into the kitchen a moment, Mrs. Finerty." And then the unctuous sojourner began "balancing" again as if nothing had occurred.

DAWN was already venturing over the edge of another day when the guests, all unconquered, sat about the middle room and chatted as they waited for the final contest between Young Barney and Rochester. While the stoveboard was being brought in again and the necessary whispered confidences with Jerry were being had, Dugan, who had been much interested in Stumpy's tale, came and sat beside him for a serious word or two.

"And ye say that ye thry to get work some-times?"

"Oh, I get jobs all the time, but not at steady work like blacksmithing. I used to ask for that once in a while, but they would n't want a stiff-legged man. It don't look so good."

"Why don't ye go down to th' Vulcan place and thry? Maybe Armsthrong w'u'd find a place for ye."

"Armstrong?" exclaimed Stumpy, coming to sudden attention. "What is his first name?"

"Well, now, I don't know—I don't know him to shpake to. I think 't is William—yis, 't is William."

"Where is it?"

"'T is three shquares down that way, an' thin wan turn to yer right an' 't is a shquare an' a half—"

The most sensational surprise of Finerty's party was the manner in which Stumpy hopped out of it, using his timber leg but three times in going through the middle room, down the steps, and out of the kitchen. A number of the guests went out on the stoop instantly to see what had happened, and the other guests came and followed the more curious ones to the front gate. The entire personnel of Finerty's party stood speechless at the gate, watching him, a block away, hopping twice with his good leg to one step with his wooden one—which was his swiftest method of locomotion. They were at a loss to account for it; and Dugan was busy protesting, in the face of his wife's accusations, that he was in no wise to blame for it.

On the next evening—a mild evening in early spring—Mrs. Michael Finerty came down the tracks of the Memphis "yards," bearing on her arm Michael's big, bright dinner-pail, which winked even *more* familiarly at the switch-lights as it passed. For Michael's pail, as remarked in the beginning, was destined to shine at night. And again she was bound for the little sand-house; for Michael had slept so late, in consequence of the festivities of the night before, that he had barely time to jump into his clothes and "take a bite" before he hurried away without waiting for his bucket to be filled. And there, sitting on the bench outside, enjoying the climate that had come into its own after the blizzard, were Michael and the one-legged man, busily talking together.

"Well, Marg'ret," said Michael, "th' bye is goin' t' get a new leg. An' 't will be no wooden leg, but 't is goin' to be an *ar-ti-ficial* wan. 'T is like thim ye see pitchers av in th' railroad magazines. Halloran's fireman has wan. 'T is th' leg he shwings on whin he throws th' coal, an' he w'u'd not thrade it for th' wan he lost, for he can put in twelve ton befure he begins to feel it. An' since he is firin' th' ould battle-ship he says he wishes he had an *ar-ti-ficial* body, for 't 'u'd take iron an' shteel to shtand it.''

"A boughten leg!" exclaimed Mrs. Finerty. "An' d' ye know they cost a fortune av money?"

"Sit down, Marg'ret," said Finerty, setting his bucket on the ground, and offering her the seat that his dinner had occupied—"sit down now, an' ye can hear th' rist av th' shtory. Tell it till her, Shtumpy.''

"Well," began Stumpy, "Mr. Dugan asked me why I did n't get a job from Armstrong at the Vulcan."

"He thought 't was Bill," broke in Finerty, "f'r his right name was that."

"So I hurried down there to see," continued Stumpy. "But 't was so early in the morning that the big double doors were closed, and there was no sound inside. I looked through the crack between the doors, and it was all dark and still; but when I got the smell of the iron it seemed I could almost see Bill working at the anvil. So I stood there a while, with my nose at the crack, breathing it in. Then I went across the road and sat down on the grass of the bluff to wait. It was all quiet as church. After a while a baker's cart began sounding on the stones in the distance and clattered past, with a dog trotting under the axle; then it seemed quieter than ever, and I looked down at the big river going by without a sound, and I imagined I could see it flow. I never heard it so quiet as it was this morning. So every once in a while I would read the front of the Vulcan again, all painted over in black and white, and saying: 'Wm. Armstrong, Machine Blacksmithing and General Repairing.' Then the *Creole Belle* came down the river, and blew the siren whistle; and it seemed like a horse whinnying with gladness to see the city again, and trying to wake it up. After a while a man in a blue shirt came along. He stopped right at the bolts of the big doors and threw them open. But it was n't Bill. I sat mighty disappointed for a minute or two, and decided I might as well go over and have him tell it to me. But before I got across the man came out with a bucket in his hand and went down street. But I kept right on and went into the place, and looked around. A horse whinnied to me back in a dark part of the place; but just as I went to look a dog ran out from somewhere around her and drove me back. Well, the dog drove me backward clear out of the shop, and I kept my peg-leg forward for the dog to bite on. The dog gave me a chance to leave; but she would go at me whenever I stopped. So I went across the street and stood a while looking at the big open doors; then I sat down and looked around at the grass, feeling disappointed. Every once in a while I looked up to see if the man had come back. And then I saw another man stooping down near the door and petting a black cat that was stroking itself back and forth against his leg. That was Bill. And maybe I did n't make quick time across the cobblestones. Bill looked up to see what was coming, and before I got to the curb he was reaching his arms out to me. Bill was glad to see me; although he ain't usually much of a man to make a fuss. But he was glad to see *me*. And when he had shook my hand again, and clapped me on the back, and stood off and looked me over from head to foot, he just said: 'I 'm glad to see you, Stumpy.' And I could see him warming up to me like an iron in the fire. And he looked sorry when I told him I was sick and could n't find him again. He had looked all over for me.

" 'And won't Eva and Nellie be glad to see you?' he says. 'They 've been worrying regular for fear you might be seeing hard times,' Bill says to me. 'And they 've been wondering if you would ever come along.'

" 'Say, Bill, which one was it?' I says.

"He gave me a kind of a look, and he said, 'Why, Eva, of course.'

" 'And how is Nellie getting along?' says I.

" 'Fat an' sassy—same as ever. But I guess we 'll be losing her one of these days. He 's a likely-looking young fellow—a clerk on the *Creole Belle*. But I 'll have to look into it a little more before I give my consent.'

"Pretty soon the men had arrived and started to work at the lathe and the vises and anvils; and then Bill took me up to the house, and we stayed there till after dinner. Bill has a fine house—a white frame-house with a porch and vines on it. Well, Eva is the same as ever, only she seemed more like Bill to me—and Nellie is just as different from her as ever. When Eva saw me she stood quiet a minute; and then she came up cool and kissed me, with a tear in her eye. But Nellie was the one that was *glad* about it. And Eva went to work setting me out something to eat and thinking of everything to make me comfortable, leaving Nellie to make me welcome. And when I saw them all at home together, it seemed strange that I did n't know all the time that Eva was the one for his wife, and Nellie for a sister to them. After dinner we went back to the shop again, and Bill took off his coat and rolled up his sleeves and banked up a fire and laid a hammer across the anvil—same as old times.

" 'And now, Stumpy,' he says, 'don't you want to finish the trade?'

" 'I was going to ask you, Bill, if you would give me a job,' I says.

" 'At helper's wages—and board to boot. And the best time to begin is always now,' he says. 'Take a length of the five-eighths rod and cut off fourteen inches for a ring-bolt. You 'll find the rule right here in my hip pocket.' "

NUMBER Twenty-four came murmuring on the rails before the sand-house. Finerty reached out and grabbed the shovel, and hurried across the tracks.

"So long t' ye," he said, waving his hand. "I have me worruk to do."